EITHER WAY DEAD

Tony Gyles

A POD BOOK

EITHER WAY DEAD

Published by P.O.D. Publishing
52 Parkwood Road, Wimborne, Dorset
England

On behalf of

ISBN: 0 9531737 5 5

This book was designed and produced by P.O.D. Publishers on behalf of the copyright holder and printed in the UK by:

**The Basingstoke Press,
Hampshire, England**

DEEP THEIR GRAVE

The Diary of a merchant ship and her crew during
the Battle of the Atlantic, 1942
(A POD Book)

In both of his novels, the author's thorough
knowledge of his subject and the clever way in which
he interweaves genuine historical facts throughout the
narrative leave the reader wondering if the story may
indeed be true.

*"The story is grippingly written. What separates this
book from the ordinary is that the narrative and
dialogue used are so utterly in the style of those times
– added to this the lively description of day-to-day
shipboard activities are full of the most meticulous
and accurate nautical terminology, which makes it
abundantly clear that the Author is himself an 'old
man of the sea'. A thoughtfully written adventure
story with an ironic twist."* **M.D. – New Zealand**

*"A damn fine tale. This book gives long overdue
credit to those who gave their lives in the service of
country without adequate offensive or defensive
capabilities. The ending, though a twist on the
expected, is consistent with the real-life theme (of this
book). This book is hard to put down."* **'Arnie' -
USA**

TONY GYLES

Born in 1925 Tony was educated at Bristol Grammar and Chard. He preferred sport to learning and dodged his final exams by going to sea in April 1942 as a saloon-boy.

Originally destined for the Royal Naval college at Dartmouth, poor eyesight diverted him instead to a Merchant Navy radio college in 1943 where the charms of the local young ladies took their toll at exam time. Volunteering for the Royal Navy he finished the war keeping temperamental Radar sets working.

After demob he took up civil flying as radio/navigating officer, finding himself in Kenya in 1948. There followed a period during which he repaired radios, wired farmhouses for electricity and sold motorcars. In 1950 he returned to sea on obtaining a coastal mate's ticket and spent a couple of years in experimental fishing before joining the Kenya Police at the start of the Mau Mau uprising, eventually rising to senior commissioned rank.

In 1961, unable to afford the sea passage for his wife and family of five children, he took them and their dog on the round trip to Britain by road through the jungles and the Sahara desert. A journey they repeated in1963 as the family finally left Kenya when that country gained its independence.

On his return to England he spent a successful period in the hotel and restaurant trade, after which he returned to sea in 1972 and obtained a Master's ticket in 1976 before joining the Fremantle Port Authority in

Australia, from which he retired at the age of sixty-five.

He and his wife built their own house 'out in the sticks' where they now live. When Tony is not writing he and Betty enjoy driving their Caspian horses in scurry events or just meandering through the forest. His incredibly full and varied life has equipped him well to write with conviction and great feeling about the subjects he knows best.

The 'Queen Mary' in her wartime camouflage as a troopship.

EITHER WAY DEAD

AUTHOR'S NOTE

In the services during a war rumours abound, some have substance others are pure fiction and depend on how disgruntled the perpetrator was at the time as to how good the story. In 1943 a rumour with substance was rife in the Royal and Merchant Navies that the giant troopship *Queen Mary* had collided with and sunk her anti-aircraft escort cruiser *HMS Curacoa*.

A year later another rumour was circulating in the merchant navy that once again involved the Cunard trooper. This time it implied that there had been an attempt to sabotage her. When this reached the ears of Naval Intelligence it was quickly nipped in the bud by a counter rumour, deliberately spread, that the incident 'was no more than that one of the ship's radio officers had been unable to take the strain of war any longer and had run amok while on duty.'

At the time of the incident, August 6th 1943, Churchill, together with the Chiefs of Staff and their retinues, one hundred and fifty persons in all, had been aboard on their way to the first Quebec conference. Naturally MI5 had been thrown into a panic that such a thing could have happened for they assumed that the Prime Minister and Chiefs of Staff were the object of the attack. What made things worse was that despite, at that time, reading the German codes and thus being able to keep tabs on current spies, they knew nothing about the agent concerned. Had there been a security leak and if so from where? They hunted for an answer and found none.

After the cessation of hostilities the *Curacoa* collision was admitted and 'human error' given as the cause. The incident with the radio officer was forgotten by all except the Intelligence service.

When in 1963 Kim Philby, who had been recruited as a spy in 1935 by the Russians, fled to Moscow someone in MI5 remembered the incident on the ship and the fact that the Prime Minister had been aboard. Since Philby had been well up in the hierarchy of MI6 at the time (to the point of being touted as a possible future head) had *he* been the 'leak' and the Germans, through their own agents in Moscow, made Churchill and his staff the real target? MI5 blew the dust off their files but were still unable to come to a definite conclusion.

The story which follows is based on a manuscript written by my father and on a chance meeting with a certain *Kapitän zur Zee* Weiner. In order to make the narrative flow more easily it has been necessary, in places, to use my imagination based on the very frank admissions made to my father by the agent concerned. Together with much research I hope I have been able to pen a reasonably accurate history of the lead up to and happenings of August 6th 1943.

All names are fictitious other than those of historical interest.

Translations for German words in *italics* can be found in the glossary.

CHAPTER ONE

THE MANUSCRIPT

Leutnant Wilhelm Schultz had paid off the taxi over an hour ago. Now he leaned against the railing, listening for sounds of the train bringing the next lot of passengers for America. Rosie in the canteen had said they had been told to be ready to dish-out the meal boxes from ten o'clock, but she had added that 'trains were more late than on time these days'.

Although he could not see her from where he stood he knew that somewhere past the pier, perhaps a mile away, swinging at anchor was that giant ship painted, like all others in this war, a dull grey besmirched here and there by a few streaks of rust. If she had been a small cargo ship like most ploughing the oceans of the world she might be more rust than paint but she was not. She and her sister ship, the *Queen Elizabeth,* were known as the 'Grey Ghosts'. She came and went with such speed and secrecy that, to those who might watch from the shore, she would suddenly appear off Staten Island out of a grey fog or, as dawn broke, be here anchored at the 'Tail o' the Bank' on a dull rain swept day – apparently conjured out of nothing during the long dark hours of the night. She would disappear just as suddenly as she had arrived. In the evening she was there busy, as like ants, people were swallowed into her vast bulk through black holes in her sides but in the morning where she had been there would just be a large empty space. Before the day was half through she would be a hundred miles out into the vast heaving Atlantic apparently, but not quite, lost to the rest of the world amidst the never ceasing waves.

It was her wireless officers, 'selected as the best of the best', who kept in touch with the Admiralty, as if by some invisible umbilical cord in the ether, never sending, only listening....constantly listening ....for the coded messages which would order the captain to change course or do this or that so they missed a known U-boat lurking, like some vicious predator, waiting to send ships to a watery grave. It was their responsibility to ensure that no mistakes were made as they received and passed those orders to the man ultimately responsible for the safety of the huge vessel and the thousands of souls in her. Now, one man would pit his skill and judgement to bring about the exact opposite of that which those on board strived to attain.

Not for the first time he wondered who had dreamed up this operation, which had so captured the imagination of the *Führer* that he had personally signed the special and so very secret order. Back in Berlin and even while in training, it had seemed more of a game he was playing. It was not until he had embarked on the U-boat that he realised that it was for real.

'Shit! Just how the hell had it all begun?' It was something he never did find out and now certainly never would.

*   *   *

To tell the story of how *Leutnant* Shultz found himself about to try to board the *Queen Mary* in the summer of 1943 and embark on the daring mission which would inevitably lead to his death, it is necessary to go back to the death of my father at the age of ninety three.

*   *   *

The ivy-covered rectory stood by the small church just past the last cottage in the village on the road out to Illminster. The garden was not looking as tidy as it could have been even allowing for the fact that it was near the end of winter. Here and there, in over-long grass, stood piles of leaves and rubbish awaiting removal. The stipendiary had ceased for a number of years and father had only been able to afford the gardener once a week whereas the man, himself no chicken, needed at least three days to keep things reasonably in order.

In retrospect the bishop had been most kind to allow father to live out the last of his days there in return for an occasional helping hand in the adjoining two parishes. It was sad to think that before the war began most Sunday Matins saw the church nearly full with country folk who believed in God, even if some questioned parts of the bible. Now with the march of time it seemed that nothing remained the same and with so many young people, myself included, leaving the country for the cities the village and its church had almost withered away.

Walking in the watery sunlight with Mrs. Glossop, father's housekeeper since the war, up the short sloping path from the decaying cemetery to the house I thought of the years I'd spent here as a boy before the war called both father and me to arms.

It seemed such a shame that something so old as the church should fall into disuse. I vaguely wondered if it might be possible for me to buy the rectory and make it my permanent home? With my new book due for its market launch later in the month I could probably afford it with only a small mortgage for I did not suppose the price would be very high in such an out of the way village. As I warmed to the thought I decided that I would broach the subject with the bishop. That worthy had insisted he conduct the service for father's interment so an opportunity would undoubtedly present itself during the wake.

I am not sure if I believe wakes are a good thing to have but I suppose they do allow those attending to get the commiseration's off their chest and for the bereaved to come to grips with the fact that life must go on. In father's case it made my approach to the bishop easy.

Dr. Cranbrook had been quite enthusiastic at the thought of at least the rectory remaining, as he put it, 'alive' and promised he would take the matter up on his return to Wells. It appeared that he was already in the process of trying to get the church itself put on the list of the National Trust.

As there had been other cases of church buildings being sold he saw my purchase of the Rectory as a definite possibility. In view of this he said there would be no hurry for me to move father's belongings and that I would be welcome to stay on there while the legalities ground their way through the bureaucracy. Nevertheless I wanted to get things done rather than possibly stir up more grief at a later date. Although the lump in my throat was slowly lessening I certainly did feel grief for I'd had a deep love and high respect for my father.

Later in the afternoon when those people who had come, it seemed from far and wide to attend the funeral, had finally departed I got down to the mournful task of going through father's papers in the large roll-top desk at which I had seen him prepare his sermons in those earlier years. The study was heavily panelled with bookshelves covering one wall and only a small window allowing a limited amount of light. At that moment it was indeed rather a melancholy place.

Meticulous in almost everything he did father had left little for me to worry about. There was a short note addressed to me and written only three months ago for, although he was amazingly healthy for his age, it seemed that he knew the end was near. It simply stated that his will was with his solicitors in Illminster, and that other than a small legacy for Mrs. Glossop, every thing had been left to me. The final sentence brought the lump in my throat to even greater pain as I read - *'Thank you son, for the life you have led. God bless you'*.

The desk was a beautiful piece of furniture and it took about an hour to go through its multitude of pigeon-holes and drawers and glance at their contents which, for the time being, I decided to leave where they were. Then I turned my attention to the wardrobe and chest of drawers, which held his rather meagre collection of clothes.

As I opened the old wardrobe there was that slight aroma which I knew as father, mostly from his old fashioned smoking jacket and I admit to a further tear or two. Now that he was no longer there I knew I was going to miss him.

Keeping aside the naval stole, his Master of Arts hood and medals (how proud I was when I'd heard he'd been awarded that Distinguished Service Order while serving in a Dido class cruiser in the Mediterranean) it did not take long to pack the two suits, various pairs of slacks and bits and pieces necessary to a man's daily life, into bundles ready to be taken to the Salvation Army. His naval blazer with its black buttons, gold pocket badge and, I noted, now shiny elbows I decided to keep. The surplices and other items directly relating to his calling I put in an old case for delivery to the bishop in case they could be used by others in the church.

By mid-morning the next day I reached up with what I had always called in my youth the 'boat-hook' and pulled down the swinging ladder to the attic. Pushing back the heavy oak trap door I entered another world.

Although the church was late fifteenth century the rectory was much younger. It had been sacked by Cromwell's troops because its then incumbent had been too 'High Church'. Rebuilt after the return of the monarchy it had been gutted by fire in eighteen ninety and rebuilt yet again. Now the attic ran the whole length above the three bedrooms and obtained its day-light through two small dormer windows. Dust and cobwebs were everywhere and it smelt so musty that I thought no one could have been up there for years. I certainly had not since I was a youngster when such places held a fascination for most young boys.

Amongst old chairs, towel rails, old- fashioned china washbasins complete with jugs and much other bric-a-brac hoarded by both grandma and mother over the years there was a large Saratoga trunk.

I had been forbidden, when playing up there, to touch this relic of a by-gone era, which must have been at least a hundred years old. Judging from the almost unreadable travel labels and faded name, it was from grandfather's days in the Indian Civil Service. Its leather bound corners and edges were dulled with age and the brass buckles green with Verdi gris.

Now I felt no longer bound by mother's constrictions and with a feeling almost of awe and some excitement, I struggled with the stiff leather straps. I was surprised to find the lock was still working and slid, albeit needing some exertion, to one side and the brass flap clicked upwards.

Opening up the heavy lid and letting out the aroma of lavender and mothballs, I found its top tray contained a mass of papers and documents. I spent several hours reading these and learned more about the previous generations of my family than I ever did when parents and grandparents were still alive and I but a mere stripling.

As I read pangs of remorse came to me for not having spent more time with father since the war but like most young people one thought that parents would always be there. Mother's death in an air raid had happened while both father and I were away somewhere doing the navy's bidding and it was left to a cousin to bury her. Apart from visiting her grave on my next leave and saying a brief hello to the vicar who was standing in for father, I did not return to the rectory until both father and I had been demobbed. Now, reading those papers I bitterly regretted the lost years.

The bundle containing the manuscript was one of the last items I came across. Wrapped on the outside in a copy of the 'Daily Express' dated October 1946, it was tied up with string. Using a small ivory-sided penknife, which I had found in the trunk's tray I sawed at the string; I say sawed because there was no edge on the knife. String cut I removed the newspaper and found two pieces of cardboard between which were a number of sheets of foolscap writing paper. Again there was more string but pushed between it and the top piece of cardboard was a single piece of folded paper. I pulled this out and saw written on the cardboard the following:

Under Official Secrets Act.
Cannot be made public before 1973.
To be opened only after my death.

It bore my father's scribble of a signature above the more legible words:

Naval Chaplain

Next I opened the folded paper and read from father's scrawl.

How I, a naval chaplain, came to be present at the execution of this German agent is a story which will only unfold after my own death.

Kenneth Brent
Naval Chaplain

September 29ᵗʰ, 1943.

Sitting there on my left haunch, which was beginning to go numb for there was no covering on the dusty floorboards, I wondered what had caused my father to write such words. From its position under the string the page appeared to have been added to the bundle as an after-thought. Putting the note down I attacked the next lot of string and with some trepidation turned back the top sheet of cardboard and found a page, again in father's scrawl, which read:

I attended as chaplain, prior to and at his execution, a German officer of the Kriegsmarine, one Leutnant Schultz. In the short time between his conviction and execution he told me how he came to be in such a predicament. These notes are the result of what he told me.

I was quite aware at the time that it was incorrect for me to write his story because his trial and the reasons for it were, of course, highly secret for which reason I was not required to attend.

To start with I was impressed by this young officer and his apparent regret at having to kill those he did. He had asked, if it was at all possible, that when the war was over I would let his family know that he believed he had served his country well and died honourably. It was only later when he got carried away in relating his escapades that I saw his darker side and wished I had never agreed to help but by then I had given my word. Because of the official secrets act I was unable to carry out this last request.

Again it was signed as on the front cover but the date was more specific:

November 3rd 1943.

A second page read:

Eventually I realised that Schultz must be typical of the arrogant brain-washed Nazi officers we had been told about. Right up to the day he died he believed in the doctrines drummed into him and maintained absolute faith in his Führer and the invincibility of the Third Reich.

Schultz was also a brave man for had he succeeded in his mission he would have undoubtedly been his own executioner and not faced a firing squad.

As he unfolded his story he became more egotistical and perhaps it was this trait which really enabled me to pen his story.

The Lieutenant was not a religious man, for religion hardly went with being an ardent Nazi and as a chaplain I was superfluous to his spiritual needs.

He had asked for a chaplain shortly after being brought down south for his interrogation which, since it concerned the sea, was primarily dealt with by the navy although MI5, as the counter intelligence agency, also became deeply involved.

As I was at the end of my sick leave and not yet posted to any ship I was handy and therefore told to report to this establishment.

I came to the conclusion that because I was only a quasi-officer Schultz did not feel the same pressure from me as he did from his interrogators. Perhaps he also felt that as a man of the cloth I might be honest and be more susceptible to his aims.

Schultz firmly believed that Hitler would ultimately march down Horse Guards Parade. However he did not trust the Royal Navy to give him the credit in the records of his trial, which he believed to be his due.

After Germany's victory he had no doubt that such records would finally fall into the hands of Admiral Canaris but to make sure that the truth was told he extracted a promise from me, in a way I suppose by trickery, to ensure the Kriegsmarine High Command was informed of his exploits.

Why on earth I acquiesced to such a proposition I do not know. Perhaps I was trying to forget Elizabeth's so recent death in that air-raid and the unusual position in which I now found myself clouded my better judgement; perhaps it was sheer bravado *and some perverse urge to 'buck the system' which made me re-write my notes in some sort of order. Once I had started I realised that I might be in all sorts of trouble for failing to pass to higher authority all that he told me. However I had made the promise on the bible and could not break it.*

Anyway, after being sentenced the man was waiting to be executed so the murders he had committed were of no real consequence other than the police being able to close their files.

Fortunately I was released from my oath by Germany's defeat but then realised that the official secrets act could still land me in further trouble so I have taken the easy, if not exactly the honourable, way out.

At the trial Schultz had apparently told only of the matters which appertained to the purpose of his mission and steadfastly maintained he was committing an act of war as a naval officer and not a spy or saboteur.

If I have erred in God's sight I ask His forgiveness.

At the bottom of the page were father's initials.

I was totally astounded by what I had read and must have sat there with the papers in my hand for several minutes as pictures flashed through my mind. Finally I re-read those first pages and turned my attention to the manuscript, if you could call it that, whose pages were many.

I knew that my father had been injured while serving in the Mediterranean in late '42 and had been sent home to recuperate. After the war we hardly ever talked about our experiences and certainly he had never mentioned anything about a Lieutenant Schultz. Flipping through the pages I now held in my hand my imagination ran away with me, conjuring up all sorts of thoughts. In my research for two other novels based on the naval war I had never heard anything about the incident of which my father had written. Even in the incredible revelations recounted in '*A Man Called Intrepid*' there was no mention of it.

As an author of moderate success I was naturally intrigued; could there be a story here waiting to be told?

I took my find down stairs and into the overly furnished lounge. After stoking up the fire, I made a cup of tea, ate one of the sandwiches left over from yesterday's wake and sat down to read yet again. How long I read I do not know, I did recall reading it at least once through but when Mrs. Glossop came in the morning she found me asleep on the sofa. There were a couple of dirty cups and an empty sandwich plate on the coffee table and the fire well and truly out. The manuscript had fallen from my hands and spilled onto the carpet. Bleary eyed and rather cold I gathered the sheets of paper into their folder and went upstairs to get rid of the stubble on my chin.

Shortly the aroma of frying bacon wafted into the bedroom and Mrs. Glossop shouted for me to come at once to the table. Over the years the good lady had lost none of her authoritative tone where father or myself were concerned and mothered us unmercifully! Together we sat down and while eating discussed her future. She would keep the place habitable until we heard one way or another from the Bishop and if my luck was in would stay on as my housekeeper.

Dear Mrs. Glossop, with her short plumpish figure, round face with those kindly eyes and now greying hair she had become essential to father in his last years. She was another who had suffered in the war; both her husband and brother, who had been in the same unit, failed to return from Dunkirk. Despite having met hundreds of potential husbands at the NAAFI canteen where she worked she never remarried.

By mid afternoon I had again read the manuscript through, making notes on various aspects of it and decided on a course of action that would keep me busy over the coming months. First I 'phoned Brenda, who with a friend ran a small secretarial business in Bristol and did my clear typing, arranging for her to translate father's pencilled scrawl into something more legible. Not wishing to risk the possibility of either loss or damage in the post I drove up to Bristol first thing the following morning and delivered the papers in person.

When, after a delay of three weeks due to Brenda having a backlog of other work to clear, I fetched the neatly typed double-spaced copy of the manuscript and read once more the story of Lieutenant Schultz I knew that there was indeed a story worth looking into and there was no doubt in my mind of its veracity.

However the manuscript had been written in a staccato form, somewhere between a diary and notes and as such would not be easy to read. I felt that it would be prudent to check as many facts as I could and then expand them into a readable story. The original manuscript I put in a deposit box at my bank since I now considered it to be too valuable to be left lying around in a desk.

According to the manuscript Lieutenant Schultz's story had begun when, he had told father, a U-boat, number 614 landed him in north Devon. From research which I had carried out for a previous story I knew that for a U-boat to have penetrated almost into the Bristol Channel in 1943 was a feat worthy of a story in itself.

The minefield, which had been laid right across St. George's Channel from north Devon and Cornwall unofficially to well into Irish waters, virtually sealed the southern entrance to the Irish Sea and Bristol Channel. In the opening stages of the war and later when the minefield had been opened for the Normandy invasion and convoys sailing from south Welsh ports, U-boats had penetrated the Irish Sea, but for them to have tried in 1943 would have been suicidal. Mines dropped by the *Luftwaffe* were just as effective.

Schultz; what sort of man was he? My father had painted a picture of a complex person and I wanted to know more about him. From his rank alone he must have had some education. Who was he and where did he come from? What had made him into the person who had died in front of a firing squad and been able to cause my father to put himself in such a compromising position and, for a time, cause mayhem in the British security services?

The most tangible thing I had on which to start my research for what I dubbed, for lack of anything better at the time, 'Schultz's Story', was the numbering of the U-boat. As I had found before, I knew that records for the U-boat command were still available in northern Germany. Perhaps there might be someone still alive who could tell me about the trip which had culminated in Schultz's landing. However, with such an appalling loss rate, eighty percent in the last years of the war, I was prepared for the worst. There were also the official records at the Admiralty and the Cunard company which might have some information.

The Bishop had been as good as his word and only two weeks after father's funeral the legal process for me to purchase the old vicarage were put in motion. With that going ahead I contacted the estate agent who originally sold me my flat in Bristol and told him to put it on the market and to send all the furniture down to the Vicarage. Although I had just started drafting another novel I had become totally intrigued with my find in the old trunk and decided to make 'Schultz's Story' my first priority.

Having made my decisions I put Mrs. Glossop in the picture and together we walked round the old Vicarage deciding where my furniture from the flat should be put and what would be got rid of to make way for it. Although I wanted to keep the roll top desk I needed to lighten up the study for it would be in there I would be spending a lot of my working time. A new lime green carpet and curtains together with my desk from Bristol and a re-covered armchair should not clash too much with the oak panelling and give the desired effect. Together we set off for Axminster and its carpet factory; thence to a drapers where Mrs. Glossop was sure we would find the right curtain material.

With the immediate things for the return to my boyhood home taken care of I packed a suit -case with what I might need for up to a couple of weeks and set off again for Bristol. There I spent a working luncheon and most of the afternoon explaining my plans with Mike Bancroft my agent and then took Brenda out to dinner and a show at the Little Theatre. The next morning, after a quick breakfast, I left her flat by half past eight and edged the car through quite heavy traffic towards the A 4 and London.

During the last two weeks I had, by 'phone, been in contact with Admiralty records where I had an acquaintance who in the past had been most helpful. However, he had been unable to find anything in the files on the subject I was interested in. After a few days of discreet questions here and there someone from MI5 had called and told him to forget the whole idea as the incident had never happened! Of course when John told me this I was more than ever convinced that it had! This left me only the Cunard company. As owners of the *Queen Mary* they might well be able to help for according to the way I read the manuscript, she had been Schultz's target.

Perhaps they might have available a record of the incident which had not been clothed in secrecy. I could have telephoned for an appointment but felt that a direct personal approach would be best. After a considerable run-around because nobody really wanted to know about something with an 'official secrets tag' I was given an appointment the next morning with the personnel captain.

I am not over enamoured with London when I am by myself so decided to catch up on the missing sleep from last night and taking a room at the Combined Services Club, after an indifferent dinner had an early night.

Captain Boulton was a small, florid plump man who looked as if he liked his beer but with a razor sharp mind which belied his appearance. Having exchanged the usual pleasantries I explained why I was there saying that I had written information, but did not mention the manuscript, of an attempt to sabotage the *Queen Mary* back in 1943.

He sat back with chin on entwined fingers and studied me hard for a moment or so before commenting that he had heard the rumour later that year when he had been a very junior officer in one of the company's smaller ships. He and a friend, Mark Lester, had finished their time as apprentices together before being sent to different ships. Mark, by mistake, had landed up in the *Mary* and was aboard her at the time of the alleged incident.

Boulton explained that the officer structure on the big ships was somewhat different from the normal run of things since, apart from the Captain and Staff Captain, there were nine other navigating officers all of whom were senior men in Cunard. Apparently one such man had the same name and initials as Mark and should have been sent as a leave relief. When young Lester had arrived aboard, the Chief Officer had hit the roof having been sent someone who, in his words, 'was still wet behind the ears!' Since the vessel sailed within hours of Lester joining the young man was aboard when the incident happened.

Late in '43 or early '44, Boulton was not sure, the two friends had met for a brief time in New York and Boulton had asked about the rumour. Lester had replied with a wink, tapped the side of his nose with a finger in great conspiratorial manner and made the sole comment 'State secret and all that sort of thing old chap!' Despite pumping by his friend he would not elucidate further. Like most others Boulton had then forgotten the rumour.

Now, thirty odd years later, memories came flooding back to the personnel captain and for a moment or two longer he mused to himself, muttered something about the Official Secrets Act then wrote on a note pad, tore the page off and handed it to me.

"That's the name and address of Captain Lester. I don't know if he'll discuss the matter with you or no. Tell you what. He happens to be home right now preparing to take up a shore post in the States. I'll give him a buzz." He looked a number up in his 'phone index and dialled out. "I must say that what you've told me is most intriguing!"

While the number was ringing out I asked if there might be something in the company's archives. He expressed his doubts, adding that he would have thought that if it had been really serious the

21

Admiralty, or whoever, would have sequestered the logbooks.

The result of the conversation with his colleague was that Lester would be pleased to see me that afternoon. Thanking Boulton I gave him my card and he promised to contact me if he found out anything useful.

Once more I hit the road but this time bound down the A3 to Haselmere. I now knew that something definitely had happened aboard the *Queen Mary* and I was firmly convinced of the validity of father's manuscript.

Captain Lester was, like his friend, in his early fifties but was still handsome in a rugged way. I could picture him as master of one of the old time clippers rounding the Horn. He and his wife were in the throes of packing up their home, a bungalow set in about half an acre cluttered with an abundance of shrubs and fruit trees. Inside they were surrounded by tea chests and newspapers. They were letting the bungalow furnished but were packing away those personal items which turn a dwelling into a home.

Mrs. Lester, a tall attractive woman, produced three mugs of tea and some fruitcake, apologising for the fact that the decent china was already packed away. On hearing my name, and ascertaining that I was indeed an author, she produced one of my books and said she had read two others by me. This seemed to set the scene for her husband to overcome his reticence to talk about matters which had been under the official secrets act.

Young Lester had been in his bunk, for his was the eight to twelve watch, when the 'incident' had happened. Next morning at breakfast there had been an atmosphere that could have been cut with a knife with hardly any of the usual conversation. Lester remembered that a junior sparks had mumbled to his watch-mate that 'the master-at-arms had at last got a real prisoner in his cells instead of just a very pissed sailor, under armed guard too!' His companion had hissed at him to shut up and looked furtively at the other officers around the table.

Before an inquisitive Lester could enquire what had happened a naval officer had come into the wardroom and told them that they were now all under the official secrets act and could not discuss or talk about the night's happenings even amongst themselves. With the ebullience of youth Lester had piped up – 'But Sir, I don't know what happened so please would you tell me what it is I shouldn't talk about?' He had not meant it to sound flippant but the withering look he had received from the naval commander had, he felt, reduced him to something the cat might have brought in.

That the Prime Minister and his retinue, together with the Chiefs of Staff and their entourage, were aboard was known by all the ship's executive officers and they supposed that their having to clam up was something to do with that august personage. However, the fact that one of the radio officers had been wounded and a Royal Marine dead was beyond doubt and could only be kept under wraps with difficulty.

In New York Lester had been taken off the giant trooper and put aboard a cargo ship as fourth officer; its chief officer replacing him on the Queen. He never did find out what had really happened but whatever it was must have been serious for just before going ashore the same naval officer reminded him of the official secrets act and backed it up with dire threats as to what might happen should he say anything about the incident. It was ironic that all these years later I was able to tell Captain Lester briefly what appeared to have happened.

On the Captain's recommendation I stayed the night at the Boar and Hounds and after an excellent breakfast, drove eastwards along the A27 to Dover; more determined than ever to find out as much as I could to confirm father's manuscript.

The crossing to Calais was by way of a Townsend ferry over a calm dull grey sea on an equally dull grey day. After a night stop in Brussels I crossed into Germany next morning and onto the autobahn, which would take me northwards to the Danish border and the town of Westerland.

Once again the people responsible for the U-boat archives were most helpful. Here I learnt that U-614 had failed to return from patrol in July 1943 so it looked as if this lead would not help. (Back in England I later found out that she had been sunk in mid-Atlantic by an aircraft from coastal command squadron 172.)

Feeling somewhat dejected I was about to leave when the librarian read a little further and saw that the boat's petty officer telegraphist had become ill and been transferred to a supply U-boat and returned to base. Ferreting further into records it appeared the petty officer never went back to sea and had not been listed as killed.

In view of his mission I had not expected that Schultz's name would have been shown on the U-boat's crew list but the Germans' penchant for keeping records showed that he had indeed been embarked on the submarine's penultimate voyage. However, it was not stated why, other than to say that he was a communications officer. The fact that there was no subsequent mention of him leaving the 'boat or in the final list of 'missing in action, presumed dead' was of interest. Presumably his landing would have only appeared in the skipper's personal journal and that, of course, was at the bottom of the sea. Possibly it was an error that he was named in the first place and some unfortunate naval clerk found himself sent to the Russian front as a result?

It looked as if I was in luck when I was given both the Lieutenant's and the P.O.'s wartime home addresses. After a lunch of *sauerkraut* and *schweinhacksle*, one of my favourite German dishes, I was once more on the road bound for the outskirts of Cuxhaven. There, as the weather turned sour on me with heavy rain, my luck ran out.

I can speak German tolerably well but I was unable to find anyone who knew of the Schultz family. Where the house should have been was a large block of flats. Apparently the original street had received a stick of bombs meant for the harbour. Further enquiries the next morning at the *Rathaus* also drew a blank, due once again to allied bombers having destroyed the relevant housing records.

Topping up with petrol I headed the Jaguar south towards a small village near Mittenburg on the border with Austria. There is one good thing about travel by car in Germany and that is a very high speed can be maintained on the autobahn system, which enabled me to reach Augsburg and stay in a reasonable hotel before the night was too old.

The village where the petty officer telegraphist had lived, and hopefully still did, nestled in a beautiful valley in the Tyrolean foot- hills and was shown to its best as yesterday's rain was replaced by sunshine. Untouched by the war years it was difficult to imagine how any one from there could have been engaged in the frightful carnage of the U-boat war. In its very remoteness and small population, almost to the point of inbreeding, lay my best hope. I was not to be disappointed. Hoping for the best I booked into the local *Gasthaus* and was soon advised where my search should start.

Kurt Oppenheim now lived a few doors down from the address given me and I found a small thin man with sharp features and a sallow skin and who was, perhaps, only a couple of years older than myself. If his looks might have frightened small children on a dark night he was kindness personified. When the Americans had broken out from the landing beaches of Normandy and made their right hook down the French coast he had been trapped in Lorient at the flotilla radio base station. Put in a prisoner-of-war cage and kept there for months after the final ceasefire he had finally found his way home in the utter chaos that followed Germany's defeat.

Using a skill taught him by the *Kriegsmarine* he had opened a small radio and electrical repair shop. With typical country hospitality he now invited me into his home and listened intently while I told him of my quest.

Sitting in the tiny garden at the back of the shop and breathing the clean crisp afternoon air he conjured up his memories for, like most of those who had been in the shooting war, his time in U-boats was etched indelibly on his mind. In his eyes I could see the pain of those days as he answered my questions and relived that voyage in which I was so interested.

The conversation was carried out in a mixture of German and English with both of us stumbling over the more technical terms. Apart from the specific reason for my visit I found it more than interesting to talk with someone who had been in U-boats at the same time that I had been a very green midshipman on a Flower Class corvette escorting convoys across the north Atlantic. For all I knew it might have been U-614 which had given me my first ducking and put me in hospital for the latter half of 1942.

During the first couple of hours and over afternoon tea, when *Frau* Ingrid Oppenheim and her son joined us, our conversation was on general topics as well as the war and our varied experiences then and now. As with many of the Germans with whom I had dealings I found no animosity for our side having won and the terrible damage done with the bombing. We all agreed on the utter futility of any form of war and

27

for the necessity for coming generations to be made acutely aware of the need for peace, but with the present bellicose attitude of the eastern block countries that seemed to be a vain hope.

As the evening closed in Kurt and his wife were pleased to accept my invitation to join me for dinner at the *Gasthaus*. I went back to spruce up while Kurt spoke with his assistant and closed the shop. After a fair meal we repaired to the empty lounge and once again, over liqueurs with our coffee, I set my portable tape recorder going.

It was past eleven o'clock when I said goodnight to the one time *Oberfunkermann* of U-614. He had explored every bit of his memory covering his last voyage and what he could tell me about *Leutnant* Schultz. His summing up of the man was that as a communications officer he was very much on the ball. The other sailors in the crew thought him to be arrogant and very much a Nazi party member and certainly not liked.

CHAPTER TWO

THE COINCIDENCE

During a light breakfast of *schinken* and a fried egg, which had hardly seen the frying pan, I decided that as I was so near to the Austrian border I would 'phone the *Gasthaus* where I stay when at Alpbach and find out how the snow was for skiing. I find skiing quite therapeutic and the cold clear air of the mountains conducive to thought, an acceptable combination of pleasure and work.

Alpbach is a delightful village up in the mountains only a short distance from Innsbruck. Its slopes are not too difficult for inexpert skiers like myself. The landlady's daughter at this particular *Gasthaus* had also, on past occasions, been more than just friends with me. True I did not have any of my skiing gear with me but I could always hire. I hoped that Gretta would still be unattached and, to be honest, I think that the thought of her was a greater influence than the snow!

I am not in the habit of sleeping around and Brenda and I had indeed thought that eventually we would become engaged. We both felt very comfortable with each other and getting into bed together had taken a long time. We did not 'hit the sack' each time we met and although there was passion there was also something else as well which made it all a bit different. She thought it was that nebulous thing called love but I was not so sure. To me the dichotomy of such a feeling is clear, there should not be any element of doubt, it must be a clear yes or no if a permanent relationship is to be established.

Gretta had happened before Brenda and had continued for a number of times since. I can truthfully say that it was she who had seduced me and I had found her quite the wildest woman I had ever gone to bed with. I suppose I was also flattered because she was considerably younger than me. There had never been any talk of a permanent relationship. It was purely a physical attraction and I had no doubt that I was one of a number, although I did not think that she was a nymphomaniac. However, she was undoubtedly the catalyst for my meeting with *Herr Kapitän* Weiner, which has enabled me to write 'Schultz's Story' in such authentic detail.

Despite the wheel-chains, which I had dutifully fitted in accordance with the notice on the lower slope of the mountain, I had to leave the Jag in a parking bay a hundred yards from the *Gasthaus*. She just would not grip on those last few yards where the gradient was that much steeper.

Thanks to the cleared path, and despite a light fall of snow, there was no difficulty in walking those last few yards to the neat double storey timbered building. With its steep roof and bargeboards recently painted with green swirls showing up against the overhanging snow it was a perfect picture for a Christmas card.

Entering the hallway I dropped my case on the floor and tapped the hand-bell on the table that served as a reception desk. Pulling the register towards me I started to fill in the necessary particulars as the door marked *Privat* opened and Gretta came to the other side of the table.

She was not what one might call beautiful but she was attractive; nor was she the typical Aryan type, in fact she was the opposite with dark hair down to her shoulders and black eyes that could flash a message and give a mere man goose pimples. Her skin had an almost olive complexion and when I had seen her naked that first time with her large brown nipples I wondered if there was Latin blood in her. At twenty-eight perhaps she now carried a little too much weight for her five foot eight or so but that mattered not one bit as I caught a whiff of her scent.

"*Herr* Brent. How nice to see you again!" Like so many Germans and Austrians her English was better than my German but her greeting was more formal than usual. "*Mutti* said to expect you. Your room number three please." As she said this she placed a hand on the corner of the register and deliberately moved a finger up and down so that I would not miss the large flashy engagement ring. Her presence had automatically given me a warm feeling in the crotch but on seeing the ring and getting its message my embryo erection halted in its stride. Obviously there would be no wild night under the duvet for me.

"You are engaged then, *Fraulein* Gretta?" It was more a statement than a question and couched as formally as her greeting had been. "A nice ring."

Actually I thought it looked hideous. "Do I know the lucky man?"

"*Ja, i*t is Ericson the instructor."

As I picked up my bag and took the proffered key there was the sound of female laughter from outside, the clatter of skis being put in the rack on the porch followed by the thumping noise of snow being knocked off ski boots. Sounds synonymous with any ski lodge, although it seemed a bit early for people to be coming in off the slopes.

My disappointment at the thought of no Gretta evaporated as the warmth of the *Gasthaus* encompassed me. One really needs to be in such a place to appreciate how each of these wooden buildings seems to have a character of its own. Even without the central heating the very timber seems to exude warmth and friendliness. The grain and colour of the planks being enhanced with an occasional picture or a small brightly dressed doll hanging on the walls. The atmosphere engendered by the whole just cannot be found in brick built places.

I had given Gretta that extra *mark* which would entitle me to a bath and soon she came to knock on my room door to say that the water was running. She cast her eyes downwards as she added: "Sorry Michael but it cannot be any more."

The system of paying a small extra fee for a bath is a funny one, which you get used to and, quite frankly, I would rather stay in these small places than the bigger impersonal hotels. I was soon back downstairs and entered the small lounge.

A young couple sat on one of the corner settles, obviously English, with accents hailing from the Yorkshire area. In an armchair near the pot-bellied stove a thin grey haired gentleman, perhaps in his early seventies and who did not look to be in the best of health, sat gazing fixedly into the flames. Like myself he wore corduroy slacks and a sports jacket but whereas I had on a light-weight roll-necked sweater his blue paisley tie was well knotted and he gave the impression that he was more used to dressing in a lounge suite or even uniform. There seemed something vaguely familiar about him although I was positive that I had never met him before. He had a pipe clenched in the corner of his mouth but seemed unaware that it was not lit.

In age I was somewhere between the young couple and the lone man. Being somewhat gregarious and probably not wanting to admit my age I would normally have tried to engage the youngsters in conversation but their attitude towards one another as they sat clasping hands was that of two people engrossed only in themselves. From the shiny rings on the girl's left hand, which she now moved to clasp the beaker in front of her, I guessed they were newly married. Deciding that they would probably resent my intrusion I nodded to them and then seated myself in a second chair by the stove. Presuming that my companion was German I said - "*Gutten abend mein Herr.*"

For a moment the man seemed not to hear and then I saw him grimace as if in pain before turning towards me and replying in English. "Good evening,

33

Mister Brent." The surprise that he knew my name must have shown on my face. "Please excuse me Sir," he said with a smile. "But I saw your name and occupation in the register. As an author, like a detective, you must surely make mental notes of what you see in case they can be of use to you later. I am naturally inquisitive and after years of having to make a note of things I find it difficult, so late in life, to break the habit."

At this moment a waitress came to ask what I would like to drink. I ordered hot *Glauwein,* that excellent warming drink, especially when one has just come in off the slopes, and asked my companion if he would care to join me. Had I behaved like so many of my countrymen and kept myself to myself my stay in Alpbach may have turned out entirely differently.

He was, of course, quite right and his few words had certainly aroused the inquisitive streak in me and made me want to know more about him. We sat in silence until the wine came and, as if it were brandy, he rolled the mug in the palms of his hands. While he did so I noted that his long fingers were well manicured. Manners kept me from asking who and what he was; I had the feeling that he would tell me in his own good time.

When he spoke again it was not what I expected. "What brings you to Alpbach, Mister Brent? Is it just for the skiing or are you also working?" Was he that perceptive or was it just an inquisitive nature?

"A bit of both," I replied leaving out any mention of Gretta. "I happened to be in Germany doing research on a manuscript concerning one of the big troopships during the war. Finding myself just the other side of the border I decided that a bit of skiing would not be amiss. And yourself Sir?" I felt that the questioning should not be all one sided.

"Me, Mister Brent?" He again looked long at the flames before turning towards me, seeming to hesitate before answering. He had put his cold pipe in his pocket and now twisted his hands together. "Me?" Again a pause. "Renewing memories of years gone past before it is too late but now I am not so sure that it was a good idea."

There was a faraway look in the eyes, which appeared to stare right through me. It was then that I saw the familiarity. Those eyes were the same as Gretta's, as was the set of the cheekbones. Later, during the evening meal, I watched as he followed Gretta's every movement in the dinning room and I was certain. She, however, showed no signs of recognition.

"Excuse me, Mister Brent, I am being rude. Allow me to introduce myself. Joachim Weiner, one time *Kapitän* in the *Kriegsmarine* at your service."

Sick though he was I am sure that had Joachim Weiner been standing he would have drawn himself to attention and clicked his heels. Such a movement would not have been ostentatious but born of the inbred Prussian love of manners.

"You say, Mister Brent, that you are researching something to do with large troop transports during the war. We, of course, had some in the Hapag-Lloyd line but none as large as your 'Queens'." Again there was a pause, a grimace of pain and that distant look.

"I once had a vague connection with one of them, although I have never seen her. I toyed with the idea of making a trip in her after the war but never did and now it is too late." He took a long sip of his *Glauwein* using both hands, which I now saw were shaking, as if the memories had somehow un-nerved him.

"Which 'Queen' was that, Sir? We only had the *Mary* and the *Elizabeth* but there was the much smaller *Queen of Bermuda*." Something inside me told me what the answer would be and my pulse quickened.

"The *Queen Mary*." The name was uttered quietly, almost forlornly. "From the pictures and plans I studied of her she was a magnificent vessel and it would have been a great tragedy if we had succeeded in sinking her."

I was now sitting bolt upright and stared rudely into the Captain's face. Coincidences did happen in life in weird and unpredictable ways; only last year I had met someone in Los Angeles with whom I had struck up a casual acquaintance during a literary lunch. On exchanging names it transpired that he had met my father in between air raids on Malta when they were both trying to rescue the occupants of a bombed house. Now I was talking to a man who might have had something to do with *Leutnant* Schultz: A man who had come to see a past mistress and his daughter. That same daughter to whom, I had hoped, I had come to make love, as he had done to her mother those years ago. Briefly I wondered if his affair had been one of love or just lust and how it had come about? My change in demeanour had not escaped the Captain's notice and he in turn seemed to be more animated.

"Could the *Queen Mary* be the subject of your research, *Herr* Brent?" Momentarily it was as if whatever had been his connection in the operation it now had shed thirty odd years off his age.

"Captain Weiner, Sir." As a one-time junior officer I had automatically become subservient. "Does the name Schultz, *Leutnant* Schultz, mean anything to you?" Although he hesitated only a moment it seemed ages before he replied.

"Willie Schultz. *Mein Gott*! *Darf ich...*" He stopped, hesitated again and then reverted to English. "So you *are* interested in the *Queen Mary*. May I ask how you got to know about Schultz?"

Leaning forward on the edge of my chair I told the Captain I had found a manuscript, but not its full purport, and that I had become interested in an attempted sabotage of one of our major troopships. Then I asked what his connections were with the affair.

"*Lieber Gott*!" he exclaimed. "After all these years am I perhaps to learn what happened to him? The last I saw of Willie was as he boarded a U-boat in Lorient. *Herr* Brent, you perhaps know something then of the operation in which *Leutnant* Schultz was engaged?"

"Captain, the information in the document of which I spoke was given to my father by Schultz before he was executed. I am trying to confirm the facts and put them into publishable form for I believe his efforts are worthy of being read about by others.

It seems Sir, that you might be able to help towards that end?"

There followed a long pause during which his face contorted in pain before he finally said. "Yes, I do know about *Operation Königin* as we called it, for I recruited Schultz and was his controller and monitor until he left for Ireland. I expect that there may well be some reason or other why I should not tell you about it but I shall be out of harm's way long before you make your book public. Frankly I see no reason after all these years not to talk with you.

After the war ended I was surprised that your naval intelligence had not questioned me about it. Perhaps your people had, at the time, hushed it up so well that they forgot all about it!" He turned from gazing into the stove and looked hard at me. "So you say Schultz was executed. I often wondered what had happened after we received his signal that the *Queen Mary* had come to anchor and, four days later, the short homing signal from her. *Herr* Brent, if I tell you all I know will you give me your word that you will tell me how *Leutnant* Schultz came to be executed?"

"You have my word Sir," I said.

"Thank you. As an English gentleman I know you will keep it. To know the full reason as to how I became involved with *Königin* I must go back to my childhood. My father was a naval attaché in Spain where he met my mother and I was subsequently born. At the age of five we were sent to London and did two tours there so that English replaced Spanish as my second language, for I was sent to an English public school. It had always been a forgone conclusion that I would follow my father into the navy, although I naturally hoped that I would go to sea and not, as they say, drive a desk.

Schooling finished I took and passed the exam to enter the *Meurwik* Naval Officer's College and finally obtained my commission in the *Kriegsmarine* where, much to my dismay – the argument being that something was going wrong with my right eye – I was posted to Intelligence and sent to the university in Bristol to take a degree in languages.

There was a Royal Naval reserve unit, H.M.S. *Flying Fox* I think it was called, attached to the university and it was somehow arranged that I would train with them. Before I left home I was interviewed by a Commander and told to keep my eyes and ears wide open and send back reports on anything of interest. Nineteen thirty-eight saw me promoted to lieutenant and although I never stood a watch I did make a goodwill cruise attached to the admiral's staff as his intelligence officer. After that I was sent to Admiral Canaris' *Abwehr* H.Q."

Our conversation was interrupted by Gretta calling us to the dinner table. I thought of going down to the car for my tape recorder but somehow felt that it might cause the Captain to clam up. I would just have to remember all he said and put it on tape afterwards.

I noticed that the Captain only picked at his food and immediately after the meal asked to be excused as he was exhausted, but he promised to continue our conversation after *frühstück* next morning. I had no idea what was wrong with the man but suspected possible cancer in advanced stages. After a schnapps with my coffee I did go down to the car for the tape recorder and then spent an hour making notes on it up in my room.

I had turned the light out about ten o'clock and was well asleep when I sensed rather than heard the door opening. I had no great valuables worth stealing and, anyway, theft was unheard of in such a small village, so the door was not locked. Perching myself up on my elbow I heard the slight click as the door closed, the rustle of a garment and then, right by the bed the greater rustling as her silk dressing gown was discarded and dropped to the floor. Then I caught her scent. Gretta!

"Vielleicht noch einmal lieber Michael," she said softly and pulled the duvet from me. After her earlier remark I had not expected a visit and was wearing pyjamas. By the time she had removed these I was well and truly aroused and, as usual, for the first time there was no foreplay. She sat on top of me and as I went into her she started to gyrate as only she could. Somehow she always managed it so that we climaxed together and very quickly. In no time at all we lay exhausted in one another's arms. Fortunately the bed did not creak and wood is a fair insulator of sound. Twice more during that night we made love and in a different way each time, and when she left just before daybreak neither of us had had much sleep.

An hour later, which seemed as if it was only minutes, bleary eyed I made myself get up and splashed my face with cold water at the washbasin. As I got ready to shave I caught sight of the magic of a new day. Although the sun had risen it had not quite cleared the mountain so that the valley was still in shadow, but in a gap through the trees the snow crystals on the ridge were caught in its rays and momentarily etched in brilliant gold, which quickly turned to silver and then became white as full daylight enveloped the village. It was one of those moments that made you feel glad you were alive, but as I scraped away with my razor my mind turned to thoughts of a grimmer nature.

One point that Petty Officer Oppenheim had mentioned which differed from Schultz's assertion to my father bothered me. He said he had been landed in north Devon from the submarine, whereas Oppenheim had been quite emphatic that it was off Ireland and into a fishing craft manned by Irish Republican Army sympathisers. While shaving I mulled over this point and decided that this would be my first question for the Captain.

Weiner was as good as his word. After breakfast, well wrapped up, we sat on the balcony overlooking the ski slopes in brilliant sunshine. Down the slope and to our left were the few buildings and the other *Gasthaus,* which comprised the small village. Below was the car park where my Jag, together with a Mercedes and a battered Morris, stood covered by a light fall of snow. About two hundred yards away was the lower end of the ski lift, which was moving endlessly up the slope towards the cafe at its peak where it disgorged the multi-coloured skiers. It is quite amazing the vast number of clothing combinations that can be seen in such a place. If you

41

are in colourful clothes and have a spill and need help then it is an advantage if you can be easily seen. However, I think it's more a case of outdoing one's neighbour; rather like the plethora of hats at the Ascot races!

My companion seemed better for the night's rest and pondered for a moment when I put my question to him.

"The answer undoubtedly lay," he said, "in the fact that he did not want to compromise the Irish pipe-line. It had been so very useful in the past and no doubt would be again in the future. Also in asserting that a U-boat had penetrated the St.George's channel defences he must have realised that your Admiralty would go into a flat spin wanting to know how such a thing could happen, and with a bit of luck a mine-sweeper might even blow herself up when checking the minefield!"

"Now I have a question Mr. Brent. How did Schultz meet his end. Was he hung?"

"According to my father he faced a firing squad, although I must admit that I thought spies were hung. But thinking about it he was not a spy as such, more a saboteur. When caught he was in the uniform of the British merchant navy and that was a civilian service. But more likely, because Churchill had been aboard, the powers that be wanted to keep things quiet and I hear that a hanging can never be kept under wraps in Wandsworth Prison, which I believe is the only place they hang people. Somehow word always seems to get around, whereas a firing squad in a military prison with disciplined men unaware who they were executing and sworn to secrecy might just keep the lid on things." I paused a moment and the captain let out a long drawn breath. "I just don't know and there is nothing in the manuscript to say why."

"*Mein Gott!* You mean to say that had Willie succeeded we would have caught Prime Minister Churchill as well?" The old man stared hard and long, again it seemed right through me, as he pondered what might have been. There would not have been enough medals in the Third *Reich* with which to decorate Schultz if he had pulled off such a coup. Without Winston Churchill at the helm who knows how the allied war effort might have altered?

I continued: "Not only the Prime Minister but also all the Chiefs of Staff, Sir. The result would have been totally catastrophic for us! In fact, in retrospect, it seems incredible that such a risk was ever taken to place almost all our eggs in one basket, as the saying goes." We were both silent for a moment as the enormity of that situation sank in.

Other than Gretta bringing us Schnapps and a coffee midmorning our talk was uninterrupted. When Gretta brought that tray and I could smell her scent once again, I realised how tired and a bit sore I was. After lunch, while the Captain took a short nap, I made more notes and was ready when he felt fit enough to resume our conversation.

Being the man he was he told the facts clearly and in chronological order with my having to ask him little. He took the whole episode right back to its beginning.

*   *   *

Operation Königin was born out of a remark made by a rather inebriated U-boat skipper in a nightclub that had become the watering hole for submariners when in Lorient. When he was leaving his patrol area he had been positive that he had sighted the *Queen Mary* on the far horizon and going like a 'pig with a scalded ass'. He had been on the surface on a reasonably calm day and had even broken radio silence to make a report.

To men who knew that the next patrol could mean death, the crowded and smoke-filled room with its scent of whores and spilled beer represented a good time ashore. Now someone said loudly that 'it was time Operations got their finger out and put a radio beacon aboard the vessel. We could then all line up for a shot at her!'

'Shit!' exclaimed a *Korvetten Kapitän*. 'Just imagine putting one up the Queen!' He thrust his gold braided arm up the skirt of the woman on his lap. There was a burst of louder than usual ribald laughter and another officer shouted the question. 'Does Royalty do *It* differently from us poor sods?'

The remarks were heard by a junior officer on the operations staff. He repeated it next morning as a joke to the Flotilla *Kapitän*, who in turn repeated it during lunch in the senior officers mess.

Somewhere along the line a wag drew a cartoon of a wolfpack, with D.F. loops turned onto a large spark emitting from an advancing ship. The ship bore the name *Queen Mary* with its forward funnel turned into the upper torso of a bare-breasted woman wearing a crown. A U-boat appeared to have just fired a torpedo that took the form of a rampant penis. The caption read - 'One up a Queen!'

As is often the case in service life the cartoon turned up on a notice board strictly reserved for important messages, in the hallway of the *KriegsmarineKommando* in Berlin. Quite how it got there no one was prepared to say. It came to the eyes of *Gross Admiral* Reader on a day, in mid-summer of 1942, when *Herr Reichsminister* Goebbels was visiting.

The astute doctor stopped to study the cartoon and saw further than the picture on the board and into the vast propaganda value that would follow such a sinking. It would not just be a case of a very large troopship going down but one that was held dear to the hearts of all Englishmen, for she bore the name of the Queen Mother and had actually been launched by her! He recalled hearing that the *Führer* had offered a considerable sum of marks for the U-boat commander who managed to sink the biggest ship afloat. As yet it had not happened. ... Why?

To make sure of getting the right answers to the *Reichsminister's* immediate question as to why such a sinking was being lampooned the Commander, who was the liaison officer between H.Q. and the *UnterSeebootenKommando*, was sent for. Fortunately the Commander was aware of the speed of the *Mary*, nearly twice that of any U-boat, and pointed out that even if she were hit by a torpedo it would probably take several to sink her since, as far as he could remember, the vessel had about a hundred watertight compartments.

The *Reichsminister* could understand the mathematics of the problem for the submarines but wondered why the *Luftwaffe* had not done the job. Surely the intelligence services must know when she was in British waters? He would have to broach the subject with *ReichsMarschall* Goering.

Although Goering had quite a reputation as a fighter pilot in the Great War and had been Hitler's right hand man in his rise to power, he was at that time, when not at his shooting lodge, more occupied with his 'one-upmanship' over his colleagues in the Nazi hierarchy by building a bigger and better palace. The day to day running of his air force he left to his General commanding the *Luftwaffe*. As usual when he had sniffed cocaine he blustered and whined his way around Goebbels' questions and promised he would look into the matter.

At his next meeting with the *Führer* the Propaganda Minister mentioned the cartoon and convinced his leader of the immense blow to the pride of the English if the *Queen Mary* were to be sunk. And so an order was issued for a feasibility study to be undertaken immediately by both navy and air force.

Thus it was that a half drunken U-boat watch-officer's ribald utterings became something to be looked into!

Captain Weiner was not aware what happened to the study by the *Luftwaffe*, if indeed it was ever undertaken, however *Gross Admiral* Reader did do

46

something. Since it was to do with U-boats the
memorandum went straight to Admiral Dönitz in Paris
who made a note on it saying he would be pleased to
drop off any agent if required but the agent was
nothing to do with him and promptly sent the
memorandum by air to the *Abwehr*. There Admiral
Canaris sent it down the line until, since he was head
of the section dealing with allied merchant shipping, it
appeared on Weiner's desk and he was told to look
into the matter 'by yesterday'!

CHAPTER THREE

THE FÜHRER 'S DECISION

Joachim Weiner, at that time a commander, had an attitude that was positive and believed anything was possible until proved otherwise. Of course he knew of the great liner, what mariner didn't, and in his particular job he had a fair idea of how and where she was plying her trade and so he set about dealing with his new orders.

First he required to know what the exact problems were which faced the U-boats in trying to sink not only the *Queen Mary* but also her sister ship the *Queen Elizabeth*.

Since the whole idea had received such top priority he opened a file, which he labelled, for want of anything better, *Operation Königin* and stamped it *Oberteilgeheim*. Then, having given his personal clerk some enquiries that could be carried out by an *Oberschreibermann* with total security clearance, he left for Rangsdorf *Flughaven*. There he boarded a *Storch* aircraft, the only plane available at that moment, from the *Abwehr's* private *Staffel* and made a very uncomfortable journey down to Paris.

Had the matter not received such high attention the pilot would have stayed on the ground, for they flew hedge-hopping almost all the way, sandwiched between tree tops and heavy rain clouds. It was only the skill of the pilot, a man considered too old for operational flying but with several thousand hours experience as a commercial flyer, that they avoided a crash at the refuelling stop.

Admiral Dönitz received the commander from the *Abwher* with his usual courtesy and sent for his staff officer in charge of operations. The *Kapitän Operations* was impressed by Admiral Canaris' signature on the top priority order shown him by Weiner but privately shrugged his shoulders and thought the whole exercise a waste of time; just another pie in the sky effort dreamt up by a bunch of desk-jockeys well removed from the real war!

In July 1929 the liner *Bremen* had won the blue ribbon of the Atlantic for the fastest crossing - 4 days, 17 hours and 42 minutes - but when this was lost in May 1933 to the new Italian liner *Rex* German maritime pride was severely dented. Hitler, now Chancellor, was affronted by something in his new Germany becoming second best. He told his minister for marine to find out how this could happen and immediately ordered a study for either the re-engining of the *Bremen*, or the building of a new vessel to regain that prestigious ribbon.

The first thing the marine engineers did was to study the drawings of the *Rex* and the new British vessel known as *Job 534*, then under construction at John Brown's yard. How these plans were obtained was open to conjecture but the result was that full particulars of the *Queen Mary* were available from the marine department and had been closely studied early in the war by U-boat command.

Job *534,* now known as the *Queen Mary*, was capable of a speed of 32 knots and, yes, there were 160 watertight doors below C deck. There were 2 engine rooms and 4 for the boilers so that even if she were hit by a couple of torpedoes there seemed little chance of stopping her. Anyway, it would be by sheer chance if a U-boat found herself in a position to fire in the first place.

Undeterred by the negative attitude of the Operations Captain, Weiner asked to speak with any U-boat captains who might be available. He was taken to the Claridge Hotel on the *Champs Elysee*, reserved for generals and holders of the Knight's Cross, where there happened to be two U-boat skippers staying for a night while en route to Berlin.

Annoyed at having to postpone their evening at the Scheherazade night-club the two submariners, still tired and gaunt from the hardships of the Atlantic and their recent brushes with death, could do little but co-operate with the commander from intelligence when shown his orders. Particularly as they would shortly be receiving the diamond clusters to their Knight's Crosses. With such high decorations the two men were masters of their trade and over a glass or two of champagne they were forthright in confirming operations' attitude that the whole idea was a joke.

'Even if we knew the exact time the liner left the Clyde,' the U-boat men responded, 'there is far too much Tommie air reconnaissance for us to lie around just waiting for her. We would have to be so far to the north or west that it's a million to one chance we would see her. After all, if we had seen her before

50

now there would have been reports of it, wouldn't there?'

After a night in a far less auspicious hotel than Claridges, Weiner returned to U-boat H.Q. and related the gist of the previous evening's conversations. Once again he received that shrug of the shoulders from the *Operations Kapitän*.

'Really, someone needs their head read to waste our time. Bloody stupid!' he said, and then realising that he did not know what the politics of this commander from intelligence might be, hastily added, 'and the *Führer's* too, on this one!'

That's all right for you my friend, thought Weiner as he left the office and headed back, uncomfortably, to the airfield in a *keblewagon*. You don't have to deal with the people who need their heads read. I do!

On the flight to Paris he'd had to make use of the sick bags in the *Storch* but heading northwards the trip had been quite pleasant, except for being buzzed by a flight of Me 109s who had somehow not been advised the aircraft was in their area.

Weiner would have liked to spend a day sight-seeing in the French capital. He particularly wished to re-visit the Notre Dame Cathedral, not for religious reasons but out of curiosity. His mother had taken him there when he was six years old and he remembered being so intimidated by the vastness of the roof – so high above him that he had been sure God must live up there. The organ had been playing and the music reached a crescendo as he had looked for God in that high place.

For the first time in his young life he had become aware of such sounds and when they returned outside, the gargoyles, which at first sight had quite frightened him and made him feel that they must be something to do with the devil, were no longer awesome. In later years he found considerable peace of mind just to sit in a church listening to organ music.

Then there was the *Folies Bergere*. He would liked to have seen that as well but there'd been no time after his talks with the U-boat men. To have stayed another day was out of the question with such a high priority on his mission. Indeed as he denied himself those pleasures he wondered, for the first time, what might happen to him if he failed to come up with a workable plan. It was rumoured Hitler could fly into a rage when his wishes were not fulfilled and the delinquent concerned banished to the front.

Back in Berlin Weiner briefly reported to the chief of the *Abwher* before he flew off, this time in the relative comfort of a JU 52 transport, for Norway. First to the U-boat base at Bergen from where the mightiest battleship in the world, the *Bismark*, had sailed a year earlier on her fatal voyage. From Bergen he went further north to Trondheim where *Kampfgeschwader 40* had a base.

Although coastal command group 40 was strictly a *Luftwaffe* base and therefore, presumably would come into any report made by the fly-boys, Weiner was beginning to believe that, if anything was to become of *Operation Königin*, aircraft were bound to be involved. Anyway, he happened to be friendly with the *Oberst* commanding there and, once again, the man on the spot would be able to brief him far better than someone back in Berlin who, rather like himself, merely read from a piece of paper.

At Bergen he talked with the base commander and then, more importantly, with three 'boat skippers back from patrols finished only days before. There was no doubt that their intimate knowledge of the enemy's air and sea patrols between Iceland and Ireland and the area of the North Channel was crucial to the proposed operation.

Questions and yet more questions with constant reference to their daily journals brought forth several points which had seemed minor when they had submitted their written reports to H.Q., but now helped to give the *Abwher* Commander a clearer overall picture.

Overlooking the *Tirpitzufer*, Weiner's office was quite pleasant even with one window bricked up and the other criss-crossed with a sticky cotton material because of the air-raids. Back there after an uneventful return trip he went through the notes made for him by his chief clerk. That done he started making enquiries within the *Abwher* of the sections dealing with New York and Scotland.

Allied ships sailing from New York were regularly reported by an operative – who until the start of hostilities had been a 'sleeper' – whose sole job was shipping movements. From his vantage point across the Hudson River, when there was no fog or heavy rain, he – Weiner discovered he had to change the pronoun to 'she' – had a clear view of Pier 90 and the other adjacent passenger berths.

Because of her vast length, a thousand feet, the *Queen Mary* had her own wharf specially built prior to her launching. Weiner smiled as he read the page in his hand; if Dr.Goebbels wanted to know he could even tell him that the Americans charged forty-eight thousand dollars a year rent for it!

The agent, by constantly shifting her communication base, remained undetected in the vast population of that huge city. But around the pier itself security was very tight; especially so since the French liner *Normandie* had caught fire and capsized nearby, causing speculation about sabotage despite the official version of an accident due to welding! Weiner knew that the *Abwher* had not been involved and wondered if it was one of Heydrich's S.D. people.

In response to a request sent to another agent – one of the *Abwher's* own men who had been put ashore from a U-boat early in 1940 – it became apparent that due to the intensive air cover given by the US Navy and Air Force, in particular that from the slow moving Coast Guard dirigibles, it would be suicide for a U-boat to lie in wait in an area where she could be sure of sighting the liner.

The 'happy days' of the first few months when the Yanks had entered the war were over. Then 'boats could get close inshore and navigate with impunity as no attempt had been made to restrict the marking of the shipping lanes and cities were a blaze of light. The American Navy had ignored the hard-won advice of the British Admiralty so that targets presented themselves with total indifference to their possible fate and the U-boat men wished they could carry twice as many torpedoes.

But now things were different and whilst any action for the proposed operation from the New York end could not be categorically ruled out it seemed unlikely. This brought Weiner back to Scotland and 'The Tail o' the Bank'; a place which had become known amongst seafarers as the 'Piccadilly Circus' of the sea it was so crowded with ships.

Sleeping on a camp bed in the office, ignoring an air raid, and working almost non-stop over the next two days, he gathered the information he required. He spent time finding out who had agents in Scotland and had upset a *Wehrmacht* Major when he had shown his authority and made the army man disclose what information he had about the Clyde area. Weiner felt that the major's reticence was due more to inter-service rivalry and petty jealousy than for operational reasons. From intelligence gathered Weiner knew that the United States forces were also plagued with this inter-service rivalry and that, although it did occur, it was nowhere near as bad in the Tommie outfits.

Slowly he built up a dossier, which was almost all in the negative from a U-boat perspective. Only in one department had he received an immediate and positive answer and that was one of the questions he had set for his chief clerk to find out.

'No problem at all,' the radio engineer in charge of the *Abwher's* workshops had replied. They made radio sets of all kinds suitable for an agent working behind enemy lines. 'Just let me know the particular situation for its use and it'll be yours in a matter of days!'

From the dossier he wrote his report and his opinion on how the operation should be conducted, if it went ahead at all, but kept some of his ideas to himself lest the hierarchy thought he might be testing the adage that 'bullshit baffles brains'!

Oberkommando der Abwher.
Subject: Operation Queen.
Security: Category one.

In accordance with your orders I have carried out an extensive investigation into the possibility of placing an operative with a radio beacon aboard the troopship RMS Queen Mary with the purpose of making the vessel easier to locate by our U-boats.

1. *The vessel in question has so far eluded our U-boats because she sails heavily escorted for the first day or so at high speed, 28.5 knots (Type VII C U-boat 17kts) before proceeding alone. (Destroyers are unable to maintain such speeds due to lack of fuel capacity). When operating within range of our bombers she also has an escort of an anti-aircraft cruiser and, while still within their range, fighters. (It should be noted that so far no successful penetration by our bombers has been made on the Firth of Clyde anchorage since 1940)*

2. *The vessel has 160 water tight doors from C
    deck downwards and would consequently
    require several torpedo hits to sink or even
    stop her.*

3. *March, 28 l942 vessel arrived Sydney,
    Australia, with 8000 American troops. Since
    her return to New York our intelligence
    confirms she is now employed in shipping
    American troops to the Clyde using Gourock
    as her terminal port on a regular basis.*

4. *Enemy air reconnaissance at both arrival
    and departure points is intense, totally
    precluding any U-boats lying in wait close
    enough to be effective.
    Any 'line' formed beyond that air cover
    would have to be at a maximum spacing,
    weather permitting, of 16 kilometres between
    'boats for visual contact and so far off-shore
    as to be impracticable.*

5. *Security of the vessel's proposed course is
    absolute and on 'a need to know only' basis.
    As yet we have no agent high enough in the
    British Admiralty to obtain this information.
    Radio silence while on passage is maintained
    at all times.*

6. *If an operative with a beacon were to be
    successfully placed aboard for the vessel's*

return trip to the States and
Kampfgeschwader 40 (Trondheim) advised
to be on standby with a flight of the newest
JU 188 (now on operational assessment
trials) fitted with long-range fuel drop-tanks,
they could be successful in a bombing attack.
The vessel's upper decks are sheathed in
wood so that any subsequent fire caused by
Incendiary bombs and bullets could cause
major damage.

Beneath the wooden sheathing the steel decks
are not armour plated and should allow
entry of suitable bombs, therefore the vessel
might well become a total wreck if the fire
burnt far enough down from the boat deck.

7. To ensure success of such an air attack it
    would have to take place only after the
    vessel was out of range of any protective
    fighter escort.

8. Assuming that some of our aircraft survived
    the attack it is likely that they would have to
    make for Scotland, Ireland or Iceland and
    the crews bale out. It must be assumed that
    none would be capable of carrying enough
    fuel to ensure a return to base.
    The use of long range Fock-Wulf Kondor
    aircraft from Kamfgeswarder 40 is not
    thought practical other than as shadowing
    aircraft once the subject has been sighted. A

fast low level attack being more likely to
succeed.

9.   The main anti-aircraft outfit of the Queen
        Mary is believed to be:-
        10 x 20mm Oerlikon cannon
        6 x 40mm Bofors
        4 x 75mm high angle guns
        Plus a number of machine guns

10.   Kampfgeschwader 200.
        It is understood that this group may have a
        Flight of captured enemy B24 Liberator
        long- range bombers. This type of aircraft is
        now in use by the British coastal command.
        Therefore if one of these aircraft were to
        lead the attack the chances of success would
        be greatly enhanced, particularly if it were
        in possession of the daily recognition signal
        and would therefore be able to approach
        undetected as an aircraft being flown by the
        enemy.
        I have had no contact with Group 200 and
        would require further special authorisation
        to do so.

11.   Operative.
        For the return voyage to New York the
        Queen Mary generally carries trainee
        flying personnel bound for the school in
        Canada; Air Transport Auxiliary crews

returning for B19 or B24s for ferrying to
bases in England; Merchant Marine crews
going to pick up either Liberty ships made in
the USA or Fort vessels built in Canada.
Also sundry civilians for one reason or
another.
There can also be several thousand of our
own Wehrmacht personnel being sent to
prisoner of war camps in the US or Canada.

12.　For an operative to board as an officer in
one of the armed services would be
extremely difficult and would probably
restrict his movements once in the ship.
However, as an officer in the merchant navy
taking passage to America he might not be
so restricted and also possibly easier to
place aboard.
Such an operative should be drawn from
either the Kriegsmarine communications
branch or from our own Merchant Marine
and not from any present Abwher agents. He
would operate separately from any existing
network.
How he would board would have to be the
subject of more research but likely to
be purely opportunistic.

13.　It is anticipated that casualties amongst those
aboard the target would be very high since it
is expected that lifeboats and rafts would be

mainly destroyed by the fire on the upper decks.

14. *The provision of a compact transmitting beacon on a set frequency and a suitable network to monitor it presents no technical difficulty. How and where it would be operated on such a crowded vessel would depend on opportunities offered at the time and liable to tax the ingenuity of the agent; hence the requirement for the operative to be a communications expert.*

15. *Because of the Atlantic's unpredictable winter weather any operation should take place in the summer months.*

    Signed: J.Weiner.
      Commander. S.O.4.
       Department K.

(In hindsight it was this insistence on not using an *Abwher* agent and his operating separately that saved Schultz from being 'blown' by MI6 who, at the time, were reading the *Abwher* code and were therefore able to keep track of most German spies in the U.K)

It was ten past one in the morning and Pieter Kummetz, the chief clerk, was dozing with his head on crossed arms over his desk when the buzzer summoning him to Weiner's office sounded. He stirred and wished to God someone would get the bloody heating going properly; having to wear a greatcoat in the office was damned annoying. He'd heard that there was a grave shortage of coal in Berlin because thirty wagons of the stuff was still burning after being bombed four days ago in the Potsdam *Barnhof*.

Kummetz, like his boss, was trilingual. Brown haired with an angular face, he was 1.8 metres tall with a wiry frame, which he kept fit thanks to his liking for football. From the small town of Landau near the French border he was born to a French mother and German father. Brought up in a household where both French and German were spoken he had also learnt English to a fair standard at school. Entering a bank straight from school he had been an assistant manager in a small branch when it was subsequently closed at the end of 1940. By nothing short of a miracle somebody in Manpower actually did the right thing and, because of his languages, drafted him into the *Kriegsmarine* and designated him for intelligence. Once in the *Abwher* he had been given the rank of petty officer-clerk as soon as he had passed the necessary exams and sent to section K, where he was soon noticed by Weiner.

Passing a thorough security check, the conquest of France enabling final clearance on his maternal side, he had rapidly risen to senior warrant officer's rank. There were those who said that such speedy promotion was due to the fact that the Vice Admiral bearing the same name, with his flag hoisted in the *Hipper*, was a relative but that was not true. He had an intelligent brain, unlike some of his contemporaries in the *S.D.* who, in his opinion, were little more than thugs, and he was happy he had got where he was purely on merit.

Pieter Kummetz considered himself to be very lucky with the extra pay both in rank and the *Abwher* allowance, and a recent mention by his boss that he was being considered for promotion to commissioned rank. He found the varied work interesting and, thank God, far from the Russian front. As he was told recently by a wounded sergeant back from the east, it seemed that in winter your balls froze off while in summer, should you be lucky enough to find a woman, your arse got bitten by a myriad of mosquitoes! Without a doubt fighting the Popovs was the worst thing going.

Until the Commander had been given this latest job they had been engaged in keeping track of information passed to them through agents abroad concerning allied merchantmen. They filtered the reports so that the agents were not compromised before handing it over to naval intelligence or, when appropriate, either of the other services. Presently there were a number of such agents in the ports of the U.S.A, South America, one in South Africa – nothing had been heard from a second man for some while – and, of course that hive of intrigue, Lisbon. Occasionally the S.D., under *Reichsführer* Heydrich, who had their own agents as well, passed information across.

It also fell to his section to interrogate any captured officers of U-boat victims. This, of course, was only possible when ships were sunk on lone voyages and the U-boat commanders able to surface and search through the survivors. Weiner liked to interrogate as soon as possible after the men were landed and before they might be subject to useless questions from escorting personnel, a journey which could sometimes take a week or more by train to reach Berlin. Kummetz had consequently visited most of the U-boat bases in France and Norway and he enjoyed such trips.

"Pieter" - in private Weiner always addressed him by his given name and to help him with his English spoke mostly that language in the office (a fact which had already been reported to the Gestapo by an over-zealous typist). "Sorry to keep you up but get this typed with the usual three copies right now. I'm going to my quarters but I'll be back before the Admiral arrives. It's probably all a bloody waste of time but who are we to query it?"

By half past seven Weiner was seated in front of Admiral Canaris while the latter read his report. Weiner had to admit to a pang of jealousy of this small man, old enough to be his father, having had command of a battleship.

"So you think there might be a slight chance of this operation succeeding, Weiner?" he said laying the folder on his desk but not really believing what he said.

"Yes Sir, but only if the *Luftwaffe* co-operate. As I have pointed out the U-boats on their own don't stand a chance."

"All right. Then I'll have to take it to higher places. Doctor Goebbels said that any report on this matter was to go through him. You'd better hold yourself ready in case of any further questions. I'll bet old Fat Boy (as he called the none too popular Georing) will have one of his tantrums when he finds out that the navy boys in our outfit want to use his people!"

Goebbels was in his vast palace, built before the war, at the Brandenburg Gate. Here he received the head of *Abwher* and read the report while a liveried footman served champagne despite the fact that it was not yet midday. The Propaganda Minister was no fool; the only one of Hitler's close associates with a university degree he was an astute politician. Having assimilated the contents of the file he was convinced that the propaganda value, if the object could be achieved, would be worth the loss of even a dozen aircraft, to say nothing of the army prisoners.

Life in Berlin at this time was beginning to get tough for the ordinary populace and there were mutterings that they resented the expensive and well-stocked restaurants patronised by the upper echelons of the Party and military. In an effort to get the people more 'on side' the propaganda minister had the offending restaurants closed, including a favourite haunt of Goering's.

Despite a compromise by changing the restaurant to the status of a private club for the air force its patron still held a grudge against Goebles, who now realised that for operation *Königin* to have any chance of getting off the deck, it would be essential to have the head of the air force with them rather than against. Fortunately the Reich Marshal was also in Berlin at his palace on *Lipziger Platz* and agreed in his most haughty manner to receive the propaganda minister.

By pointing out the accolades which the air force and therefore its commander, might receive for having had his 'fly boys' execute such a daring operation – no mention was apparently made of the operative who would make such a thing possible – Goering finally condescended to the use of his planes but insisted that he would see the *Führer* with Goebbels and, on the latter's insistence, reluctantly agreed that they would have to make the journey by air. Strangely the ex fighter pilot preferred to use his luxurious train where possible.

Having insisted that a dinner party and night at the opera already scheduled could not be altered, the two men, accompanied by the admiral, departed two days later for the *OberkammandoWhermacht,* temporarily situated in the Ukraine. Here the *Führer* eventually received them at five in the evening, in none too good a temper having been informed of further Russian gains on the central front.

Hitler did not need to be reminded of the feasibility study for the proposed sinking of the *Queen Mary.* He was known amongst his senior commanders, who at times were considerably irritated by the fact, for the considerable amount of trivia which he could assimilate while often failing to grasp the greater overall picture of things. This was a very small operation in the greater scheme of winning the war, but it had caught his imagination and he overrode his air force commander, who now protested against too many aircraft being used and the fact that he, the

Reich Marshal, would not be in charge of the planning and execution of the scheme. At this juncture Hitler began to get annoyed with his air force commander, almost screaming at the man.

"If junior officers can come up with plans like this why can't you and the Generals do so! Why am I beset with idiots?" And then, as if to further humiliate Goering, in a more reasonable tone of voice asked of the admiral. "This man of yours, Weiner, he is capable of organising the operation?"

"As competent as any, *mein Führer*"

Hitler paused for a moment as he contemplated whether he could involve himself with the planning but thought better of it. "Then see to it. He is to be given full co-operation from wherever he needs it. *Reichsleiter* Bormann will write the necessary orders this evening. See that I am kept informed. Now it's time for the evening briefing!" He dismissed them with a wave of the hand.

Back in Berlin Canaris sent for Weiner. The commander entered and clicked his heels. Unless it was obviously asking for trouble he used the raised arm of the Nazi salute as little as possible.

"Take a seat Weiner and a glass of schnapps for we have something to celebrate." The flag lieutenant handed over a glass while the admiral raised his and continued. "I give you our latest *Kapitän*. *Prost*! And good luck Weiner for I think you'll need it! Look at the signature on these orders; one for you and one for me. As you see, as far as 'Operation Queen' is concerned, you are almost God and answerable through me to the *Führer* himself. That bit of paper and an extra stripe on your arm should give you all the clout you need. Now all you have to do is get the damn scheme operating! As I predicted, Fat Boy didn't like it at all; wanted to run it himself but, thank God, was overruled. You even have access to *Kamfgeschwader 200* and that certainly didn't please him!" It was ironic, he thought, that in the early days he had assisted Goering to set up the secret flight group!

Weiner read the order and let out a slow whistle. "*Holle,* Sir, I didn't think they would go through with it; not a *selbstopfermanner* effort."

"Well, suicide mission or not they have and you had better get cracking." The admiral turned to his flag lieutenant. "See that someone takes over the captain's present job," and then back to Weiner. "What staff do you want Weiner?"

"At the moment, Sir, just my present chief clerk but I would prefer a more secluded office off-limits to all but yourself".

"See to it Karl." The small admiral stood up and held out his hand. "Again good luck and God be with you, I think you'll need his help on this one. Keep me informed."

Back in his own office the newly promoted captain showed Kummetz the orders and gave his first command as overlord of *Operation Königin.* "Pieter have my steward get a tailor to put a fourth stripe on all my uniforms!"

CHAPTER FOUR

THE PLANNING

Kapitän Weiner sat in his new office, and in due deference to his new rank, in a chair that was just that bit more comfortable than the one in his previous office. His chief clerk was doing the handover to the commander hurriedly summoned to section K4 who was none too pleased at having been thrown in at the deep end and not being briefed at length by Weiner himself. Since the orders for Operation Queen had stressed top priority Weiner himself, rather than the flag lieutenant, had gone to the office administrator to sort out the new office and was well pleased with the result. It had been quite amazing how fast people could move when the name of the *Führer* was invoked. The trouble was, he thought, could he move as fast?

The new office was at the end of a corridor on the same floor as the admiral. There was a communicating door into another smaller office while another led directly out into the passage and this he had given orders to be boarded up so that the only entry would be through what would be Kummetz's office. It was all a bit small but at least it would not be as cold as on the floor below whence the previous occupant had been quickly banished.

It was not only the operation which was starting from scratch, but so was Weiner. In his time in intelligence he had never had to act as controller for an agent let alone organize a whole operation. Of course, like everyone else, he had attended lectures on anti-espionage so that now, in theory at least, he should be able to spot a Russian spy or a British double agent as soon as he clapped eyes on one. Perhaps he was being too cautious here in the heart of the *Abwher* building but if anyone said anything he had that bit of paper!

He had ordered charts covering the area from Norway to Iceland and as far south as the German Bight and westwards to include Ireland and well out into the Atlantic. He also obtained a British one – for they did produce the best – of the Firth of Clyde, all of them to be fixed to one wall. A new filing cabinet for Kummetz, a safe in here and an armchair for the admiral should he visit at any time, and a larger desk. By tomorrow all should be in place and in the meanwhile there was already a fresh blotter on the desk and a full inkwell; freshly sharpened pencils and a large pad of ruled paper. It was all there ready for him to start writing, but where to begin? Unable to make up his mind he filled his fountain pen, a Parker still with him from that last cruise when they had visited Portsmouth.

This evening in the wardroom he would have to stand drinks all round to celebrate his fourth stripe, but the reason for that stripe?

He re-read his memo on the operation. It had seemed so straight-forward while he had been compiling it; just a paper exercise which, as the U-boat men had said, was crack-pot and a waste of time just thinking about. When completed it would no-doubt find its way into the shredder. Now it had rebounded on him and he was beginning to wonder if he was up to the job? Sure he was a senior naval officer engaged in intelligence work but quite what qualification did that give him to play with men's lives? The thought that he might be directly responsible for the deaths of several bomber crews, to say nothing of the man he would have to find who would be the center-pin of things, sent a peculiar feeling through him.

Until now he had virtually been a 'desk jockey', doing important work true but far from the reality of a submarine commander, bomber pilot or anyone else who had the lives of others in their hands. His abstract war was finished, now it was real but what if he failed? It was known that the *Führer* could go into terrible rages and more than one staff officer who had failed in his job had found himself posted to the Russian front. Perhaps there might be disadvantages in being known in higher places?

Weiner was not married and had no close family. His mother and father had been killed in 1941 near Duisburg when a British bomber had jettisoned its load in a vain attempt to keep flying. He had been engaged just before the war started but a *Hauptmann* in the *Waffen SS* had claimed her so that now, when a father or wife could have offered him solace as he came to grips with his new position, he had only his mistress to talk to and he felt she was not the sort he could confide in. Certainly she was warm and rewarding in bed and, Weiner thought, in love with him but he did not think that he was in love with her. As he lay close to her late that night, after another air raid had ended, he wondered if they did get married whether love would come. Perhaps after Operation Queen was over?

The carpenters arrived in the new office about mid-morning and started to put up the soft-board backing for the charts, which had already been delivered and now stood neatly rolled in the corner by the window. When the two carpenters had entered the room Weiner stopped writing and closed the file. Leaving the room to the sounds of hammering he sat in Kummetz's chair, re-opened the file, and looked at the 'shopping list' he had been making out.

1. Operative. Send telex to naval personnel H.Q requesting files on all unmarried communication officers prepared to volunteer for special detached duty. Must have good knowledge of English.
2. Ditto above to mercantile marine head office on radio officers.
3. Visit Air Force H.Q. re range of JU 188 with drop tanks. What bomb load carried? Arrange visit to K.G. 200.
4. Discuss radio beacon and range etc with chief radio engineer.
5. Obtain British school atlas.
6. Discuss with relative Abwher department current situation regarding all types of movement within Britain. Documents required for an agent. Cash requirements. Feasibility of agent being a lone operator.
7. Entry into Britain. Air, sea or what?
8. Operative's background and cover in England.

Clothing, uniform.
9. *Training program and where.*
10. *Set up final 'delivery' and monitoring stations.*
11. *Codes.*
12. *Whatever else I've forgotten!*

He read the list through and changed the word 'requesting' to 'requiring' and added, 'To be given top priority', in item one. He then read it several times more trying to envisage every possible problem, realizing that everything really depended on the man who would finally do the job. What sort of fellow was required? The technical side was the simplest part. Weiner wanted a fully trained radioman so that if things did not go according to plan he would be able to extemporize. A fully indoctrinated spy per se was not required but rather a man who understood ships and was capable of pursuing his objective single-mindedly.

Since it was quite possible that he would not survive he obviously needed to be dedicated to Germany's cause. A Party fanatic perhaps? Weiner knew that at this time there were some who were beginning to doubt the reasons for this war, particularly now that Goering's boast that 'no bombs would ever fall on Berlin' was being proved a blatant lie.

What did he, Weiner, feel about the politics of the war? Basically he was a military person brought up to accept discipline and the teachings of the Catholic Church. The latter he had shed when he joined the navy, although he was far from being an atheist. What motivated him? Certainly he would rather have been at sea, even if that meant he would, air-raids discounted, be at the 'sharp end'. At least he had progressed up the promotion ladder and the standard of living in the wardroom here was undoubtedly better than the general run of things. In fact he was almost cocooned in *Abwher H.Q* by the parameters of his particular work, which kept him from seeing, apart from those trips to the coast, the darker side of war and also the implementation of the Nazi doctrine.

He had never joined the Nazi Party, although there had been times when he had thought about it. Certainly it appeared that Hitler had done wonders for Germany and, as far as the war was concerned, up until now, made all the right decisions. The recent, virtually Canadian, assault on Dieppe had turned into a disaster for the allies while in the east the *Whermacht* advances had been phenomenal, although there now appeared to be some setbacks. The Tommie air raids were also becoming more than a joke. Had the *Führer* perhaps bitten off more than he could chew?

Weiner, like most of the general population, had not really taken in the contents of *Mein Kampf* – in fact, because it made stuffy reading, he had only glanced through the book. Of course he was aware of the persecution of the Jews and their deportation to the east, but again, like so many, it did not really affect him and so he shut his mind to the subject. Of greater concern was the more apparent silencing of

74

those with views opposing the party doctrine, but then perhaps that was necessary because of the war.

Had he been privy to Hitler's declaration to the party hierarchy in October '41 when they had been told 'now was the time to implement the doctrine of *Lebensraum'* and which was, at that moment, being carried out with such terrible thoroughness by the *S.D. Einsatzgruppen*, Weiner might have thought seriously about where his loyalties lay. By nature, he was not a violent man. It was this 'soft' approach to the ideas of the war, together with the report about his use of English, which later nearly cost him his life.

After Operation Queen had finished he became a general staff officer to Admiral Canaris, retaining his secluded office and thus became suspect as a participant in the July 1944 attempt on Hitler's life. He was closely questioned by the Gestapo and narrowly escaped being hung along with his admiral and hundreds of others. That staff officer position also brought him to the notice of the Allied War Crimes Commission but he was cleared of any crimes.

"Alles in ordnung, Herr Kapitän."

The carpenters emerged from his office carrying bits of left over board and timber and reported the job finished. Now he could occupy his office and get down to the job in hand. First get those telexes off. He finished the draft just before Kummetz joined him, the handover complete.

"Pieter, get this down to the typing pool and have it sent 'priority'. No need to code it up. I'm off to see

Colonel Ulbrecht. If I'm not back before you are, start putting up those charts."

He placed the file with the 'shopping list' in the safe along with the original of the memorandum, thinking they looked rather lonely in the otherwise empty safe.

That 'bit of paper', a photograph of which now reposed in the original file, he had carefully folded and placed in a separate wallet to be carried with him at all times. As he walked along the corridor and down the main stairway he thought of the things he could do with those orders; even do a 'Hess' and demand a 'plane and jump out of it over Scotland!

Oberst Ulbrecht's official position in the *Abwher* headquarters was that of *Luftwaffe* liaison officer but in reality he was more than that. He was a personal 'plant' by Goering – there was at least one in most branches of the services and civil departments – and had direct access to the Reich Marshal with orders to by-pass normal channels when the situation demanded.

This had come about because he had, in the last war, joined the squadron of Richthofen, the famous Red Baron, just after Goering had taken over command. Apart from flying they had spent many drunken nights whoring together until Ulbrecht was shot down.

He had managed a crash landing behind his own lines but broke a leg in two places and suffered much facial damage, which had left him hideously scarred so that now he was far from a pleasant sight. It had also scarred his mind while the leg, which had been badly set making it impossible to wear the boots and breeches that went with rank, gave him much pain. Some years after the end of that war Goering had passed a beggar in the street and taken pity on the man he had once known. Now that man was repaying the dept to his mentor.

Ulbrecht had already been sent word from above about *Operation König in* and was surprised by Weiner's visit so soon. Weiner had only once dealt with the air force man when one of their rescue seaplanes had picked up an allied sea captain from the North Sea. At the time he had not been very impressed with the man and had tried to make allowances for the colonel's objectionable manner due to his afflictions.

Reaching Ulbrecht's office Weiner entered and an air force sergeant, seeing the rank of the visitor, pushed back his chair and stood rigidly to attention, as the captain announced the reason for his visit.

The inner office was thick with the smoke of cheap French cigarettes, which the colonel smoked incessantly much to the annoyance of other officers when he did so in the wardroom. His supply of the weed seemed inexhaustible and was flown in to him on the 'mail' run. Vaguely he recognized Weiner as he blew smoke rings into the air before uttering a guttural, "Yes?"

"You are aware *Herr Oberst* of *Operation König in*?" Weiner coughed as the smoke caught at his throat.

"*Naturlich.*" The sneering and pompous intonation of the reply raised Weiner's hackles, so he dropped any pretence of protocol.

"Well I'm just informing you that I shall be visiting the headquarters for Special Operations Group 200."

The *Abwher* had used the services of *KG 200* several times before when agents had needed to be parachuted into enemy territory, although Weiner had not been personally involved. Apart from protocol, if Ulbrecht was genuinely helpful it could save a lot of legwork but the man's retort dispelled any thoughts of co-operation.

"Anything you require from them you will get through me, Weiner," he snarled.

Except for a few at *Abwher* H.Q. Ulbricht was totally disliked and Weiner now joined the majority and decided there was no longer need for pretence. Weiner, who had not been asked to take a seat, leaned with both hands on the edge of the desk.

"If you know about the operation I…" and he repeated the pronoun with emphasis, "*I*, am running then you must also be aware of the orders I carry. Do you wish to see them Ulbrecht? Or should I report to their source that I am not receiving the co-operation that they say I should!" He stood back a pace and looked directly into the furtive eyes before him.

"Of course not, of course not," the misshapen mouth spluttered. "Do as you please! Go and see them yourself for all I care!" He dabbed at the spittle dribbling from the corner of his mouth with a white 'kerchief.

Walking back to his office Weiner felt more sure of himself after overcoming the first hurdle. If he had submitted to Ulbrecht he would have been subservient to Goering's paranoia for wanting to know everything that was going on. No doubt, somewhere along the line, the Fieldmarshal would have tried to get his own back on Canaris by making things difficult for Weiner.

The next morning, which happened to be fine and relatively warm, Weiner took the short walk along the *Tirpitzufer* to naval H.Q. He showed his *Abwher* pass to the sentry outside the main door and, crossing the spacious entrance hall, showed it again to an *Oberbootsmannmate* seated behind an oak desk with a large ledger before him. The captain's name and reason for his visit was duly entered in the tome and a nearby sailor, wearing a wound stripe, no doubt given for the loss of his left hand, was duly summoned to show Weiner to the senior operations officer's office. Here the atmosphere was totally different to yesterday's meeting with the air force liaison officer. It was also here that he discovered the first mistake in his planning.

Had he seen time as a seagoing watch officer or a navigator he would have realized that there was a considerable difference in the latitudes of Northern Ireland and New York. The first was roughly on 55 and the other on 40 degrees north. He had made the assumption that his proposed bombers would operate from Norway, but now he was not so sure and hoped that nobody higher up had noticed his mistake.

The operations captain and Weiner had previously dealt with one another on several occasions. After cigarettes were lit and Weiner had explained about Operation Queen, they stood looking at the Atlantic Ocean charts spread before them by a junior officer, who was then dismissed. Weiner felt that, until absolutely necessary, the fewer people who knew about the operation the better.

From his colleague he wanted to know what the time frame would be, bearing in mind the present state of the U-boat war, for an agent to be embarked at a U-boat base to being landed in Ireland, should it be decided that was the way which had to be taken for entry into England. He already knew that such a route was used from time to time and now made it known that he might wish to use it. The operations officer promised he would let Weiner know as soon as he had contacted *Unterseebootenkamando*.

Of course Weiner could have done that himself but felt that protocol should be followed just in case more help might be needed in the future from Naval H.Q. However, as he studied the charts and discussed the war at sea in general terms it became more obvious than ever that it would be from the air that the coup de grace would come.

The meeting with a major from the operations section of KG 200 at their base outside Berlin a day later proved to be, as the saying went, 'the planting of the acorn from which the oak tree would grow'.

Security at the base was very tight and even with his *Abwher* identity card Weiner had to wait at an inner guardhouse for the Major to escort him to the operations room. There a colonel and a captain, both with pilots insignias on their otherwise plain *Luftwaffe* uniforms, sat without being introduced listening as Weiner unfolded his overall plan of action after having shown his special orders. He soon felt that, as with his meeting with the U-boat captains, here were men who were at the top of their profession.

They were the elite of all aircrews; volunteering, knowing that there was little chance of their exploits becoming public. Not for them the receptions and personal awarding of the Knight's Cross with Diamonds from the *Führer*. These men were in a grey area of the war who readily undertook flights at the very thought of which ordinary fliers would quail. Their dedication to their job was ultimate and their contribution to the war effort at times immeasurable.

Major Stricher heard the naval man through without interruption and then spoke into a phone to request the presence of the *Gruppefermeldeoffizier*. Whilst they waited for the signals expert, schnapps was poured for all those present from a cut glass decanter reposing on a dark oak sideboard, the only non functional item of furniture in the operations planning room.

Sipping the schnapps Weiner explained the time frame of the operation. According to what little information an agent could glean the Queens sailed from their anchorage at the 'Tail o' the Bank' mainly, but not always, during the hours of darkness so as to be out of sight by day-light. At a guess, allowing for anti-U-boat zigzagging, after twenty-four hours the target could be expected to be five to six hundred miles out into the north Atlantic.

Because of the poor weather in winter it was hoped that the operation would take place some time in the summer and probably at night. This was because of the anticipated difficulty of the agent being able to operate his beacon without discovery in daylight. It was thought that with the vessel totally blacked out access to the upper deck would be easier. Of course it was appreciated that this would make a bombing run more difficult.

Major Stricher nodded. He was not a striking man to look at and except for his immaculate blue uniform with its yellow facings he would not have been noticed in a crowd, until he spoke. His voice demanded attention from his listeners no matter where he was. Now he spoke.

"*Herr Kapitän,* we are here to solve problems!"

Picking up a piece of string he measured off a distance from the latitude of the chart and then pinned one end just off the Mull of Kintyre and with a pencil at the other end drew a semi-circle with a radius of six hundred miles, which stretched in the north from almost at the Faroes Islands and then southward to the bottom of Ireland. Next followed two similar semi-circles but centered from Nantes in France, first at a thousand miles and again at fifteen hundred. The latter ran roughly from Iceland to the Azores.

"The smaller circle represents where you estimate your ship could be at nightfall. The second is the range for our JU 188s to be able to turn after the attack and make Ireland. The third will be the point of no return." To emphasize that he paused and finished his schnapps just as there was a knock on the door. A *Hauptmann* entered who, seeing the seated colonel, saluted in the military style before turning to the operations officer.

"Sir?"

"Klaus a question for you. A ship somewhere out here." He made a gesture with a finger. "Has a low-powered, low because it is portable, beacon on her and I want to find her. Are our present radios good enough to locate and fly on to that beacon?"

"Well Sir, it would depend on the distance away from her, the frequency and how much static is around. Under good conditions no problem but I could not guarantee it."

"Klaus I want that guarantee. Given whatever you need, can you do it? Keep the technicalities out of your reply."

A broad grin spread across the younger man's face, for in the mess he was known as the 'Professor'. He would talk on the technicalities of radio with anyone who cared to listen. After a short pause while he thought the problem over, he nodded. "Yes. Given an extra R/F amplifier with pre-set tuning to the signal frequency I should be able to do it. What is the priority on this?"

"From the very top Klaus, the very top, as is the security rating."

"Right. Then I would build a separate set for each aircraft but still retain the ordinary sets as back up." He looked at the chart. "Flying down the beam, as you well know, will not give you a range but I could do that as well. Similar sets used at shore D/F installations such as at our Merimac 'field, another around the Friesian area, and one at Trondheim would give us a good triangulation for a fix. We could then plot any movement of the vessel in question. It would be better still if we also put a set into that weather base we supply up in Greenland. Is the beacon already in place, Sir?"

Stricher looked at Weiner and introduced him for the first time. "Klaus this is *Kapitän* Weiner from the *Abwher*."

The signals expert had tossed his cap on a nearby chair after his initial salute so now stiffened slightly and clicked his heels. "You see Sir, it would help a bit if I knew more about the beacon."

"It has yet to be constructed by our workshops. Would it help if I placed their facilities at your disposal? Indeed, perhaps if you were to work directly with them from the start? The time frame looks as if it will be two or three months."

"That would be excellent *Herr Kapitän* if my commander agrees!" He glanced at the seated colonel who nodded his acquiescence.

Three hours later Weiner left, well pleased with his visit to KG 200. It had been agreed that three of the new JU 188s and a single Liberator would form the strike force. The Liberator would carry the latest, although still to be proven, radar and if it were dark would illuminate the target with flares. She would drop depth charges set to explode on contact with the water with the hope of damaging propellers and rudder and thus slow the vessel up, making it easier for the low flying 188s.

After the attack the larger aircraft, with its greater range, would shepherd the others until they were forced to ditch, pin-pointing their position to a follow-up *Kondor* which would drop a collapsible life raft and hopefully advise the nearest U-boat. If the weather was good the downed crews might even be able to be rescued by flying boat.

At no time during the discussions was the thought of failure even contemplated. With the flying side of the operation now on the right rails it rested with Weiner to ensure the other pieces of the jigsaw fell into place. It seemed to the *Abwher* man that the hardest part of all was going to be finding the right man for the job as the saboteur and how he was going to be able to operate his beacon.

Weiner wished he knew more about the intricacies of wireless. At this stage he was sure that locating the beacon and its aerial on the upper deck of the liner without being discovered would be by far the most difficult part of the whole operation.

Back at H.Q. he made arrangements with the chief radio engineer to liaise with *Hauptmann* Swartz from KG 200 and then turned his attention to the five telex resumes of possible agents, which had arrived in his absence.

CHAPTER 5

THE OPERATIVE

Rain driven by a sou'westerly gale beat at the two windows of the small conference room on the second floor of naval headquarters in the *Tirpitzufer*. The dull grey light emitted between the anti-blast paper gave the room an air of gloom as if it knew that soon one of the men waiting outside would be chosen to die for the Fatherland. The two large red flags with the black swastikas in their white circles hanging either side of the equally large portrait of the *Führer* and the gold braid of the major occupant of the room did little to disperse the gloom.

Seated at one end of the highly polished oval table was Captain Weiner. In deference to the occasion he wore his number one uniform, for he felt acutely that he was about to become the quasi executioner of one of the officers now waiting in the passage way. Whilst there was a slim possibility of the aircrews from KG 200 being picked up from the sea after ditching, he was sure that the man who was chosen as the saboteur would most likely be one of the first to die on the upper decks of the *Queen Mary*. If he failed to get aboard the trooper and was captured then he would be hung as a spy. Either way he would be dead.

With a deep sigh Weiner turned to his chief clerk and nodded. Kummetz took the top file from the pile in front of him and placed it before his captain, at the same time issuing an order to the seaman who stood to attention by the double doors at the far end of the long room. Turning on his heel the man opened the double doors and called the name of the first man to be interviewed for the position as kingpin of *Operation Königin*. As that man entered so the seaman left, closing the doors behind him.

The first candidate was in his early forties, plumpish and of medium height. Wearing the uniform of a radio officer in the mercantile marine he slouched slowly towards the table as if he felt that his presence there was a bore, before making a naval salute of sorts. Although he already knew the contents of the file in his hands Weiner read it again, deliberately keeping the man standing and in suspense. The file said that the applicant had been a senior operator on the liner Bremen but now, since Germany's liners were virtually laid-up or taken over by the Americans, was in charge of a watch monitoring the British naval Morse transmissions at a wireless station near Cuxhaven.

"Firstly, we will speak only in English," Weiner said opening the interview. "Secondly, Mr. Spreckles, why have you volunteered for special duties? You're doing essential work where you are with *B-dienst.*"

Kummetz looked sideways at his boss who had sounded quite belligerent. It was not at all his normal manner but then this new job was not exactly normal.

"*Kapitan*, I'm a seaman and totally bored where I am. May I ask what the special duties are?"

"No. I'm sorry Spreckles but at this stage all I can tell you is that it is highly dangerous and that you would be operating on your own behind enemy lines for possibly two or three months. The officer I require needs all the qualifications that, according to your file, you have. Good English and top radio and telegraphy knowledge as well as a familiarity with merchant shipping. Can you tell me what this circuit is about?" He passed over a diagram prepared by the senior technical officer in the *Abwher* radio workshops. The diagram had no figures or notations on it.

Spreckles looked at it for less than a minute before replying. "A small fixed frequency Morse transmitter, battery or mains operated."

"Correct. Tell me, have you ever killed anybody in cold blood and could you do so if required?" At this juncture in the operation Weiner could not foresee such a requirement being necessary but one never knew and it would be no use having an operator who threw in the towel because he would not defend himself to the end.

Spreckles frowned and thought about the question for a moment. "No, but I bloody near did when I came home unexpectedly and found some bastard having it off with my wife! I suppose if it were me or him I could do it but I'm not sure I'd know the best way."

Weiner felt that not being addressed as 'Sir' together with the man's way of speaking and laissez faire attitude, showed a certain lack of respect for authority. True, once embarked on the mission the man would be on his own and subject to no one, but did a lack of respect for authority also mean a lack of self-discipline?

Undoubtedly as far as wireless was concerned this man had all the necessary attributes and would be totally at home both in the ports of England, which his file showed he had visited numerous times, and on any enemy shipping. On those points he would be ideal *but* was there the self-assurance and initiative the man being sought must have?

The *Gruppefermeldungoffizer* back at KG 200 with his quick and positive decisions would have been ideal had he been a sailor rather than a flyer. Before leaving the briefing room that officer had suggested he fly in the Liberator to ensure the co-ordination of all the radio stations involved and he would, 'if the *Herr Kapitan* would agree, like to write out the communication orders for whatever operation was planned.' A suggestion to which Weiner had agreed to with alacrity.

Now, in this dismal room, Weiner looked at the file again and then up at the pallid face in front of him. He noted how there were two or three hairs on the right eyebrow curling upwards. He also thought that the fellow did not look very fit. 'Damn it, I should have put a fitness requirement in the telex,' he mused.

"You're not married?" His telex had stipulated single men. The file said Spreckles was just that but he was aware of the possibility that some unscrupulous commanding officer might use the occasion to get rid of an unwanted man and tell a little untruth in a file to do so.

"Not any more. She couldn't do without *it* if I was away too long so she went off with some guy from down the road. Women! Poke 'em and leave 'em is my motto now. Anyway, what's the point of being married while this bloody war's on?"

'What indeed,' thought Weiner as he made a notation on the file, which read - 'Technically all that is wanted, but character?'

"Who's going to win the war, Spreckles?" he asked quietly.

The radio officer looked surprised by the question. "I suppose we will if all we hear on the radio and read in the papers isn't just propaganda."

"Right. Thank you. Wait outside, Spreckles." Weiner had already decided that the man to be chosen should have no doubt as to the Fatherland's victory even if he himself was beginning to wonder how much longer it would be before that happened.

The second volunteer was also in the mercantile marine but considerably younger than Spreckles and was presently serving in a tanker running much needed fuel oils up to Norway. He had tasted action, having been torpedoed by a British destroyer during the Norwegian campaign and was lucky to be alive since he'd had to swim almost a kilometre to the shore in next to freezing water. Sodden and shivering, he had hidden for a day to avoid capture by the Norwegians and was almost at death's door when found by a panzer patrol. Had his ship not sprung a bad leak in its stern gland and was now in Whilemshaven for repairs he would probably never have seen the call for 'volunteers for special duty'.

Not a very tall man, one point seven metres, he was wiry in build and said, when asked, that he kept fit shadow boxing. His eyes were a soft brown and rather prominent which drew attention to the crow's feet wrinkles at their outer ends in a face that looked far too old for his years; but then Weiner had noticed that for those who fought the real war, not from behind a desk like himself, they became old before their time and it invariably showed in their faces.

To the question as to whether he could kill in cold blood the radio officer leaned forward in his chair as if to emphasise his words, replying in a voice that held a trace of a Bavarian accent. "If I had to Sir, yes. When they damn near killed me I know the Tommies were only doing their duty, just as I would be doing mine if the necessity arose!" Although Hashagan did not have as much experience as the older Spreckles he would be, Weiner knew, a far better choice.

Weiner had made out a set questionnaire for all the candidates and one question was - 'Do you know any part of Holland'. He had thought hard about a cover story for the operative since he was aware that, unlike himself, most Germans had a give-away accent when speaking English. Posing as a Dutchman was less likely to arouse suspicion.

"Yes, sir," the candidate replied promptly and with confidence. "I know Harligen, put in there in a coaster a few times and of course have been to Amsterdam and Rotterdam." He had also, with the same confidence, identified the circuit diagram.

"Thank you, Hashagen. If you would wait outside please." As the officer rose and saluted Weiner wrote on the file - 'A definite possible'.

The next candidate was called and entered with absolutely the correct bearing required of an officer of the Third Reich. Coming stiffly to attention he gave the Nazi salute with a loud *'Heil Hitler'*. Weiner made the required reply with less enthusiasm.

When he had first seen the telex on the third applicant there had seemed something about it that did not gel. There was no background to it other than to say the man had transferred from the *Waffen SS* with qualifications in the Signals branch. Now, studying the file in front of him and then looking hard into the officer's eyes, which he was sure showed contempt, Weiner again thought that something was wrong. The man was too sure of himself, and only grudgingly gave Weiner the deference due to his rank. The possibility occurred to Weiner that this man might be a *Gestapo* plant.

Himmler, the most feared and hated man in the Third *Reich*, with control of the *Gestapo* was scheming to oust Admiral Canaris with the intention of absorbing the *Abwher* into the external spy network formed by his former deputy Heydrich through the *S.D.* (Something which would be achieved the following year after the failed attempt on Hitler's life.) The *Reichsführer* of the *SS* had heard only vaguely about *Operation Königin* and was eager for more information.

The file said that this officer, a *Leutnant* Schultz was stationed in the communication centre of naval headquarters here in Berlin; a perfect position from which Himmler could keep tags on what was going on in the navy. What if Weiner did choose Schultz? The *Gestapo* would have to find a replacement and that might not be so easy bearing in mind the technical qualifications required. The thought of causing the *Gestapo* some inconvenience, as long as it did not rebound, amused Weiner. As he mulled over the situation he continued to hold the other's gaze. What if?

All members of the *SS*, no matter which branch, took an oath swearing absolute loyalty to the *Führer* and his ideas. They would die for the fatherland if required and without asking the reason. If chosen would this member be too brash and arrogant to pass himself off as someone who had chosen to leave his country and fight against the Third *Reich*?

Rapidly Weiner fired the pre-ordained questions at Schultz and received the answers required. To that of - 'Why are you volunteering for unknown special duty', the reply was: "It is my duty to the *Führer* that my rank and qualifications are used to the maximum!" The way it was so punctiliously said made Weiner sure that he had the man's background right. "And you would be prepared to die for the Fatherland alone and unseen by your comrades?"

"*Naturlich Herr Kapitan!*" he replied forcefully, as if it was a bloody silly question,

"You were told to speak only English Schultz!" snapped Weiner. "If you were behind enemy lines and used German it would be the end of you and the whole operation!"

Schultz was not the type of man to be cowed by the rebuke but it did hurt his pride to be found wanting in anything. Now he covered his annoyance by saying in the most punctilious English manner he could muster and taking it almost to the point of sarcasm: "What *is* the operation, Sir?"

"Should you be chosen you will find out in due course. The fewer people who know about it the better the security, with that you have to agree, Schultz."

"Yes Sir." When he had found out who the interviewing officer would be Schultz had, by devious means, been appraised of the contents of Weiner's personal file. He considered anyone who was not a member of the party to be inferior to the likes of himself so he was indeed contemptuous of the naval captain, but for now he would have to bite his tongue. "Of course Sir, you are quite right."

Weiner came to the conclusion that he definitely did not like this man but then personal likes could not come into the equation. Schultz's grasp of English was not as good as the two merchant officers and neither did he, it transpired after further questioning, have their knowledge of merchant shipping, but he did have the self assurance that would be required to carry the operation through to its conclusion.

On being told to wait outside, *Leutnant* Schultz rose from his chair, clicked his heels and once again gave the party salute. This time Weiner merely nodded. If the man was going to report back to his bosses he would go away knowing no more about

'Operation Queen' than he did when he came. If Schultz was chosen he would know soon enough.

The other four volunteers, all from the navy, were interviewed in turn and although all possessed the basic qualifications required the Intelligence captain decided on Hashagen, the second and younger merchant officer, and the man from the *Gestapo*. Almost but not quite two opposites, one quiet and self-effacing but nevertheless positive in his way of thinking whilst the other was effusive in manner but left Weiner with the thought that he would kill his own grandmother if necessary. Originally Weiner had not thought of training two men but now that seemed to make sense since there would be a fallback if anything went wrong; or was he just being perverse in accepting Schultz? Whether they would both be sent on the final journey remained to be seen.

Weiner went into the corridor and thanked the waiting men for volunteering for special duty but regretted that only two would be required. Checking that they had the necessary travel documents to return to their units he then dismissed all but *Leutnant* Schultz and *Funkeroffizier* Hashagan. Back in the bleak room he asked Kummetz if he had brought the schnapps as requested.

"Of course, Sir," replied the chief petty officer as he gathered up the unwanted files. "What shall I do with these?"

"Keep them in the office safe for the time being. How many glasses have you?" As four were produced he commented: "That's lucky. In a moment

I want both men in for drink. Have you realised that Schultz might be on the *Gestapo* payroll?"

"Is that it? Thought something was a bit off." Kummetz put up the glasses and half filled them from a large pocket flask. "We'd better be on our best behaviour then. Shall I call them in now?"

"Yes please and tell that seaman he can go for a coffee."

The two officers entered the room and as Hashagen was about to give a naval salute he saw the other's arm being raised and changed to the party salute. Weiner studied both men. The sub-lieutenant in his immaculately pressed uniform, no doubt looked after by a 'guest worker', as the foreign forced labour was euphemistically called, for the *Gestapo* could wangle anything. One point eight metres tall, lean featured with cold blue eyes and blond hair, Schultz was almost the perfect Aryan. Weiner wondered whether the man was being used as a 'stud' in one of the *Führer's* rumoured baby farms and therefore doing his 'bit' for the Fatherland in more ways than one!

Hashagan, with short curly dark hair and round face, which at nearly midday was showing a shadow of stubble, certainly had not the outstanding appearance of his companion, but there was something about him which gave an impression of reliability. His file said he was not a party member although in his younger days he had attended the huge Hitler youth jamboree at Lansdau.

"Be seated gentlemen and take a glass of schnapps with me." And to his clerk: "You also Pieter, for you are a part of the team." Weiner saw

Schultz's eyebrows go up at the thought of a chief petty officer taking a drink with officers but it did not appear to worry Hashagan. They sipped their drinks and looked enquiringly at the captain.

"I have chosen you to be the knife thrust of 'Operation Queen'," he said, breaking the silence. "An operation which is the direct order of our esteemed leader and one over which, through Admiral Canaris, I have sole command.

You will note that I am speaking in English with no reference to German niceties concerning rank etc. This is because, on your ability to both speak and to think in that language, will depend not only the success of the operation but on your ability to stay alive! Chief Petty Officer Kummetz here is totally cleared for this top-secret operation and a request from him is an order from me. Is that clearly understood?" He paused and both men nodded, although Schultz had started to say something in German, but he bit the words off.

He paused again to sip at his drink, all the while keeping his eyes on the two officers in front of him. "For security reasons, and because undoubtedly you will get drunk at home, you will be told no more about your future except that I am granting you a fortnight's leave from this evening." He glanced sideways at his clerk who nodded in understanding.

"On your return you will report back to my office in *Abwher* H.Q which, until otherwise advised, will be your base. From then on your service life will totally change." He shifted in his chair, marvelling at how easily he seemed to be slipping into his new roll.

"Your commanding officers will be informed that you will not be returning to your present duties. When we have finished our drinks you will go with Pieter for the necessary paper work to be filled out. I will now show you the orders which allow me to place you on this special duty and which also will mean you will obey no one but me. I repeat, no one but 'me'. "

He took the order signed by the *Führer* from his inside pocket and showed it to each in turn. On seeing the signature Schultz sat rigidly to attention for momentarily he could not think of a suitable expression in English. Hashagan drew in his breath and then let it out in a low whistle.

"So you see gentlemen we are a chosen few and although probably only one of you will have the honour of the final stage of the operation, you will both be known to the *Führer* because of his personal interest in it. Your special order placing you under my command will be carried at all times. Of course I do not now have to remind you that total secrecy will be required from you at all times. Indeed you will only be told about what you will be required to do as the plan unfolds. I repeat what I said earlier, the operation and your lives will depend on it. Do I make myself clear?"

"Of course, Sir," both men replied in unison.

"Since this will be your last shore leave make the best of it." He paused again to let his words sink in.

"I note, Schultz that you are due for promotion to full lieutenant; take that as read from today. You, Hashagan, will be given a temporary commission as a sub-lieutenant in the communications branch of the navy. Pieter will give you the necessary authority to visit a tailor this afternoon for a change of uniform. Now, for the last time until the operation is over I give you a toast. To the fatherland and good luck!" Standing up he downed the rest of his schnapps and, feeling that it might be appropriate, raised his arm and gave the party salute. "*Heil Hitler. Deutchland über Alles*! Dismiss."

Two chairs squeaked as one as they were pushed backwards and their occupants rose to repeat the toast and salute with arms outstretched.

During the interviews Weiner had gradually warmed to his subject but now that they were over and the decision made he felt somewhat deflated. The knowledge that this was the first time he had organised anything like this operation still made him a bit unsure of himself. He was certain that Schultz had *Gestapo* connections and that was enough to worry anyone.

He went off to the wardroom for lunch and then back to the office where Kummetz waited for him to sign the leave passes and the special orders. Those orders read that the bearer was on detached duty as a member of the *Abwher* and under the direct orders of *Kapitän* Weiner; as the final stamp of high authority he took them to the Admiral for signature. The die was cast!

Captain Weiner had been correct in his assumption that Schultz had associations with the Internal Security Police. After being dismissed

Kummetz had told him and Hashagan to go and have lunch and then to report to reception at H.Q.

Making the excuse to Hashagan that he would have to cancel an evening date Schultz reported the basis of the interview with his contact, one *Standartenführer* Muller, who foresaw the difficulty of finding a replacement for Schultz. Getting him placed at *OberkammandoKriegsmarine* had taken some while to arrange without causing suspicion.

"No. You should stay where you are and forget the heroics," he told Schultz.

The 'phone box had half the glass missing so that the gale blew the rain onto Schultz as he argued with his superior. He pointed out that the operation, whatever it was, had been approved by the *Führer* himself and to be chosen was a great honour.

"I am sorry *Herr Standartenführer* but I have already accepted!" Schultz had been transferred to the navy from the communications branch within the *S.S.* fairly early in his career but now he wondered if it was wise to argue with one so high up.

Muller exploded and told Schultz that he would be sorry, realising as he spoke that telling the man to apply for the interview in the first place had been a mistake. If indeed the orders had come from so high up then there was probably little he could do about it.

He swore again after putting down the 'phone, deciding that when the time came he would get even with this bloody unknown naval captain. (This he did later on when Admiral Canaris was 'disposed of' after the attempt on Hitler's life. Out of sheer spite he saw to it that Weiner was transferred to Estonia where he learnt what real war was about. When the Northern Army was evacuated Weiner was one of the last to leave the small port of Pal Diski, near Talin, in a *Schnellboot,* but not before he had received a minor wound from the Russian bombardment.)

Having sent Hashagan and Schultz on leave Weiner sat once more at his desk and wrote down the programme for when the two returned. First, he would send them to *Milag Nord*, the prison camp near Bremen where allied merchant seamen, being civilians, were interned.

There they would learn something about the men they were going to impersonate and their ways. For Hashagan it would probably not be much different from his own ways in the German merchant marine but Schultz would, no doubt, have much to learn. Again Weiner began to have doubts about the choice he had made.

While in the camp they would need a cover story and the commandant given a reason to pull them out. A few days should give them a chance to assimilate the current slang and some of the idiosyncrasies prevailing in the enemy's merchant ships. Then there would have to be familiarisation time for their background in some Dutch town near the German border. He also wanted them to do a week on unarmed combat – just in case!

A spare beacon was being built so that they could practice repairing it should any fault occur. On the suggestion of the Signals officer from KG 200 they must also spend time sending brief messages so that the carefully chosen wireless operators, who would be manning the monitoring stations, got to recognise their Morse 'hand'. A necessity should things go wrong and the enemy get to know of the plan and use the set instead of Hashagan or Schultz.

As Weiner wrote and realised how the whole operation seemed to be growing by the hour he found that he was sweating despite the stormy weather outside.

They would need as much information as could be mustered as to how things were in England if they were not to stick out like sore thumbs. If it became impossible for them to board the liner then at least they should be given the chance of finding a possible escape route back to Ireland.

When the time came for them to be told of the target and given the plans of the vessel to study, a secure billet must be found. Perhaps the best place for that would be with KG 200. Yes, that would definitely be best, he mused. Quarantine them where the security seemed infallible, and since the whole success of the operation depended on good communications all the personnel concerned could be grouped directly under the control of *Gruppefer-mideofficer* Klaus Swartz. God, the list seemed endless!

Weiner called Kummetz in and told him to fix another meeting with KG 200 and a day after that a flight to Bremen, then he picked up the 'phone and after much delay got through to the Commandant of the P.O.W. camp. That done he finished his notes for the future of the operation and made up his diary.

After carefully locking everything away in the safe he reported to his Admiral on the progress so far.

The Admiral raised his eyebrows on being told that Schultz was probably connected with the *Gestapo*. He warned his subordinate to be very careful indeed.

CHAPTER SIX

PROBLEMS

During the fortnight the two men were on leave Captain Weiner tied up the loose ends for the execution of Operation Queen. The Colonel commanding KG 200 readily acquiesced with the plan to use one of his group's aerodromes as a base when the time came. Indeed it made sense for the more the saboteur and the group's communications officer worked together the less likely it would be for misunderstandings or mistakes to occur.

At *Milag Nord* Weiner had to re-think his ideas. It appeared that to put the two men in as P.O.Ws would be unrealistic as far as background was concerned. The commandant thought more would be gained if Schultz and Hashagan just wandered around in their uniforms as pseudo intelligence officers. Not being service personnel as such many of the inmates were quite happy to chat with the camp officers and guards.

The two agent's leave expired at 1400 hours and while Weiner waited for them to report he mused on how they should be categorised. Presumably the enemy would call them saboteurs rather than spies; perhaps the French would say they were agents provocateur. He'd be damned it he'd call them operatives for, after all, whoever went would be the lynchpin of the whole operation.

Schultz was on time, despite having had one drink too many in the wardroom over lunch, but by

1600 hours there was still no sign of Hashagan. When Kummetz reported to his boss at 2200 that the man was still adrift Weiner became concerned.

He was sure that the merchant navy officer was not the kind to go AWOL. Had the man been injured or even killed in an air-raid? He had not heard of any major raid on Hamburg, which Hashagan had given as his address for leave; but then Goering only admitted raids that could not be hushed up. Apart from having Schultz hanging around doing nothing, except to take the school atlas and learn something of the geography of the British Isles, it delayed their departure for *Milag Nord*.

What really started to worry Weiner was the identity paper Hashagan had in his pocket.

As there was still no sign of the missing man by 0800 the next morning he ordered Kummetz to get hold of the senior operations officer at naval headquarters. As soon as they were connected he told Captain Fackler to 'scramble' and having adjusted his own 'phone came straight to the point.

"Klaus, you remember the subject we discussed when we last met, well I've struck a problem. One of the fellows I've selected for the job hasn't reported back off leave. Apart from not being able to get on with his training I'm worried about the orders he carries. Of course there's no mention in them about the operation but in the wrong hands they could prove embarrassing. Rather than me trying to throw my weight around could you get hold of your senior security type in Hamburg and have him make discreet enquiries at the fellow's home? Of course this has to be done by yesterday." He shifted in his chair as if trying to hide his embarrassment. "Damn it, what a thing to go wrong so early in the operation! If they find Hashagan skulking at home have him placed under close arrest and keep him incommunicado until I can send a plane for him. What else to tell you apart from the address?" He paused for a moment "Yes. I'm not sure what uniform he'll be wearing, could be merchant or ours since he's been inducted into our mob."

Weiner fumbled with the file in front of him and then read out the address. "One other thing Klaus, have your fellow contact me direct and many thanks." He put down the 'phone. "Hell's teeth," he said out loud. "Have I made a wrong choice? I could swear the fellow was OK."

It was just after ten o'clock when Kummetz told Weiner that Hamburg was on the line; what he heard from them made him swear. The radio officer had been reported missing to the civil police by his mother on the third day of his leave. Then, three days after that, his body had been identified by her, having been taken from the steps of the gasworks landing opposite the *Segalhafen*. The police had reported that there were no papers or identity discs on the body. They also said that the man had been garrotted to death not drowned.

Weiner was now totally perplexed and decided to go to Hamburg himself just in case there were any clues that the civil police had missed. Leaving his clerk to hold the fort Weiner, after reporting to his admiral, made the short and disagreeably bumpy flight

106

to Hamburg. There he commandeered a *Keblewagon* and driver from the airport transport pool and drove to the port's naval security office. After seeing the commander who had been detailed to find the missing agent he went on to the fellow's home.

Here *Frau* Hashagan said that her son had arrived home at teatime. Over the meal he told her he had been put on special duties and that after this leave he would be away for some considerable time and probably unable to write or 'phone her. That evening he was going out on the town with a colleague who was on similar duties.

Mrs. Hashagan was a fairly liberal minded woman and although she did not like her son picking up any woman off the street she understood his needs. Since he had no regular girlfriend she accepted that a night on the town undoubtedly meant ending up on the *Rieperbahn*, so was not too worried to find that her son had not slept at home. However, when he failed to come home for a second night and had not made contact with her she became worried, for it was totally out of character.

When on leave from his ships he had always spent time with her. Since she could not ask her husband for advice, he being somewhere in France with the *Luftwaffe,* she went to the police.

Not knowing what the special duties were she was of little help to them, other than to say that she knew the name of his last ship and that he was wearing a new *Kriegsmarine* officer's uniform. Three days later she was sent for on the off chance that a body taken from the docks might be her missing son.

That it had turned out to be Bengt had devastated her for several days and as she spoke with Weiner she had difficulty in keeping back the tears.

Thanking the good lady and promising to keep her informed of any happenings Weiner called at the local police station where he interviewed the sergeant who had dealt with the case.

The man was on the defensive and a little over-awed by the officer from the *Abwher*. He made the excuse that with all the extra work caused by the air-raids and with an acute shortage of manpower a murdered man, even one in an officer's uniform, was treated with some disdain. Even so, a couple of photographs had been taken of the body. Someone being garrotted was unusual; stabbing or a crushed skull done with a handy piece of iron being the more common form of murder.

"Yes, of course the *Herr Kapitän* may see the 'photos and then I would like to close the case file. The murderer is probably some disgruntled 'guest worker' and with thousands of them around it'll be almost impossible to investigate successfully."

Weiner was noncommittal for the moment and queried again the fact that no identification papers had been found.

"None at all," the policeman repeated, handing two 'photos from the file to Weiner. These clearly showed the thin weald around the neck. Yes, it was Hashagan.

"Post mortem?"

"Good lord, *Herr Kapitän*, there's a war on. With so many dead after the 'raids this one was lucky to be identified and buried properly. Damn lucky!"

"I don't give a shit what you think sergeant, you will tell your superiors I want this case fully investigated! Should anyone turn up trying to use the papers carried by *Leutnant* Hashagan he is to be arrested and I am to be informed immediately. I repeat, *at once*! Do I make myself clear? In fact, you had better circulate all stations that we, *Abwher*, are interested. Understood? One other thing, I presume that after my officer had been identified you notified naval headquarters here?"

"Of course *Herr Kapitän*."

Since Hashagan had only just been put on the naval payroll it could be weeks before the administration caught up with themselves and notified intelligence that one of their men was now a statistic. There were times when being a secret organisation obviously had its drawbacks.

"Right. Thank you." Weiner turned and strode from the room, his heavy leather coat brushing a file from the table as he did so. He could almost feel the sigh of relief from this old and tired policeman who had not been at all happy with his first contact with the secret service.

Weiner wondered how the man would have been if it were someone from the Gestapo here and not himself. He had the feeling that he would hear nothing more about Hashagan's death. Criminal investigations such as this one were not normally his concern but he did need to know, if at all possible, how his fellow had met his end. Yes, there was a war on and it did make life bloody difficult. Outside he found it almost dark and a fine rain starting. He turned up his coat collar and ran down the steps to the waiting car.

Back at the airfield the pilot told him the weather had closed in over Berlin and anyway it was doubtful if they would switch on the runway lights for a night landing. The Brits might take that very moment to pay a visit despite the rain. Also, even if he filed a flight plan there was a real possibility that it would be delayed in the system and that they could be shot at by their own ack-ack guns! No, they would be a lot safer to stay here the night so they might as well see what accommodation could be found in the officer's mess. Grudgingly Weiner agreed.

After a meal of sorts, rye bread and an *eintopf,* which left one wondering quite what was in it, washed down with a *steiner* of indifferent beer, they were told that there were no spare beds even for a captain from the *Abwher*. After listening to some desultory conversation about flying, most of which Weiner did not understand, he tried to make himself comfortable in an armchair and began to feel that his job back in section K 4 had had its advantages.

Cold and aching after an uncomfortable night they took off at daybreak. Weiner, dishevelled and unshaven, reported to Canaris soon after nine-thirty.

Since Hashagan's death did not seem to compromise Operation Queen in any way the admiral was not too perturbed and he reminded his subordinate that it was his 'show' and what happened was up to him, the results resting squarely on Weiner's shoulders. A statement that did nothing for the captain's moral!

Only a few days before, a commander in naval H.Q. had disappeared with his gear in a matter of hours. Rumour had it that he had made one God-awful cock-up in which the high-ups were involved and that now he was a lowly second lieutenant in the labour corps. Quite frightening!

Shaved and in a change of uniform, Weiner sat in his office contemplating his position. To call in the next on the volunteer's list would not be difficult but it would take two or three days. Time, with the requirement of mounting the operation in the summer months, was not on his side. The trouble was there were no naval regulations or book of words, which would tell him what he should do now and, since this operation was a one-off, there was no one to ask as to how it was done last time. *Scheisse*!

He called Schultz, who was sitting on the spare chair in Kummetz's office reading a book on Holland.

"Willie," he still did not really like the man but if they were going to be in close proximity over the next month or so he felt that using a given name might help things along. "I've got to tell you that Hashagan is dead. Murdered in Hamburg! You were with him in Hamburg on the first night of your leave?"

Schultz sat bolt upright in his chair. "Good God. Yes, Sir." And then, after a moment's hesitation: "Although you said before we went on leave only one of us would be going on the actual operation, whatever it is, I thought we should get to know one another so suggested a night on the town. Home's a bit dull and since I had to change trains in Hamburg why not a visit to the flesh pots?" The younger man shrugged his shoulders and began to relax again. "I thought something was wrong. Anyhow Sir, how'd you know I was with him?"

"That's immaterial, Schultz." Had Weiner seen a flicker of worry in those eyes? "What happened when you parted ways?"

"When Bengt went home to see his mother I 'phoned a girl I knew and was in luck as she wasn't doing anything for the evening. I called for her and then we met up with Bengt. We had a few drinks here and there before my bit went home. She had the rags up so it was no go on that score. Bloody waste of marks! Anyway, we split and I went off to the station and that was the last I saw of him. Damn sorry he's copped it though; I was getting to like him. 'Still I suppose now I'll be the one to go on the op, so for that I guess I should thank him."

"Perhaps." Callous bastard, Weiner thought to himself! Something did not quite gel in Schultz's reactions but he couldn't put his finger on it. Needing a moment to think without the distraction of those eyes he turned in his chair to study the charts on the wall. He looked at the mouth of the river Elbe and then lowered his sight to Bremen. *Milag Nord.* Yes that was the way to go.

"All right Willie, you're on your own now. Go pack a bag, uniform not civies, for a few days away. Bring those books with you. Be back here in an hour. Got it?"

"Right Sir." As soon as the man had left the outer office Weiner called Kummetz in.

"Pieter, did you tell Schultz about Hashagan's death?"

"Certainly not Captain. Is there a problem?"

"I'm not sure but his reactions to the news didn't seem quite genuine. Almost as if he knew he was dead."

"Gestapo connections?"

"As far as I could tell they weren't involved, only the civil Police. A leak through naval security up there perhaps? Jesus, we've got to be careful!" He felt worried despite the orders from on high. Was someone trying to throw a spanner in the works, and if so, why?

"Pieter, I've changed my mind. We'll go to the P.O.W. camp at Westertimke today and then on to Groningen, but keep that name between us, for Schultz's background cover. Since he's from lower Saxony accents from just across the border into Holland might not be too far apart. I want you to come as driver. Can't trust pool drivers from now on but also I'll need your help to keep an eye on Schultz. Don't want anything happening to him! Get a limo from transport, those bloody *Keblewagons* are too damned uncomfortable for a long drive. Make out the paperwork for at least a week. Yes, I think it might be an idea if you draw a sidearm. Right, off you go. I'll see the admiral and tell my steward."

As they set off Weiner told Schultz where they were now going and that ultimately he would be impersonating, as a Dutchman, a merchant naval

113

wireless officer. That was all he required to know for this part of his training. They would be wandering around the P.O.W. camp on the pretext that, as the interrogating officer for a number of the interned captains Weiner was interested in how they were being treated.

When Schultz had absorbed some of the atmosphere and the way the seamen talked and felt, they would go on into Holland. As a Dutchman he obviously needed some background and therefore must have some knowledge of that country.

Should he be unfortunate enough to be unable to avoid questions on his past or a conversation with any Dutchman serving with the allies, he would say that he had been a radio operator with the underground. When his cover had been blown he had only just managed to get out and to England one step ahead of the Gestapo. Weiner smiled to himself when he mentioned the Gestapo.

Because the German monitoring service knew his Morse hand Schultz could not work as a contact radio operator for the underground from London. Therefore, he would say that he had volunteered for sea duties where it was unlikely he would have to send any messages. Naturally he could not talk about his previous activities and it saddened him to talk about Holland and where he came from, so he would clam up. That was to be his cover story and he must stick to it.

As Kummetz drove the Mercedes through the countryside Weiner made Schultz go over his cover story time and again. He consulted the school atlas, a

114

concise Oxford so he would be able to take it with him to England, and made sure Schultz had an idea of where the principal towns and their railway links were.

Such memorising for Holland would be easy but for England it was different. So as not to give any indication as to where Schultz would end up he was told to learn far more than would be required on the assumption that he could end up at any of the ports. When asked by Schultz where and what the target was Weiner replied that it was for his own safety that the operator did not know until the time was right!

By evening they were only a few miles from Bremen and stopped at a village *gausthaus,* whose owner was most surprised to see who was requesting three rooms. He quite often let rooms to naval officers accompanied by their wives, at least that is what the register said they were, but it was apparent these men were not out for a dirty weekend. He wondered why they were not staying in some mess up in the port city.

Weiner wanted to avoid the larger hotels or military messes where possible as he did not wish to have Kummetz billeted separately because of his lower rank. Also it avoided mess talk as to why they were there, which undoubtedly would have had to be held in German just when Schultz was, at last, getting used to speaking only in English. It was the use of that language which spoilt their night's sleep.

The *gausthaus* seemed quite popular with the locals, probably because the landlord's brother had a farm, which meant that occasionally there was that little extra on the menu. This evening the restaurant was fairly full but the naval men managed to get a table in a corner, ordered whatever the landlord recommended and three beers. The local policeman, his craggy face resplendent with a well cared for Hindenburg moustache, was among customers sitting at a table where he could hear snatches of the naval officer's conversation.

His knowledge of English was limited to asking peacetime tourists for their passports, but now he thought it odd that a chief petty officer should be sitting with two officers and he the only one who spoke in German when giving the waitress their order. Like the sergeant in Hamburg he was old and overdue for his retirement. He was weary of the war and the extra work it caused but nevertheless he still knew his duty. The navy men spoke only occasionally between mouthfuls of food and swigs of their beer so that he had to unobtrusively lean towards them to hear what they were saying. Yes, it was definitely English but he could not make out what it was about.

Why were they here and not in Bremen? It was most odd. His mind went back to an incident last year when an order had come through to look out for some escaped prisoners-of-war. Could these three be on the run? Their uniforms looked genuine but why should two of them talk only in subdued English. Had they stolen the staff car and uniforms and were being so brazen that they might really escape? He finished his beer and went to the 'phone.

Weiner was in that area when sleep had not quite claimed him but wakefulness was a blur when he heard the door handle to his room turn and the door being shaken when whoever it was found it locked. *"Auf machen! Polizi! Schnell!"* a gruff voice ordered.

Reluctantly he swung from the bed and pulled on his jacket, asking in German what the hell was up and hearing from down the corridor shouts of - "Tommie, the game's up!"

Opening the door he was confronted by a military policeman whose badge of office reflected the dull hall light. He held a Schmisser machine pistol at the ready. *"Paperien bitte!"* In the background stood the village policeman.

The corporal glanced at the naval I.D. card and studied at length Weiner's *Abwher* pass, which was something he had not seen before. He called to his men now scrutinising Kummetz's and Schultz's papers who replied that everything appeared genuine. The corporal was not so sure and asked why the three were here and not in a mess in Bremen?

"Because I bloody well choose to be here! We're on special detached duty proceeding to *Milag Nord*. If you don't understand that pass you can check with *Abwher* H.Q. transport pool that the car outside is on issue to me! Now Corporal, my men and I want to get some sleep!"

He snatched back his papers and closed the door in the man's face. The last thing he wanted to happen was to end up having to explain to the provost marshal what they were doing here. He hoped he'd called the corporal's bluff and as he got back into bed was relieved to hear the village policeman being told his fortune in no uncertain terms.

The night passed without further incident and they reached the POW camp before midday. Here they were given rooms in a requisitioned farmhouse a few metres from the main gate. Weiner found he had no option other than to take their meals with a couple of other officers billeted there and he had to order Schultz to answer any questions put to him with facial expressions or gesticulations with his hands. Weiner would explain that his companion had a serious problem with his larynx and was forbidden to talk for the next few days. Schultz had not liked this at all, for he was naturally garrulous, but did as he was told.

Weiner found that he enjoyed the next two days. Several of the captains, upon seeing who the *Kriegsmarine* officer was, came over and shook his hand and engaged in easy conversation with both he and Schultz while Kummetz made appropriate notes of any reasonable requests.

He had gone out of his way to speak to several men who wore the braid of Wireless Officers and introduced Schultz as a radioman himself. He was well pleased, and somewhat surprised, to find him quite at ease and asking pertinent questions, such as the Morse speeds required for them to pass their exams. Schultz even said that he would see what he could do to get them a couple of keys and a buzzer so that they could keep their hands in. Without compromising equipment used in the German navy he discussed the merits of various types of transmitters and receivers, most of which was, like the conversation about flying back in Hamburg, above Weiner's head.

In Groningen Weiner took the bull by the horns and went straight to the town Major and informed him that they would be cruising around 'familiarising' themselves. It was as well he did for their naval uniforms and the black Mercedes were conspicuous where only army and the SS were to be seen. Indeed, on the second day when they passed a patrol for the fourth time they were waved down and politely asked if they needed help finding whatever they were looking for?

Weiner was noticing a change in Schultz's attitude. Following their first night in the billet by the POW camp he had lost his surliness and seemed to be identifying more with the job in hand.

Weiner had asked the camp commandant to provide a sentry outside Schutlz's room with orders to keep him in and let no one enter other than Weiner. Willie Schultz, like anyone else, had a need to go to the toilet but was told by the sentry that he would have to use the chamber-pot under the bed. Annoyed, he confronted Weiner on this in the morning.

"Willie, we have already lost one man and I do not want to lose you. A few people know we're here so I'm taking no chances. At the moment you are an important fellow and if all goes well you will undoubtedly get an Iron Cross of the highest order. Once you have embarked on your mission your name will be known to the *Führer*, I shall make sure of that, believe me!" Weiner had said that in all sincerity. He believed that to go alone behind enemy lines required a special kind of courage, different from that needed when fighting alongside your comrades.

"Yes, Sir. Thank you," the young lieutenant had merely answered, but he had thought about it a lot. He had taken a risk in arguing with *Standartenführer* Muller and an even greater one in Hamburg to reduce the odds on not being chosen to go on the operation. He'd had a feeling, which now seemed correct, that the operation would take him out of the doldrums of his previous job and into glory.

"This operation, whatever it is, *Herr Kapitän*. What are my chances of getting back?" he had then asked Weiner.

"That my dear fellow," replied the *Abwher* man, "depends a lot on Lady Luck and your own initiative." But to himself he had added - 'about zero. Either way you're dead'.

Willie Schultz had been a young and ardent Nazi when Jew baiting had first begun. He had been stationed in Dresden at the time and gone on the rampage of the Jewish quarter with others from his unit. They had taken a girl down an ally and after raping her one of them had calmly killed her using a garrotte.

Since that time Schultz had carried a suitably made up piece of wire inconspicuously in his right jacket pocket. It gave him a feeling of power to know how easy and quiet it was to use!

By the time he and Bengt Hashagan had arrived at Hamburg station Schultz had come to the conclusion, from the type of questions asked at the original interview and conversations between the two on the journey up, that the merchant navy man would be the obvious choice to go on the operation. He knew ships backwards and many of the Tommie ports and had shown his courage under fire off Norway. Schultz knew he could not match these attributes and would definitely be only the running mate for the training period. Unless? And he had fingered the wire in his pocket!

It had been no problem to persuade Bengt Hasshagn to stroll down to the water's edge as they had some while before picking up Willie's girl friend. A half moon had occasionally appeared through scudding clouds, making it right for an enemy bombing raid somewhere or other.

Looking back on it all he was surprised that getting rid of the other fellow had been so easy. The offer of a cigarette in the shadow of the anti-aircraft tower; the suggestion of 'what's that over there'; followed by the slight turn which had given him the opportunity to slip the wire over the man's head and quickly pull it tight. The slight noise of heels kicking on the flagstones, a gurgle and then the struggling body had gone limp. All too easy, but even so he had found he was sweating, not from exertion but fear at the realisation of what he had done.

CHAPTER SEVEN

THE JOURNEY

Lorient was a bleak place in nineteen forty-three, even on a summer's day, but in late March it could be even less inviting. That it was not raining was the only good thing which could be said about the day that *U-614* returned from her first patrol of the year.

The rust-streaked and damaged submarine cast off the tow line from the escorting mine-sweeper well inside the harbour and proceeded, using her one functional motor and aided by a new line from a docking launch, up the narrow channel past the conglomeration of ships and small craft which make up the requirements for a naval base in wartime.

It was a dull and listless scene with about the only colour being from the numerous red, black-crossed swastika-daubed ensigns of the German fleet and the many white crested waves, which slowly diminished as the boat neared the lee of the gigantic U-boat pens.

On the sub's minute bridge *Leutnant* Strater stamped his feet in the cold, watching anxiously as a back eddy of wind threatened to slam the bows into the wharf wall. Giving the order to increase the revolutions on the starboard motor and putting the wheel hard over he thwarted the wind of its ill intentions; it was almost as if the French Resistance had conjured up the bloody wind just to make him look incompetent in front of the Admiral.

When the first heaving line snaked on to the wharf and willing hands grabbed it, the welcoming home band struck up, 'Hail the Conquering Hero Comes', or at least the bandmaster's version of it. Rear-Admiral von Friedeburg, commander of the U-boat Fleet since Admiral Dönitz had taken over as C-in-C of the *Kriegsmarine*, came to attention and saluted the U-boat and her captain. At the same time the launch cast off its line and the U-boat was warped by hand into the safety of the bomb- proof pen.

Now that the *UnterseebootenKamando* had shifted to Paris the admiral could not always get away to welcome back U-boat crews, but when he could he did his best to follow on Dönitz's custom. Before the British had raided St.Nazaire, and he had his H.Q. where his men were, Dönitz had been able to say that he attended every sailing and return of the 'boats under his command. Such a boast was not made from self-aggrandisement but because he wanted to let his men know that he at least, unlike some of those bores in Berlin, did respect them for their part in the war at sea. His men had by far and away the toughest job in the *Kriegsmarine* and Dönitz fought tooth and nail to see that they got the best of things when ashore.

If only the damned boffins could sort out the faults in the torpedoes, things would be much more profitable for the U-boat crews when at sea and they would not be so discouraged when, looking like underfed scarecrows, they came back to port.

The crew of *U-614* had been glad to be back in Lorient, for their patrol had been more than very unpleasant. The weather had been exceptionally bad with the bridge, when surfaced, almost continually awash with green seas. The resultant static had made it near impossible for the petty officer telegraphist and his junior to receive anything on the short wave bands although they could still receive the powerful long wave w/t transmissions.

Also, when they transmitted their short position reports, at best only guessed at by the chief quartermaster, they were asked time and again for a repeat because of the breaking seas shorting out the aerials. Then there was the difficulty of trying to use a Morse key with the 'boat behaving like a bucking bronco or, in the more graphic terms of the mess deck, 'a nymphomaniac having a double orgasm!'

They had seen one small, fast and well-escorted convoy. Their reward for firing four torpedoes at it was an hour of depth charging. Whether the torpedoes had failed to explode, or just missed they did not know, for the seas running at the time had beggared the question. But being in the right position for an attack on a fast convoy comes rarely to the U-boat commander so fire he did.

Later in the patrol they had sighted another convoy, which was making its pathetically slow progress from Halifax to Scotland. The weather was still against them and they hit nothing, but an escort had somehow managed to get an asdic contact on them and called up a consort so that they were, this time, hunted for three and a half hours and almost sunk, such was the severity of the damage from the depth-charging. With one engine out of action and the other only just functioning due to a bent stern shaft, it was only thanks to the acumen of the chief engineer and perhaps a little bit of divine intervention, that they made port.

If the weather out in the Atlantic had been rotten to them it became more perverse, dashing their hopes of a calmer passage as they neared Cape Finisterre. The wind had increased from a mere gale to force ten and the seas, in the shallower water and on the rebound from the coast of Spain, became even worse, which was something they had not thought possible. If the chief quartermaster could not see the shore through the blinding rain and spindrift and say exactly where they were then it also meant that it was unlikely the enemy air patrols would find them. Better to be damned uncomfortable than be sunk.

Since the elements had been against them from the second day out into the Bay of Biscay, the 'boat had never had a chance to dry out, with the result that their fresh food stores became mouldy sooner than normal. With clothes, bedding and everything else aboard constantly damp; to say nothing of the stink of stale unwashed bodies, and to start with, vomit, their tenure on the wish to live became borderline. No one, other than perhaps those men in the trenches in that other war, could appreciate that humans could survive such conditions.

Hunched up in that foetid atmosphere in the minuscule space that passed as a radio room, the duty telegraphist was their only contact with the outside world existing beyond those grey-green, or at night black, foaming seas which thundered at them in a seemingly endless procession.

Hollow-eyed and sallow-skinned it was not until they had got to their barracks, showered, changed into clean uniforms and had a meal sitting normally at a table, did they begin to feel that they were indeed part of that world.

Afterwards, for those not lucky enough to be on the first leave roster and who knew no better, or for those who did but needed to forget the war, there was the French wine, or the weak beer they called 'maiden's piss', to get drunk on and the local whores to be patronised. For the very few who did neither there were walks through the town or countryside – but not too far afield lest the resistance decided to slit one's throat – and letters to be written. Petty Officer Telegraphist Kurt Oppenheim was one of the latter type.

Country youths tend to learn at an early age from the animals what 'makes the world go round'. Having literally rolled in the hay with several local girls, Oppenheim, on his last leave, had finally married his first childhood love, a daughter of the local butcher.

Since it was only four months since they had shared the nuptial bed Kurt felt no reason why he should go whoring; particularly as in one of the letters waiting for him she had written that she had missed two periods.

With a child on the way he needed to husband rather than squander his hard-earned pay on too much drink and debauchery. He increased his allotment to her, leaving only enough for an occasional meal and glass of wine ashore. Of course there were those in the crew who chided him for his abstemious ways but he accepted such taunts with good humour.

It took six weeks to carry out the repairs before the 'boat could do her sea trials, and even then she was not right and required another two before she was ready for her next patrol.

The day of their departure dawned with a promise of an improvement in the weather. A few clouds tried their best to stop the rising sun from spreading its life-giving rays but for once they were on the losing side. As those rays came slowly over the town buildings and finally lifted over the cavernous submarine pens, the upper edges of the small waves on the dirty, garbage strewn water were turned to silver, giving momentary colour to the otherwise still sombre scene.

The first that any of the crew knew they were to carry an extra person on their next patrol was when they were fallen-in on the 'boat's casing. They had been inspected by the captain and were awaiting the arrival of the Admiral while the band was playing 'The Ride of the Valkyies'.

Instead of the Admiral, a captain none of them had seen before, and who was accompanied by a civilian dressed in a shabby rain-coat and cloth cap well down almost to his eyebrows, walked briskly along the wharf and stopped by the gangway. They were followed by a chief petty officer.

The civilian switched the small attaché-case he was carrying to his left hand and, exchanging a few words, shook hands with his companions before coming gingerly across the brow and was then shown below. The chief P.O. followed and handed a canvas ditty bag, which he had been carrying, up onto the bridge and then returned ashore. As the crew waited for the admiral's inspection more than one muttered, 'who the hell was that fellow?'

Inspection over those seamen required on deck took up their stations for leaving harbour. Amidst the usual saluting and the playing by the band of 'Deutchland Uber Alles', U-614 sailed once more for the wide Atlantic to play her part in bringing Britain to her knees: A part that all hoped would not bring upon themselves too much of the awesome 'pinging' sound of the enemy's asdic as it searched beneath the waves seeking a 'kill'. A 'kill' which would be preceded by the terror of the crump, crump and nerve shattering jolts to the 'boat of exploding depth charges until the final one which would send them to the bottom. In the compartment where the water tightness was first shattered and if the force of the explosion did not kill them, drowning soon would; whilst for others there would be a few moments of realisation that they were about to die before the deep pressure shattered the rest of the 'boat and their bodies split asunder as if they were kippers!

On the wharf knuckle a flock of seagulls, disturbed by all the activity, finally gave up their preening and, vying with the band, flew off screeching towards the near-by rubbish tip looking for their first meal of the day.

To some of the U-boat's crew the noise of the birds was preferable to that of the band, whose large brass instruments were playing a flat note or two due to the damp air. To mariners, birds generally meant that they were near to shore and therefore, perhaps, relatively safe: a false assumption but it helped to dull their fears. Most of them being normal men they did have fears; they would do their best to help win the war but would like to be alive at the end of it.

"Alles klar, Kap'tän!"

The last of the ropes were flung back aboard and as they were stowed under the casing the captain gave his first orders.

"Langsam achteraus backbord!"

When there was the possibility of visual signalling, Petty Officer Telegraphist Oppenheim's place was on the bridge standing behind the officer of the watch and the captain, ready with his lamp. At this moment he had nothing to do or occupy his mind and, as always, on hearing that first command and then feeling the tentative movement of the U-boat beneath his feet, he felt slightly sick with apprehension - that this could be the last sailing he would make.

When he had first joined the U-boat fleet things had gone well for the submariners with the sinking of allied merchant ships one after another and almost with impunity. But now things seemed to be changing, the boot was beginning to shift to the other foot!

As radio operators he and his underling heard the repeated calls from base to 'boats which failed to make their scheduled contacts. Between them the two men had counted at least five during January alone and there had been another five during December.

How soon would it be before they also failed to respond to their call from base? Would he ever get to see his yet to be born child? He shivered uncontrollably, which had nothing to do with the cold of the dawn.

Clear of the short groin the submarine swung quietly around, her electric motors below filling the vessel with a subdued hum. On a nearby buoy a black shag, wings spread out to dry, turned its head to keep a beady eye on the 'boat, not sure if it was a threat. When the motors were replaced by the noisy diesels, blowing a cloud of black smoke as they started up, the bird decided all was not well and, squawking its objections, flapped away.

Four hours later, with the low pressure system which had passed over Lorient the day before, moving well to the north east and the sun's mastery of the heavens complete, *U-614* was making a sou'westerly course out into the Bay of Biscay. The wind had backed and was now from the north west blowing a force five, causing the 'boat to corkscrew on the cross seas and whipping spray over those on the bridge.

Their escorting mine-sweeper had bidden them farewell and been replaced by three Ju88 fighters, an unusual happening so close to their own coastline, for no lumbering enemy bomber would risk a daylight raid. It was, of course, because of their special passenger that *KG 40* had been ordered to provide total air cover until maximum range was reached. When they realised what was happening, the crew of *614* blessed this unknown man in their midst.

More of a problem than the enemy at that moment was sea-sickness. There are men for whom the pangs of 'mal de mer' are unknown, while others suffer for the first few hours no matter how many trips they have made. Willie Schultz, having never been to sea before, found he was one of the unfortunate men who suffered. Dockside parties had been his only previous contact with ships and he could hardly blame them for the subsequent puking over the rail because of his over-indulgence of schnapps and too much beer. Now he was not allowed above decks and into the clear air but had to retire to the space, euphemistically called a wardroom, with a bucket!

Petty Officer Openheim noticed this and wondered what their passenger's background really was? The captain had introduced Schultz to those in the control room by his rank and as a communications officer and no more. At that juncture in time even he, the captain, his sealed orders yet to be opened, did not know why their passenger was aboard or for how long, although he had made an educated guess.

In the wardroom, when he had finally nothing to vomit but bile, Schultz began to wonder why he had volunteered for this crazy scheme. Since there was a good chance that he would die anyway why not now and to hell with the Fatherland and all in it. Surely nothing was worth how he felt now? Where were the Tommie 'planes which would help to put him out of his misery with a well-aimed depth-charge?

Fortunately for Schultz he was one of those who recovered quickly and his head started to clear once he had got used to the un-natural movement which had caused his predicament. By dusk he was allowed on the bridge to smoke a cigarette and as darkness fast approached, leaning against the periscope standard, he was feeling considerably better and listened to the conversations taking place between the lookout and officers.

The day had passed quietly as far as the enemy was concerned. They were still too close to their own coastline and the consequent fighter cover for the enemy planes to venture into the area. The chief engineer had been satisfied with the trim dive – a few minutes relief for those who were being sick as the boat went deep – and the captain satisfied with the various drills he had ordered. With only a couple of new hands aboard there was no-one to trip over their own feet and foul things up.

The subject of the conversation on the bridge was mostly centred around certain parts of the anatomy of various whores and hostesses back at the base who, as so called collaborators, would eventually be called to account by the Resistance and have their heads shaved. In the meanwhile they had to live and German sailors paid well. For those women who were unfortunate enough to produce German bastards their humiliation would last much longer than it took for their hair to re-grow.

Three days later the U-boat was well out into the Bay and thoughts were no longer on the pleasures of the flesh but on the possibility of attack by enemy aircraft. Now there was little conversation as lookouts and officers alike concentrated on the tasks at hand.

The relay of escorting Ju88 fighters had left them along with the daylight. They were alone on the sea, accompanied only by the constant throb of their diesel engines and the swish, swish of the bow wave as it travelled outwards until it finally fell over itself.

The previously boisterous wind, which had turned the blue-green sea into a myriad of tumbling white-topped waves, had finally abated. It was now but a zephyr hardly reaching force one as a high-pressure system edged its way over southern Europe. Whilst the wind made no more than an occasional ruffle on the placid sea, far to the south west another front foretold of its approach by sending a long undulating swell, causing the 'boat to rise and fall in a subdued, almost gentle and caressing, motion.

Schultz, having been given permission to come up topside, drew on his cigarette. He was at last beginning to feel that, after all, life was not too bad. Down inside the 'boat privacy was an impossibility. Even in the lavatory there always seemed to be someone knocking on the door, telling him to hurry up. But up here, as he had watched the setting sun back-light the few streaky clouds, first with silver and then gold through to orange and finally dull grey, he was able to think.

The chief quartermaster quietly preparing to take a star-sight before he lost the 'hard' horizon in the fast approaching blackness from the east, failed to distract Schultz in his train of thought. Thoughts which went back over the happenings of the last two months since their return from *Milag Nord* and his incarceration at the *KG 200* airfield. His reason for being there was known only to a very few and contact with the outside world forbidden.

He had to admit that his training for the operation had been both very thorough and intensive. The days had started with physical training and a run around the 'field perimeter track, which finally left him the fittest he had ever been, even if the first three or four runs had left him panting with the stitch. There had been unarmed combat sessions and a half hour's Morse practice with a dozen air force telegraphists. Much time was spent with the wireless wizard dismantling and then re-assembling the beacon transmitter/ receiver, until he could almost fault find with his eyes closed.

Eventually Weiner had disclosed the reason for all the training, after which he and the captain spent hours, often well into the evenings, studying the plans and all other relevant material that was to hand on the liner *Queen Mary*. Even to such trivia from a magazine called Handicrafts and dated May 1936, which described the incredible amounts of equipment aboard her. Half a million pieces of linen, two hundred thousand pieces of earthenware, china and glass, sixteen thousand pieces of cutlery and, almost unbelievable, four thousand miles of electric cables! The mind boggled at such huge figures; but day after day they had studied, until he would know his way around the upper-decks without thinking. Providing, of course, he would be able to get aboard in the first place and therein lay the nub of the whole exercise.

Realising that he had come to the end of his cigarette he wet his left thumb and forefinger with spittle and then squeezed its lighted end as he had been shown. A lighted 'dog-end' thrown overboard could be, he had been assured, seen at quite a distance. Its momentum gave it a glow as if in defiance to its smoker having made the last draw. The cigarette was half way to the black sheen of the sea but four metres away, a sheen whose surface was broken only by phosphorescence bubbles sliding along the casing and a little farther out their bow wave, when a look-out shouted.

"*Achtung, Flugzeug!*"

Almost before he had completed the warning, a brilliant light appeared about halfway to the hardly discernible northern horizon, revealing a very naked looking submarine heading in the opposite direction to themselves.

"Dive, dive, dive!" shouted the officer of the watch as those on the bridge were galvanised into action. Schultz had been told he was to be first down the hatch if the order, 'clear the bridge' or 'dive' was given. Since boarding the U-boat speaking only in English had gone by the board so that now he responded to his native tongue with alacrity. He leapt the two paces to the open hatch and jumped feet first down it. He grasped the upper ladder rung with both hands to arrest his fall before transferring them to the side and commencing the short slide to the deck. As fast as he was he was not quick enough and a heavy sea-boot from above thudded painfully on his left hand. He had learnt a small but painful lesson as to what the war at sea meant to a submariner.

Once below he took the few steps to the wardroom on, to him, an alarmingly tilting deck, and out of the way of men closing up to their stations. Within thirty seconds the sub's conning-tower had disappeared beneath the surface as the enemy, a 'Leigh Light' equipped bomber, swooped in on her target with guns blazing and the sea around it illuminated as if it were daylight.

Levelling out and returning to periscope depth the commander of *U-614* watched as the sea erupted around their now diving comrade. Faintly, except for the hydrophone operator, they all heard the sound of the exploding depth-charges and thanked God it was not them being attacked. For the men in the elite corps of the *Kriegsmarine* the difference between life and oblivion at the bottom of the ocean was, in this particular part of the world, a very tenuous one.

When the movement of the crew had subsided Willie Schultz edged his way back to the watertight door to the control-room and marvelled how anyone could know just what all the myriad of valves, pipes and gauges were for.

He was perfectly at home with the most complex of circuits in the wireless world and had even delved into such peculiarly named things as 'saw toothed triggers', 'push-pull oscillators' and other phenomena to be found in the new radar sets; but this cramped and almost over-filled control-room left him in awe.

Calmly and almost casually, the chief engineer gave his orders for this and that to be done so that the U-boat remained at the required depth. Momentarily lost in a world of technicalities he forgot that only a few miles away a U-boat and the sixty odd men in her might be dying and that it could happen to him even before he got anywhere near his quarry.

Aboard *U-614* watch followed watch as she headed first sou'west, then west before heading north and finally eastwards towards the Irish coast, as required by her captain's secret orders. Orders which said that no one in the crew was, in case of premature capture, to be informed of their contents. For navigational purposes the chief quartermaster could be advised of the co-ordinates of the course changes but only as they occurred. Until they acknowledged the final rendezvous position signal they were to keep absolute radio silence.

Captain Weiner had done his best to keep security to the maximum using the adage of 'on the need to know only' basis. Indeed, the French Resistance had advised London by the evening of the day she had sailed of *U-614's* time of departure and that she appeared to be carrying a civilian passenger. MI5 and MI6 already knew, from monitoring signals in and out of the German Embassy in Dublin, that the IRA were to help an agent get through to England in early May. When S.O.E. advised them about *614's* sailing the necessary steps were taken to monitor the situation. It was unfortunate for counter-espionage that a further signal giving the position and date of delivery to the Irish was mislaid somewhere along the line.

As a further precaution Weiner had arranged for the final exact instructions to be transmitted to *614* the day before the first rendezvous date. So it was that Willie Schultz's landing in Ireland went undetected.

CHAPTER EIGHT

FOREIGN SOIL

U-614 came cautiously to periscope depth even though they were in Irish waters. If U-boats could consistently use Spanish waters by Cape Finisterre and then creep around the coast almost under the cliffs and where the Tommie aircraft, being under orders not to antagonise the Spaniards, could not go; who was to say that here the boot might not be on the other foot?

"Up periscope!" Bending nearly double the captain seized the handles and followed the instrument up so that as soon as it was clear of the water he started a rapid sweep around the horizon at sea level and then repeated it for aircraft. It appeared clear but just in case he went through the whole sweep again more slowly – momentarily a wave might just have obscured a waiting corvette put in the area as the result of a careless signal from intelligence or U-boat command. But their luck held – "Stand by for the bearing. Mark!"

A petty officer read off the figure indicated on the verge ring as the periscope steadied on the distant lighthouse, perched, it seemed almost precariously, atop the high black cliffs. The chief quartermaster, ready at the chart table with pencil and parallel rulers, drew in a position line. "Distance three point four Kilometres! Down 'scope."

The captain came to the chart table and rested an arm on his navigator's shoulder, seeing their position now clearly marked. "Damn good Klaus. A mile from where you reckoned." Then turning to Willie Schultz. "Now all we need is that fishing boat, Willie, and we'll have you ashore in no time, and the sooner the better. It's too damn shallow for good health if the Tommies catch sight of us. Right Klaus, take her out to deeper water and we'll wait for dark. Say twenty kilometres, better safe than sorry! Let's hope the weather doesn't worsen."

The seven-day journey since witnessing the 'Leigh Light' attack to where they were now, just west of Tralee Bay, had not been too onerous by comparison. Their air escort had come back the next day but, since the JU88s had reached their operational limit, the sub was then on its own. Despite the air cover on that last day, they had still had to crash dive twice.

On the first occasion the lumbering Sunderland flying boat took off for the nearest cloud cover when they saw the JU88s, but not before the fighters had got in several bursts of cannon fire. However, it must have sent a w/t sighting report because an hour later they had to go under again.

Two Beaufighters streaked in at wave-top level before the '88s had time to come down from about two thousand metres. In both instances the 'boats Metox radar warning sets had failed to give any indication of the enemy planes and it was only the alertness of the lookouts which saved them from damage or destruction.

His sealed orders had clearly stated that he was not to engage the enemy until after his passenger was transferred and the Captain had no intention of deviating from them. Staying on the surface and fighting it out with their new twenty millimetre anti-aircraft cannons was not an option. The orders had given him a point to sail to fifty kilometres south west of their present position and there wait for the final rendezvous signal. In case the weather was against them for an immediate transfer they were to wait for two nights before taking the risk of coming right inshore and hope they could get him to the beach in the lee of Brandon Bay – an idea which definitely did not appeal to Captain Strater. With an unseasonable low-pressure system approaching and the wind increasing from the south west, he was worried.

The evening before sailing he had been called to a meeting in the operations room and been very surprised to find the admiral there. With him and the flotilla commander had been a naval captain from the *Abwher* who had shown him an order signed by none less than the *Führer* himself, which implied that the requirements of his passenger transcended all other operational matters.

On paper it was all very simple; meet a fishing boat and transfer your man. Unfortunately a submarine does not have nice flat sides against which another vessel can lie in safety except in calm seas. Ok, it's too rough and you are rolling too much so you float off a dinghy with the fellow in it; and if it is too rough even to do that?

'Shit!' The captain exclaimed to no-one in particular. 'Why the hell did they have to choose my 'boat to land some bloody agent and his radio!' He definitely did not fancy having to go into any bay at night and without a decent chart – base could not find one – just so that calmer waters would enable this spy, or whatever he was, to get ashore without getting his feet wet. The 'boat and everyone in her would be jeopardised!

When the last shred of daylight had left the cloud-strewn sky to the west, *U-614* surfaced and started slowly towards the rendezvous position. She corkscrewed her way over three metre seas with the wind and spray wetting the bridge crew. Even before the hatch had been opened Strater knew from the motion of the 'boat that a direct ship-to-ship transfer of Schultz was an impossibility. He doubted if a dinghy was practical either. It started to rain so that it took some while before they could fix their position from the lighthouse.

Schultz sat doing nothing in the wardroom, wedged in a corner against the violent rolling motion. His mind flitted from one subject to another but all connected with his imminent future. At the moment uppermost in that thinking was the glory for the Fatherland and the accolades he would receive if he succeeded in his mission, then creeping in where he knew such thoughts should not be, the seeds of doubt about his own future.

Around him men came and went, orders were given and repeated to ensure they had been heard properly. The noise of a bilge pump whirring away joined every now and then by another, pumping water from one trimming tank to another as the chief fought his battle to keep the 'boat level in the boisterous sea. Dominating all other noise was that of the diesel engines as they drove the vessel forward and sucked much needed fresh air down below, where it vied with the pungent stale odours generated during the last fourteen hours below the surface.

He had already dressed, to ensure that all was as it should be, in gear designed to keep him dry during his trip to the shore. Then, because the heat threatened to cause him to collapse, stripped back to shirt and slacks. That gear comprised of an exposure suit which had once belonged to an allied seaman. Perhaps its bright yellow colour might be conspicuous but it fitted loosely over his civilian clothes from his shoes upwards and although cumbersome it was considered ideal for keeping him dry. Hopefully he would not reach the shore looking like a drowned rat.

He had also exchanged the now creased and sweaty clothes in which he had come aboard for new ones. His underwear bore labels proclaiming they were made by Marks and Spencers (who would expect a Nazi to wear anything made by Jews?) while his sports jacket and slacks carried the well know name of Burtons.

The all-important case containing the radio and his toilet gear was ready to be fastened around his waist with a short piece of cord once he was out on deck. At the moment it was wedged between his ankles to stop it sliding around with the unpleasant motion of the 'boat. It was a motion that first lifted the stern almost out of the water and then, as the swell moved forward, rolled the 'boat thirty degrees to port before doing the same to starboard while pushing the bow upwards towards the low clouds.

Schultz, with tension rising in him, began to feel queasy and hoped he would not start throwing up again. On the seat beside him was an RAF May West life-vest to be worn over the exposure suit, a last minute addition taken from the body of an allied airman. If things went wrong he might just pass off as a survivor from a crashed 'plane. Having seen him all togged up and ready to go, the chief engineer, although almost bereft of humour himself, thought that in different circumstances someone must be able to make a joke about how the fellow looked!

Up on the bridge the captain was not worried about the noise of the diesel exhausts giving them away to anyone on the shore. The howling wind and swish of the breaking waves dissipated it long before it could get near the jagged cliffs.

Having reached the rendezvous position they lay bow to sea with just an occasional touch ahead on the engines to keep them where they should be. With an extra two men as lookouts all strained their eyes, which soon became sore and red from the constant spray, but saw nothing except the darker blackness of the cliffs and the phosphorescence of the breaking waves. Above them, through breaks in the cloud, an occasional star could be seen together with a new moon well past its zenith.

An hour before the first signs of the forthcoming day broke the eastern sky, *U-614* went to 'slow ahead' and corkscrewed her way back to deeper water and another day of waiting, in negative buoyancy and silent routine, doing their best to conserve their air and battery charge.

By midday everyone aboard was sure that the clocks had stopped ticking and must be slow. Surely time could not really drag like this? Conversation, on orders, was kept to a minimum but even so tempers started to get short and remarks normally seen as facetious became tinder-boxes for arguments.

More than one crew member in the particularly cramped forward torpedo space started to blame that 'fellow' back aft for the slightest thing that went wrong. Conveniently they forgot that his presence had been the reason why they'd had a relatively untroubled passage across the Bay; an area fast becoming a very perilous part of any patrol.

By sixteen hundred hours the captain decided that come what may they would come up for air and battery charge; having convinced himself that the enemy would not expect to find a U-boat so close to the Irish shore. If they had known about *614's* intentions the 'boat would surely have been attacked by now.

Once more they came slowly to periscope depth. Being thrown around on the surface was preferable to the stifling heat and atmosphere of the calm waters down below. Once more they turned and stemmed the seas just enough to maintain their position, but well out of sight of any prying eyes from the shore, to await darkness.

Yes, there it was again, a small green light heralding the presence of another occupant of the sea. *U-614* came slowly around to bring the light ahead; the rolling almost ceased but the pitching increased as the swell was brought more astern.

"Man the cannons!" Strater was taking no chances even if the rough weather would make accurate firing almost impossible. The captain could feel the tension rising in those around him as they closed the distance to the other vessel, the light now being constantly visible instead of disappearing in the troughs of the waves.

The fishing boat was about twenty metres long, its bluff bows riding high up the waves as it stemmed the sea. Carefully noting its drift Strater brought his own craft as near alongside as he dared. A voice, just audible above nature's noises, hailed: "Follow me into the bay. Did you hear dat? Follow me!"

Strater waved and shouted, "Ok, Ok," his worst fears confirmed but at least he had someone to follow, providing of course, the fellow showing them the way realised the sub had a deeper draft than they did! The fishing boat turned away, rolling violently as she did so causing Strater, unnecessarily, to tell his own bridge crew to "hang on" as they too turned beam to sea before putting the waves once more astern.

The fishing boat had switched off its sidelights but now showed a small white one for the U-boat to follow. Two black shapes only marginally blacker than the sea on which they rode. Strater ordered the starboard cannons to train aft just in case it was a trap with an Irish gunboat coming up astern.

146

"Shit, Klaus, I hope to Christ these Irish are as friendly as we've been told or we're in trouble!"

The chief quartermaster nodded his sou'wester-clad head, not wishing to break his concentration. He noted the approaching headland's bearing as he etched in his mind the reciprocal of their course in case they had to turn and run for it. Below, the chief engineer was having scuttling charges laid in position just in case they ran aground and could not get off again.

The chief, at thirty-two, was the oldest member of the crew and the only professional amongst them, having come across from the merchant navy. He was glad that he was not a skipper. He did not like the idea of sinking any ship and drowning most of their crews, let alone having to watch it through the periscope. Whilst the other officers would take a look when offered he steadfastly refused. He knew they had a job to do but that did not mean he had to like it.

Now, as he gave his orders, he wondered what an Irish prisoner-of-war camp, if they had one, would be like. He'd been to Dublin in his ship just before war was declared and spent a few evenings ashore acquiring a taste for their Guinness beer. No, he really could not see the sense in this war.

He and the first watch officer had been the only ones aboard when the final rendezvous signal had come through and who had been told why they were where they were, although he had guessed days ago that they would be landing their passenger somewhere. He wondered, once again, what drove a man like *Leutnant* Schultz to do whatever it was he was going to do behind enemy lines. He shuddered as the last charge went into position and the engine room petty officer was told how to arm it if the worst came to the worst.

The rain showers were becoming less frequent so that those on the bridge could now see a headland on both sides as the two craft changed to a southerly course and entered Brandon Bay. To their south west a couple of lights on the shore indicated the sleeping village from which the bay took its name. When the lights bore due west the fishing boat turned towards them and the calmer waters in the lee of the land.

U-614's speed dropped right off, there were only two metres under her keel and her captain was not prepared to go any closer to the beach. True there were no waves in here, the land broke the power of the wind, but there was still some swell bouncing off the shore behind them. Almost silently, for they had changed to the electric motors before turning into the bay, Strater turned the boat short around so that they were heading back the way they had come and then took the way off her.

The fisherman went on for a few minutes and then must have realised the U-boat had stopped and came back. There was the sound of ropes squeaking in blocks as a dinghy was hoisted out. Vaguely a dark shape could be seen as it left its parent vessel and came towards the submarine. Schultz, now fully clothed and on the bridge, watched in awe as the small boat clawed its way to them. He was totally unable to say how he felt or why but he did know that a very cold shiver went through him.

A seaman threw a heaving line to the boat and as the men shipped their oars they were hauled alongside aft where the tumble-home of the U-boat's side was not so great.

Schultz shook hands with the officers, climbed down on the deck and, grabbing the jump-wire, made his way to the dingy. Quite what went wrong he did not know, perhaps he did not jump quickly enough when he was told to, perhaps his cumbersome survival suit got in the way but he ended up face down across the stern sheets, his faced lapped by the sea as he did so.

Unceremoniously one of the two men in the boat hauled his legs around and told him to sit up properly. He then took the proffered case from a seaman and handed it to its owner. Shultz tied its lanyard around his wrist; it was a good thing he'd not done so before but let the second watch officer carry it for him. Damn it, he hurt right across his chest and for a moment he closed his eyes, hearing as he did so the noise of *U-614's* motors go to full throttle.

The sound made him forget his hurt as he realised the stark reality of that moment. He was now totally alone, and his stomach muscles twisted at the thought. His last link with the Fatherland and all that meant was gone. No longer would he speak his native tongue or taste German cooking ... 'Jesus, he mustn't think like this or he'd be a failure before he started!'

The next he knew was the sound of the dingy bumping alongside the fishing boat and a voice telling him to hand up the case. Doing as he was told but with an admonishment to the voice's owner to be careful with it, he stood up and took a firm hold of the gunwale, which was level with his face. He felt two strong hands grabbing him under each armpit and he was hauled rather than being allowed to climb the short ladder up the boats side. Someone said, "Begorra but you're...." the rest he could not understand, then another voice said, "an' the top o' the morning to you, Fritz. Come into the wheelhouse now, n 'tis a bit of the hard stuff I'm thinking you'll be needing!"

The wheelhouse was almost in total darkness except for a subdued glow from the compass which barely made any impression elsewhere. Schultz was told to sit on a settee behind a small table and took the heavy glass tumbler offered by one of the men who had fetched him. Someone said - "Here's to the damnation of the bloody English." To which the man at the wheel replied.

"Now that's what I'll be thinking. To be sure, the Mother of God," and he crossed himself, "should see they all rot in hell!"

Schultz raised the glass in both hands and took a gulp of its contents and spluttered, almost choking; it smelt like whisky but was stronger than anything he had tasted before. Hearing him the helmsman quipped - "nothing like a drop of the malt to cheer you up, Fritz! Give the man something to eat Paddy. I doubt he'll say no after living in that sardine can for a week or so." And with that he got the boat underway.

Twenty minutes later the waters around Rough Point lived up to their name, making the boat roll so that once more Schultz had to brace himself behind a

150

table before they eventually were again under the lee of the land and heading down Tralee Bay towards Castlegregory, where the skipper put her deftly alongside what appeared to be an old jetty.

"Right Fritz, away you go. Paddy here will take you ashore and see you on the next stage. When you get on to the jetty take that exposure suit off and leave it with us. You may be among friends but no sense sticking your neck out. You'd look right daft walking down the road in that lot!" He held out a large grime-stained hand and as Schultz took it, continued - "Good luck and may the Blessed Mother go with you, to be sure."

Schultz handed up his case to the man who had preceded him and commenced the short climb up an old iron ladder. With the tide half out he was very conscious of the odours from the barnacle-encrusted piles and the seaweed hanging from the struts connecting each pile. The rungs in his hands felt slimy so that he gripped them more tightly lest he fall backwards. In front of his eyes all was a dank blackness until several rungs later he was suddenly head and shoulders above the top of the ladder.

Again there was that hand under an armpit as he came unsteadily to his feet; the days at sea in a small craft playing their usual tricks on the human body as it tried to re-adjust its equilibrium to the unmoving land. Quickly he shed the Mae West and exposure suit and threw it down onto the deck below, inwardly cursing at the pain in his chest as he did so. The boat started to move away from the jetty as he heard the order to 'come!'. Picking up his case he followed meekly.

The jetty was a short one and just as his feet had got used to walking on the boards they had to re-adjust to the loose gravel of a wide path that curved sharply upwards. The strong smell of seaweed gave way to the scent of wet grass, bushes and damp earth.

"Welcome to God's own blessed country. 'Tis the best there is to be sure now." The Irishman enthused, but the German was not so sure.

A fortnight ago he had been a fit man but now his bruised chest hurt and his breath was beginning to come in short pants due to the steepness of the path. He grunted 'thanks', his eyes, although attuned to the dark, now barely able to see the man in front of him as clouds obscured the faint moonlight and a fine rain began to fall.

They reached the top of the path, which petered out and became a narrow roadway. Had he been able to see it the topography of his surrounds had changed to rolling farmland and with it, although it had nothing to do with the change in the countryside, the wind was rapidly dropping.

After the cacophony of sounds in the U-boat and the steady thump, thump, thumping of the fishing boat's slow-revving diesel the low moaning of the wind became almost threatening in a ghostly way.

Coming from a town where even in the deepest hours of the night, when silence was supposed to be golden, there had always been some sound to break it: a distant train or passing truck, a dustbin lid knocked to the ground by scavenging dogs or the yowling of a tomcat on the prowl. Subconsciously this totally different noise, or lack of it, began to percolate his thoughts to how, from now on, his life was rapidly changing.

The *KG 200's* airfield had, perforce, been a big open space and there had been an eerie feeling about the early dawn mist. During the short times he was allowed on the bridge of the U-boat, the sea, with its unreachable horizon, had seemed boundless and he had been impressed. But now? Willie Schultz was aware, here on foreign soil for the first time, that this place and its atmosphere was changing something inside him. He did not know what it was and he felt he had no control over it. He had been party to killing a Jewess and, calculatedly on his own, murdered a man. Was this feeling 'fear', now taking a physical form at the realisation that he was totally dependant on this one person in front of him?

'Scheisse!' He could no longer see the man and quickened his step, then realised he was making the ultimate mistake of thinking in German. 'Never ever do that', had been his instructions. 'You let slip one word of German and you could be a goner! English, English, English!'

They walked for perhaps ten more minutes – he had not looked at his watch once since leaving the wardroom, but it was still dark with a gentle hint of grey to the east just visible – before the Irishman opened a farm gate and, increasing his pace, arrived at a small, dilapidated cottage.

Without knocking they entered. His companion struck a match and applied it to a hurricane lamp so that Schultz saw by its flickering light that they were in a room, which was both kitchen and living space.

153

To the left was a bed, partly obscured by a faded curtain of almost indistinguishable colours as was the one tightly drawn over the only window. The back wall was taken up by a large earthenware sink with a well chipped upper front edge, a wooden draining board and an equally old wood-burning stove. A battered cupboard, table and two upright chairs were the only other furniture. The room smelt damp, which was probably due to the fact that the hard packed earth floor was only an inch or so above ground level.

"Right, Fritz, make yourself at home. If you need the bog 'tis out the back but make sure there's no one in the lane first; otherwise stay indoors 'till I or one of the lads gets back to you. To be sure now don't start the oven fire either; there's bread and pickles and a bit of cold meat in the cupboard. Right I'm off. You're safe enough here so don't worry." With that the Irishman disappeared out of the door.

After the crowded U-boat Willie Schultz was now totally alone. The rain had stopped and the wind died down, the only noise being that of the crickets outside. It was the first time since reporting back to *Abwher* H.Q. that there was no one to keep an eye on him; always there had been a sentry or that damned chief writer nearby; almost as if he were a prisoner.

"I need a piss!" he said out loud as if his solitude were suddenly oppressive. Carefully he opened the door and peered out. No sounds of people or a light. He took three paces down the path and urinated long and hard into the grass. As he did so, reaction to the trauma of his situation started to set in and he began to feel desperately tired.

Back inside he locked the door, took off his outer garments so that they would not become too creased and collapsed onto the bed. Although the mattress was hard and lumpy it felt infinitely better than the bunk in the U-boat.

CHAPTER NINE

AMONGST FRIENDS

Willie Schultz woke with a start. He'd been dreaming; his hand was moving up the girl's thigh, pushing the navy blue skirt with it, when there was a knock on his cabin door. '*Himmel!* Can't they give me a moments peace?'

The *Führer* had invested him with the Knights Cross with Diamond Cluster only two hours ago and now here he was kissing this adoring typist in his cabin. Five minutes more would be all he'd need and she would have had his lot. He could see that being the *Reich's* latest hero was going to open the floodgates!

An Irish voice again demanded he open the door. He sat bolt upright, the blissful dream shattered as he realised where he was.

"Ok I'm coming." He scrambled off the bed and pulled on his trousers; the thought flashing through his mind that if this fellow was not a friend he'd be a laughing stock to be caught without pants! It was broad daylight and Willie could see that the man silhouetted in the doorway was not one of the fishermen of last night.

"Top o' the morning to you Fritz. You got some sleep then? Good. Finish dressing there's a good chap, while I stoke up the old oven. A cup of tea wouldn't go amiss. 'Tis fortunate we are that the grocer man is one of us and knows how to get round the rationing now and then."

"I was told not to light it," Willie retorted, still halfway between the dream and reality and riled by the man's dictatorial attitude; surely as a German officer he was due some respect?

"Now that was last night. To be sure it's today. This is a fisherman's hut and often used during the day." He went to the window and drew back the curtain so that Schultz saw there were several nets hanging from wooden bars, two or three wicker baskets and much other paraphernalia of the fisherman's world; just as he would have seen back home on the banks of the river Elbe.

The Irishman was not someone who would show up in a crowd. Dressed in dirty blue overalls, heavy black ankle-boots, which had not seen any polish for a long time, and a blue shirt with no collar, he was not meant to be conspicuous. The stubble on his chin was dark, like his uncombed hair and in build he was shorter and thinner than the German. His eyes never seemed to be still; dark and inquisitive they now took in Willie Schultz from top to bottom. "So it's yourself then."

Schultz failed to understand the Irish idiom and remained silent.

"Now, when we've handled you fellows before we have known a bit about you but of you we know nothing." The rich baritone voice had taken on an even sharper, authoritative note.

"We've been asked to land you in Wales rather than to just get you on the packet for Fishgard. I take it that your case there is the important thing. True it is that the Brit's customs an' police have cracked down

157

at all the ferry ports when before you could just walk ashore. To land anything that is a bit suspicious is definitely risky! No doubt it's all something to do with these Yanks that are arriving." The stove fire, already laid, was now going well and he lifted the lid on a blackened kettle. "Good, enough water for tea." He looked quizzically at his companion. "Could you be using a bite of hot food now? I make a good scrambled egg to be sure. Tea over we'll boil some water and you can get rid of that beard."

Automatically Schultz rubbed a hand over his chin but was given no chance to utter a sound before the other continued, totally in command of the conversation. "Now, what do your papers say you are because in those clothes I can't pass you off as a local fisherman? Although getting you across our sea will have to be by one of their boats." He took down a saucepan from the shelf and tipping it upside down gave it a tap on the stove so that its inhabitant, a large cockroach, fell to the floor and was promptly squashed under a boot. "Right, my friend, I'm listening."

Without realising it Schultz drew in a deep breath, the time had come. "I am Wilhelm Schultz, a Dutchman from near the German border. I was a radio operator in the resistance but had to leave in a hurry because the Gestapo were on to me." How easy it was to tell it even for the first time. "I am now serving in the Allied merchant navy as a radio officer and am carrying an experimental lifeboat wireless transmitter. I am in possession of all the necessary papers to prove it." He tapped his sports jacket over the inside pocket.

"Hmm! Merchant navy eh? We'll see," was the Irishman's only comment, and for the next few minutes there was silence as he burned, rather than toasted, two bits of bread in front of the flames and made tea. The eggs did taste rather good, Wilhem Schultz thought; using his real name instead of having to think that he was someone else made things so much easier.

Meal over, which was eaten in silence, the Irishman went outside to the old iron hand-pump and brought in a bucket of water. "Right now, there's water for you so, except for using the bog, no need to go outside." He crossed to the door. "I've things to organise now I know what you are so I'm off. And mind you're not after opening this to anyone unless they say that 'Small Paddy' sent them. To be sure now, I or someone else'll be back some time or other!"

Once more the German was on his own and realised that he needed the bog and right now. It was the usual country 'long drop' and he could smell it from five metres away. 'Jesus, don't these people know about the use of lime?' he muttered.

He spent the rest of the day in solitude, reading a Fisherman's Times, various bits of newspapers, all old, and a couple of English magazines called, 'Men only'; expecting at any moment that someone would join him but no-one did. From time to time a man or woman passed by down the road riding a bicycle and once there was a farm cart loaded high with lobster pots but no one seemed interested in either the cottage or its occupant.

By dark he had finished all the ham and most of the mutton from the cupboard while the bread was beginning to feel stale. But it was better than he'd had over the last few days on the U-boat so he knew he could not grumble on that score. He longed for a cigarette, something he did not have.

At eleven o'clock he wound his watch and went outside to empty his bladder, just getting back inside before it started to rain again. He was beginning to feel agitated at still being on his own. He locked the door, noting that, due to age, the lock and the door could well part company, he put one of the chairs under the doorknob. It would not stop a concerted effort from anyone trying to get in but it would make a noise and give him warning.

He felt too nervous to take off his trousers but hung his jacket across the other chair, taking from its right hand pocket his garrotte and placing it handy by the pillow. He had managed to conceal the bit of wire with its toggles from everyone right up to the final evening when there had been a dress rehearsal of all his gear. That damned chief writer had seen him swop it to the coat from the air force overalls he had worn during the training period.

The man had said nothing to Weiner at the time, although the look he had given Schultz was as good as shouting from the rooftops that he now knew who had killed Hasahagan. Perhaps if it had not been only a few hours before embarkation time but several days, would Schultz have been arrested and now be in some cold prison cell and someone else be here? He lay on the bed but sleep eluded him until the early hours.

It was late afternoon when the door rattled. He had fallen asleep again when a woman's voice called for the door to be opened. Another one from the typing pool, or would she be from the signals centre? God, being a hero was going to be bloody wonderful! Despite the qualms about his present position his dreams had followed the same pattern as on the previous night.

"Wilhem Schultz, please open the door. Small Paddy sent me." He'd fallen asleep with arms under his head, leaning across the table, a week old copy of the 'Dublin Times' under him. No this was no dream – it really was a woman calling to him.

"Ok, ok I'm coming." Hell's teeth his neck ached. Perhaps he had been dreaming, but the woman who stood in the doorway was everything he would have liked to have dreamed about.

In her late twenties she was dressed in a brown and green tweed suit, the jacket of which hung loosely open showing a tightly fitting cream blouse from which her breasts seemed to be trying to force their way out. Over her brown pageboy haircut she wore a deer-stalker type hat, which he thought looked ridiculous. Realising she was being mentally undressed her hazel eyes froze and the smile on the red lips disappeared.

"You can forget all that for a start, Mr. Schultz. This is strictly business! I'm here to take you to Tralee and then through to Waterford by train where someone else will take over."

She pushed past him and in doing so caught a whiff of his unwashed body, which still held some of the U-boat stench. "Holy Mother of God but you need a bath!" She grimaced and backed away from him to the other side of the table. "Show me your case."

He pulled it from under the bed and put it on the table, watching the rounded face as he did so. "Small Paddy was right. It'll fit into a pannier nicely. Now Willie, that's easier to say than Wilhem, this is how it will be. You and I have just become engaged and have been to Castlegregory, that's the place where you came ashore, to see an aunt, my only relative, but she wasn't at home and doesn't have a telephone. We are now going to cycle back to Tralee and stay the night with friends before catching the train tomorrow. Got that?" She showed him an engagement ring on her left hand. "We met in the Toc-H club in Dublin when your ship was in for one night last year. We corresponded and you've come on leave and asked me to marry you. It's a whirlwind romance as are so many in this day and age. Should we get caught up in unavoidable conversation I'll do the talking for us. My name by the way, is Eileen O'Flaherty. Got it? Eileen O'Flaherty, and I'm from Dublin."

Like Small Paddy before her she seemed used to giving orders but her speech was more refined. "Small Paddy left his bike here yesterday so you'll ride that. You can ride a bike of course?" He had not done so for years but he nodded his head, almost dumbstruck by the way she rattled on. In fact, he could only just keep up with her, the word 'bike'

162

momentarily eluding him in his mental translation. His time with the submariners had undone much of his training to think only in the enemy's language.

However much he'd like to bed her he was glad he wasn't really going to marry her; she'd wear the pants too often.

"Right, come on then. It's too warm to wear your mac so you'll put it across the handlebars the same as we all do if we don't have a cycling cape with us!"

She went outside to her bike, looked around to make sure they were on their own, and took a pile of folded newspapers from one pannier and replaced them with his case. Then from her pocket she gave him a pair of cycle clips, which he looked at without comprehension. "For God's sake man they're for your trousers!" Damn it, of course, did this woman have the power to make all men feel like lost schoolboys?

They wheeled the bikes to the gate and then rode off. Of course she was as majestic and totally self confident on a bike as she was on the ground, whereas he wobbled, rather than rode, the first kilometre until he got used to keeping his balance.

The weather was kind to them and the sunshine held all the way until, just before they reached the village of Blennerville, it set across the bay behind them. In other circumstances the sixteen-kilometre ride would have been idyllic. Now, upon seeing a faded stone with the distance in miles, he realised that he was still thinking in metric measurements.

He swore under his breath, aware that he needed to get his wits about him and forget the fact that his guide was a female. He'd tried to talk to her but was told to save his breath and just listen while she described to him the Toc-H dances and a bit about how to get there from the Dublin docks. She gave him some background about herself, whether true or not he could not decide.

She was obviously very fit and talked as if she were nonchalantly sitting in a chair rather than peddling hard. It was all he could do to keep up with her, which did not help his ego one bit. Indeed he seemed to trail behind her by a few yards most of the way but that at least enabled him to watch those legs and wonder, when she wasn't snapping at him - "did you get that now? You must concentrate on what I'm telling you,"- about how it would be at the top of them.

It was twilight when they stopped outside a pub near the bank of the River Lee. From its open windows, for the evening was still warm, came the sound of fiddle and drum accompanied by rough voices and the stamping of feet. After three years of war he'd almost forgotten what it was like to see lights everywhere.

They put the bikes in a yard, taking the cases from the panniers. She linked her free arm with his and they walked into the noisy smoke-filled room as if without a care in the world. At the bar she said something to the man behind it in a language Schultz did not understand and then, dropping her hand into his, lead the way through a door marked 'private' to the accompaniment of a wolf whistle. A man seated at a near-by table winked up at Schultz and muttered, "Lucky bugger."

They crossed the nondescript hallway and into the dinning room where once again there was cold mutton but with fresh salad stuff and a large crusty loaf on the table. It was a long time since he had seen such an abundance of food. He supposed, as they tucked into the food before them, that he could get used to the plain brown bread instead of the darker German Rye. He was also not sure that he liked the heavy Guinness beer they were given to drink.

Meal over, most of the time bereft of conversation, she led the way up squeaky stairs and pointed to a door. "That's your room. Bathroom's that door down there. The train leaves just before eight so I'll call you at six and for God's sake have a good wash-down. I'm damned if I want to spend the morning in a train with you smelling like that!" As if she was reading his mind again she added, "this is my room and the door will be firmly locked!"

The bed was comfortable and to his surprise he slept well, having backed-up the locked door with a chair and stripped back to just underpants, placing his money belt under the pillow. Here in this pub, as she had called it, he felt more relaxed than he had at the cottage and these Irish really did seem quite friendly.

The night passed without incident or dreams of the woman next door or any others. As promised she called him at six with a cup of tea – another thing he supposed he would get used to, tea with milk – and, miracles of miracles, a warm smile. By the time he had shaved and come down to the breakfast table he felt almost back to his old self. He had preened himself in front of a mirror and made sure his attire was as neat as could be as befitted an officer of the Third *Reich*.

Breakfast over, which to him seemed over-cooked compared with the continental way of doing things, they cycled further into town. Leaving the bikes at a hire shop they caught a tram, which took them along Ashe Street to the station.

Tickets purchased, she found an empty compartment, told him to sit opposite her – did she never stop giving orders? – and then placated his annoyance by offering him a cigarette. Automatically he drew out the box of matches he had in his left jacket pocket and went to light the cigarettes.

"By all that's Holy, Willie, you're the most useless spy I know. Look at those matches!"

He did. German! Dear God, he must have picked them up in the U-boat. Thankfully the compartment was empty, but the feeling of well-being he had experienced earlier quickly evaporated and he slumped back into his corner. Those cold blue eyes of his must have shown some of his feeling for she stretched across and patted his knee.

"Don't worry Willie. No harm done but get rid of them. You'll make out all right with whatever it is you have to do."

Promptly at five minutes to eight the train came to life and huffed and puffed its way towards the other side of Ireland and, for him, what lay beyond. Once clear of the town he tore the offending matchbox into little pieces and scattered them out of the window. The last piece of anything that could identify him with his homeland was now gone.

As they travelled, stopping at the occasional station, she went over what she had said the previous afternoon and this time he took a lot more notice.

Two hours later they were in Mallow. He wanted to buy cigarettes for himself but the vending machines were empty for, as she told him, they were strictly rationed; plenty of good Irish Malt whisky but not cigarettes. Anyway, with only twelve minutes to change trains there was just time to visit the gents before they were off again.

On this part of the journey there were no empty compartments so Eileen O'Flaherty sat beside him and, head on his shoulder, pretended to go to sleep, thus avoiding any possible conversation for the time being. As she made herself comfortable, clutching her hat in her free hand – the other holding his - he could not resist a kiss to the top of her head. Momentarily she looked up into his eyes and the look she gave him hardly went with a girl in love with her man! 'To hell with her', he thought, 'she's made of ice, but her hair did smell rather nice'.

Unlike trains back in Germany, where air raids could make a mockery of schedules, this one ran to time. By midday they were in Dungarvan, where she came to life and he realised that she really had been napping. She sat up and smiled at the woman seated opposite them, deliberately showing off her engagement ring as she pushed her hair back in place. Outside the carriage it started to rain.

It was still raining when they reached Waterford and she took him to a terraced house near the harbour, which had a 'Bed and Breakfast' sign in the window. Here it was obvious that it was a 'safe' house for the IRA, the owner fussing around them as if they were very important people.

They'd had nothing to eat on the train so the inevitable tea – despite the rationing, which was taking some getting used to – and thick wedges of jam sandwiches appeared. These were devoured in silence. During the last few hours he had given up trying to converse with his minder. When the meal was over all she said was, 'We've come this far without incident so there's nothing to discuss. What happens next will be told you in due course. I'll stay with you until we've had supper at the fish and chip shop up the road after which it'll be someone else's turn to look after you. In the meanwhile there are magazines and the paper to look at and the radio to listen to!'

And so it was for the next hour *Leutnant* Wilhelm Schultz of the *Kriegsmarine* sat with apparent impunity in the hands of the IRA and began to be lulled into a false sense of security in this totally ordinary Irish living room. They had seen a Garda policeman outside the station but he was not in the least bit interested in them.

After an hour of silence, other than the rustle of pages being turned, Schultz became bored, got up and went to the radio. It was a Bush, a model he had not seen before but that was of no consequence since he was, after all, a radio expert. He fiddled with the controls and, without thinking, tuned to long wave and Bremen radio. He turned the volume control too fast and the room was suddenly filled with a very loud-voiced German newsreader.

"....*nachtrichtendeinst aus Bremen. Heute die Luftwaffe hat London wieder gebombardieren!..*"

Before he could gather his wits she sprang for the wireless cord leading to the power point, pulling the plug from the wall. Almost in the same movement she turned and slapped him hard across the face. He reeled back, not so much from the stinging hurt but from total surprise!

"You bloody fool! The people next door or outside could hear that. D'you want to get me arrested for helping a German agent? Christ, you want to 'have it off' with me? Why you probably wouldn't know where to put it, you stupid idiot!" She took a deep breath and was visibly seething with rage. "I've only dealt with two of your kind before but at least they knew what they were about. God help you when you get to England and are on your own!" She flopped down in an armchair as there came a knock at the door and the landlady came in.

"Is everything all right?" she queried looking from one to the other, obviously anxious.

"Yes, thank you Mrs. Patrick. Don't worry."

Holding his smarting cheek the German sat down in the other chair saying nothing but desperately worried as he realised his stupidity. She was of course, once again, quite right. 'God help me indeed'. A moment or two passed and then he felt he needed to explain.

"Look, I'm sorry but I'm not just an ordinary spy, in fact, I'm not a spy at all. I'm..."

"For God's sake shut up! I don't want to know. You're just making it worse! Shut up. Shut up!" She kept her voice down but it was full of venom. He suddenly thought of *Standartenführer* Muller and decided that he'd rather be balled-out by him than this woman, but at least she could not have him sent to the Russian front. Nevertheless, his position was almost as perilous for what if he annoyed her too much and she walked out and left him stranded?

Eileen O'Flaherty, if that was her name, did not walk out but duly, and without a word to him, left when a nondescript man called to take over. He gave Schultz a large pair of overalls to put on over his clothes there and then and a canvas ditty-bag to hold his coat and case. Thus attired he accompanied the man through the dimly lit streets down to a wharf where they boarded a fishing boat with two others, who seemed to have been waiting for them. As soon as they were aboard the vessel cast off and sailed into the night.

"Well Willie, there 'tis, enemy territory for you and all true Irishmen. Mind you some of these Welshmen think like us but they're few and far between and although they cry 'home rule for Wales' they don't do much about it, mores the pity. "

The skipper, a big heavily built man with flaming red hair, and Schultz were looking out of the wheelhouse window at the now rapidly approaching island of Skokholm to their north east and on the bow,

170

Saint Ann's headland. Out on deck two of the crew were still busy with twine and large wooden needles repairing various holes in the cod-end and wings of the trawl, while another two had just finished some welding on one of the otter-board shoes.

They were all, like the skipper now talking to him, nameless Irishmen. This crew, like that of the boat which took him off the U-boat, just called each other 'Paddy' if he was within earshot. The woman was the only one to have used a name and he did not know if that had been real; somehow he doubted it. Other than to her, Small Paddy and this big skipper, he was just another 'Fritz'. He supposed that it would be the same for an allied agent. Names were never true so that if you got caught you could give little away.

Behind the boat their wake stretched out clear and white on a blue sea, which now showed little of the nastiness of last week's gale. Under their feet the big diesel engine throbbed away, pushing them relentlessly towards the land. The sun was starting to lower itself in an almost cloudless western sky but there was still plenty of daylight left for them to have made an accurate landfall.

When he had boarded the *Leprechaun* in Waterford the night before last, Willie Schultz had no idea as to where he was to be landed, other than it was somewhere in Wales. It was only now, as they came close to the land, that the skipper said it was to be Milford Haven.

Thanks to those hours spent studying the school atlas he could visualise roughly where it was but he would check nevertheless, the atlas being the only book he had with him. The humiliation over his mistake with the wireless became a thing of the past as his second transfer to land grew nearer and he became apprehensive as to how this would take place. He felt sure that going past police and customs at a dock gate would be the real test for himself and his papers. He had to maintain his composure at all costs.

'All in good time, Fritz, all in good time, 'tis too impatient you are to be sure!' the skipper replied to his question as to how he was to be put ashore, adding as they sat down to a tea of fried fish and mashed potatoes. 'Eat well my friend for it could be the last good meal you'll see for a while, dat's for sure!'

On leaving Waterford the *Leprechaun* had steamed to the south west for a couple of hours and then shot the trawl over a ground which, said the skipper, was particularly good for plaice. The boat needed more in her hold to make the landing of their catch in rationed Britain really worth while; for although prices were considerably better than Ireland the cost of the fuel to get there had to be covered.

The man had been a fisherman most of his forty odd years and reckoned that with the closing off to fishing of a large area of Saint George's Channel due to the minefield – and he knew the eastern limit as well as any of the navy men who had laid it – had created a new spawning ground giving better trawling either side of it. Of course, as he had said, "It can only be fished in good weather so's you know exactly where you are. Catch one of those mines," he said

172

pointing sky-wards, "and 'tis Himself up there you'll be talking to!"

They had trawled, with fours hours each time between shooting and hauling, throughout the day and night and well into the next morning before setting off for the Welsh coast. The skipper wanted to arrive off Saint Ann's Head and the anti-submarine boom by teatime so that they could dock and get ashore before the pubs closed. Had today been a Sunday he would have trawled some more since having the pubs open was critical to landing this German chap.

The meal finished, the skipper relieved the man on the wheel so that he could have his tea with the others who came in off the deck. Looking out of the window once more Willie Schultz found it difficult to understand the conversation going on behind him at the table. Having listened to and only spoken Oxford English he had found the Irish brogue hard to follow and even more so when spoken through mouths full of mashed potato!

After a few minutes, while he finished his mug of tea, the skipper spoke. "Now this is how I think it'll be Willie. All you'll do is to walk with us when we go to the pub and if we're asked then you'll be after coming off one of the ships at anchor and we've just given you a lift. To be sure the bobby and customs man on the gate will be wanting their fish fry and bottle of the real macoy as usual." He paused to fill and light his pipe, stuffing the tobacco well into the bowl with a gnarled finger.

"There happen to be several Dutch manned Norwegian whalers operating out of the port and two scows used for loading. Of course the whalers are now armed and used for convoy work being fine sea-boats but the scows now, there're different. When you people took Holland quite a few of them ran for the English shore. To come all the way around the north of Scotland and down here in a flat-bottomed inshore boat calls for fine seamanship. I hear there're a number being used up in the Clyde too. The whalers often call in at 'Derry or the Clyde so you could have joined one up there. Anyway if you do get stopped at the dock gate your Dutch cover will fit in nicely. That's why we chose Milford and not Fishguard. By the time they find out, if they ever do, that you're not off one you'll be long gone and so will we; this tub won't be coming back here again just in case. We'll see what's in after we clear the boom."

CHAPTER TEN

ENEMY TERRITORY

The *Leprechaun* arrived off the boom and joined three other fishing vessels waiting to enter the estuary anchorage. Upon seeing the tattered Irish flag the duty motor-gunboat came fussing around them, taking note of their name and number, its crew glad to have a diversion from their boring patrol up and down the anti-submarine net.

After about fifteen minutes an ancient coal-burning tug with patches of red lead over most of its upper works, slowly pulled the boom gate open. The gunboat stopped by the opening, gently rising and falling on the slight swell as its crew scanned the water for any sign of an unwanted visitor, while the fishermen entered the anchorage. There had not been a U-boat in this area for near on a couple of years but orders were orders and God help the young skipper if he failed to carry them out. It would be more than his single wavy bit of gold braid was worth!

Out of sight in the corner of the wheelhouse Schultz felt a surge of excitement and, again, fear. What was it some fool in the bible had written about 'Daniel in the Lion's Den'? Here he was in Milford Heaven Sound and well and truly in enemy territory. If his guise as an escaped member of the Dutch Resistance, now serving as a Chief Radio Officer on Allied merchant ships, was not accepted he would undoubtedly be hung as a spy. Involuntarily he felt his neck as if the 'noose' were already in place. The fact he was an officer in the Germany navy would not matter one iota for he was in civilian clothes. He knew the same would apply for a British officer trying to land in Holland.

Now he watched, fascinated as various vessels came in sight, the skipper vigilantly watching for the red, white and blue flag of Holland in the waning afternoon sunshine. The last forty-eight hours had brought back his confidence. The time had, in fact, been quite pleasant with the war seeming a long way off, other than the Irishman listening to the radio news from Cardiff, which made reference to the numbers of prisoners taken in Tunisia after the Africa Corp had surrendered. He doubted such a thing could be true but if it were his mission was all the more important.

"Right, Willie Schultz." Using his name for the first time. "We're in luck. See, there's one of the whalers and its not too far off the fairway." He pointed to a group of small vessels fine on the port bow. "Just what we wanted. We'll go slowly up to her and you take a good look while we do. That's the one you'll be after being aboard."

He steered the *Leprechaun* to the side of the fairway and pretended there was something wrong in the engine room, gliding to a stop almost alongside. So close that there was a shout from a man in a petty officer's uniform at the side of her small bridge to 'watch what you're doing you Irish git!'

"'Tis Irish I am to be sure, but I'm no git." Deftly the skipper stopped with the whaler between him and any prying eyes from the far off control room for the lock and officialdom. He waited a few minutes before getting slowly underway again, explaining to Schultz what was in his mind.

"Now Willie, I have to admit that I've never put one of you fellows ashore before so it's a case of trial an' error, hopefully without the error! I want to loose a bit of time so we'll continue to go slow and miss the lock-in with those other two boats. If we get alongside too early it only increases the time you'll have to kill. Once tied up we may start to unload straight away or have to wait awhile until the porters and what have you are free to handle us. Anyway, you can start to act normal and show yourself if you want."

Act normal? What was normal for a fellow about to go behind enemy lines? He stood at the wheelhouse door as they finally entered the lock and the gate swung shut behind the *Leprechaun*. As it squeezed the last bit of water out of its way Schultz suddenly felt insecure again, as if the gate closing was the final straw on what had happened to him so far in his life but was now locked out forever. Ahead lay only *Operation Königin* and all that implied. A shout from the shore made him start.

"Your last port Skipper?"

"Waterford"

"Fish to land I presume?" The man was in a uniform that Schultz had not seen in those shown him on the recognition charts during training.

"That's for sure now."

"Good. I'm from Port Health. No diseases aboard?"

"Not unless one of the lads has the clap and not told me!" the skipper replied with a chuckle.

"Right you are Skipper. Who's your passenger then?" The official was standing on the opposite side of the lock to the boat but not more than a few yards from Schultz, who now smiled at him and gave a half wave.

"He's off one of the Dutchmen; they got trouble with their motorboat so I gave him a lift in."

"That's Ok then. In those clothes he didn't look like one of your boys!"

Just like that! Surely it wasn't going to be as easy as that all the time; if it was, then it was no wonder the Tommies were going to lose the war! One of the crew had left a packet of Woodbines on the mess table so he asked the nearest man if he could take one. With a cigarette going he felt less apprehensive and was sure he looked more like a man acting 'normally'.

The boat rose a couple of feet as water was pumped into the lock and levels equalled with the harbour. Gates opened; lines were let go and they started forward, towards the long quayside where already a dozen other trawlers were tied up; some unloading and others waiting to start, whilst a couple were taking ice before going back to sea. It was a long quay with an equally long and cavernous shed behind it with doors opening onto the railway siding behind where wagons stood with doors slid back waiting for the harvest from the sea.

It was a scene of activity typical of any fishing port but the import of it all was lost on the German

178

officer standing on the deck of the drab, green hulled trawler with its net piled on deck and the otter-boards hauled tight up to the gallows. With plenty of practice behind him one of the crew threw the fore-line over a bollard and made fast inboard so that with the wheel to port the vessel came easily to rest alongside.

He had arrived and, strangely as he thought about it, he found that he was calm and collected. No longer was he *Leutnant* Schultz but Chief Radio Officer Schultz of the Allied mercantile marine.

"Now Willie, just help yourself to more tea and a sandwich. I have to talk to a man up there and fix for our catch to be handled and sold. After that me and one of the lads'll walk you ashore to a pub and find somewhere for you to sleep the night." The skipper left the wheelhouse and clambered up the iron ladder to the quay. On deck the lads started to rig the derrick ready to hoist the baskets of fish up when the porters were ready. Roughly sorted after being caught and gutted by the crew the agents would re-sort and grade them ready to be auctioned or sold straight on.

Schultz did as he had been bid, made a sandwich and heated up the kettle then lounged, cup and sandwich in hand on the small after-deck gaining confidence as the minutes went by and no-one paid the slightest attention to him.

The walk with the red-haired Irishman and his deckhand seemed endless to Schultz but, again, other than someone off one of the other trawlers calling a greeting they were ignored. At the dock gate there was a policeman and a customs officer standing by a hut, exchanging their thoughts in the growing dusk.

"Evening Red, had a good trip?" It seemed the policeman recognised the skipper. He went inside his hut followed by the Irishman who passed over a paper bag. The customs man smiled wanly at the German and asked what he had in his case.

"A new type of lifeboat radio we've been testing. Got to take it to the Ministry in London. Want to see it?"

"No, that's Ok. Good luck."

Schultz had been quite prepared to show the set because all the labels and instructions on it were in English for such a moment as this. In bold letters across the top of the set was the inscription MARK II LIFEBOAT TX\RX, followed by the serial number 00015. Weiner had left nothing to chance. The skipper rejoined him and together with the deckhand they left the dock; the small boat yard to their left with a gun boat on the slip minus one of its propellers reminding him of the one near his home in Cuxhaven.

Red pointed out the railway station not a hundred yards away to their half left and then crossed the road and entered the Albert Hotel. The Albert was really no more than a glorified pub but it did have a few rooms. Here he enquired if they had anywhere for his friend for the night, knowing very well that they, as were all the other hotels and guest-houses, would be booked out. However, he felt the need to keep up the pretence that Schultz was only a passing acquaintance.

Milford Haven was bursting at the seams with extra people making it a far cry from the sleepy holiday town of peacetime. Civilian workers for the increased workload in the docks, fishermen and their families from the east coast who could no longer use their own ports because of air attacks, to say nothing of the wives of many service officers. Accommodation was, indeed, at a premium, all of which helped to make Schultz totally inconspicuous.

They went next door to the Victoria, where Red was greeted with considerable friendliness by the barmaid. "Gwen. Willie here needs somewhere to put his head until the first train out tomorrow. To be sure now, the town seems bursting at the seams! Perhaps you've got a suggestion?"

"Nowhere that I know of but there's the armchair in my place if he doesn't mind that, my love?"

Willie sensed that this was meant to happen and just said, "Thanks." Remembering the idiom, 'beggars can't be choosers'. "An armchair will do fine."

"Right, now there's an end to the matter. Three halves of Mild please, Gwen. By the Holy Mother of God I'm dry! Just time for a quick one then Paddy and me must get back aboard."

Schultz, knowing he had to stay stone cold sober from now on, had only half finished his drink when the others finished theirs, got off the bar stools and nodded to the barmaid. Red looked him straight in the eyes. "Just do what Gwen says and you'll be right."

The others gone Gwen suggested he move to a vacant stool at the end of the bar where there were fewer customers who might engage him in conversation. She smiled at him. "Not long 'till closing time love. 'Spect you'll be tired after coming off a ship." And she moved away to serve a blousily dressed woman who eyed Schultz speculatively on hearing he was a sailor. When she caught his eye he turned away as if to look out the window. The Irish girl was one thing, but definitely not this one!

Half an hour later a man, presumably the landlord, whom Schultz had not noticed before, called a loud but gruff, 'Time Gentlemen please. Drink up now.' Obediently Schultz downed the last of his beer, then looked enquiringly at Gwen who reached across the bar and put a hand on his arm.

"You sit tight my love and give me a hand with the glasses when the others have gone."

So it was that a serving officer in the German navy helped to collect and wash glasses in a Welsh pub and was given an extra half pint by the landlord for doing so. Was that man party to the help Gwen gave to the IRA, or just grateful for the help? Schultz did not know the answer and when the work was done and they walked the half-mile to her flat he forbore asking, almost feeling that the whole evening had not been real!

Her flat was on the second floor of a terraced house two streets back and up a hill from the Victoria. It consisted of a bedroom, lounge with kitchenette and the use of bathroom down the corridor. Nothing in the place was pretentious but she had done her best to make it comfortable. She took a pillow and rug from a wardrobe and threw them on one of the two armchairs in front of a tiled fireplace containing an old gas fire with its adjacent meter.

She asked him if he wanted a hot drink? On receiving a negative reply she said, "I'm off to the lav, make yourself at home. Back in a minute."

When she came back he did the same, leaving the case behind and out of his sight for the first time since leaving the U-boat. He somehow felt he could trust her with it. When he returned she had changed into a light dressing-gown and brushed her hair down. For a moment she looked into his cold blue eyes, then held out a hand. "Willie, please?"

The woman stirred beside him as the alarm clock went off with its insistent clanging demanding immediate attention. She stretched out an arm from under the quilt and fumbled at the rear of the clock. The noise ceased and she became fully awake.

"Right my love. Time to dress and have a bit of brekkie before you get on that train. If you need to get away from here as soon as possible then that seven ten is the first one out." Her voice, with only a slight trace of the Welsh lilt, sounded strained.

He looked hard at her naked body as she swung her legs over the side of the bed and suddenly he felt something for her. No, it certainly wasn't love but at least gratitude for putting him up for the night. If the police found him here she might be in serious trouble, unless she was able to persuade them he was just a 'one night stand', and a rather good-looking one to boot. The feeling was replaced with one of emptiness and perhaps apprehension when she was no longer intimately close to him but dressing on the other side of the room.

He realised he was not thinking positively. She was far from attractive, with a small midriff tyre of fat starting to form and almost old enough to be his mother. Her nail varnish was ragged and her mousy coloured hair stank of stale cigarette smoke from last night in the pub. But she was still a friend and not an enemy and maybe she'd be the last one he would ever speak to. As she put on her bra he had a sudden longing to have her again; not as he had wanted that girl back in Ireland but for the pure comfort of just being close to a mature woman. It was, for him, a totally new feeling and one he did not quite understand.

Yes, he was apprehensive because within an hour he'd leave this dreary room and be out there in enemy territory without help. Until now he had not quite realised what it would mean to be alone in enemy territory. Back in the U-boat he was with comrades and if they had been sunk he would not have died alone. What was it Wiener had said to him at the interview, which now seemed years ago? 'Are you prepared to die alone and without a comrade at your side?' or something like that. Well, now he knew what the captain had meant and what it could feel like; if he did not get a hold on himself he probably would get caught through his own carelessness.

He followed her off the bed and momentarily stood there, fear replaced with the thought of what he must look like. He'd kept his vest and underpants on because there was no way he was going to take off the silk money belt with its carefully folded five pound notes. She must have wondered, or guessed, what it was but had said nothing.

'Shit,' he thought, 'fancy shagging a bird with a thousand pounds strapped round you!' He grinned, starting to unwind. He pulled on his trousers and shirt and went into the small living room where she had a kettle on the stove and bread under the grill. He needed a shave and unlocked the case – the spare key hung around his neck and its loop of string had got around one of her boobs at a crucial time during the night, causing them both to laugh amidst their panting! In the case there was just room above the wireless for the school atlas, a spare set of underwear and socks plus his toilet gear.

She gave him a cup of warm water and he got on with his shave, his fair beard hardly showing even if the bristles did feel rough.

Having returned the shaving kit to the case he drew one of the brown ten shilling notes from his wallet – he had changed a fiver in the pub – not knowing if that was enough for her services and offered it to her. She smiled and pushed his hand away.

"No, my love. I only do it when I want to and you needed relaxing. Anyway I enjoyed it and the Paddies already paid me for putting you up. They look after me well enough, 'though it's always been one of their own when I helped before. Come on, sit down, 'fraid it's not much of a brekkie. Rationing you know; get plenty of fish of course but there's not really time to cook the bit I got." She made the tea and put the toast and a pot of jam on the table. "You'll be able to get a bit of cake and a cuppa on Cardiff station when you change for wherever it is you're going."

The meal over she walked him to within sight of the railway station, pecked him on the cheek and wished him luck, adding 'fix a couple of the bastards for me'. He wondered what the Brits had done to a Welsh woman that she could say those last words so vehemently?

There were only a few people about by the station entrance and they were mostly in uniform. He remembered part of his briefing: 'walk and look positive even if you want to ask the way or whatever.' He slung his raincoat over his right shoulder, making sure that the silver badge with its castle-crown and the letters MN; a genuine one from some survivor who no-doubt now languished in the P.O.W. camp in Bremen, was conspicuous in his left jacket lapel.

That badge was his reason for not being in uniform; young and looking very fit someone was bound to ask why he was not. There were still people in Britain who did not know that M.N. stood for Merchant Navy and that, generally, only officers wore uniform and then not always. In fact, most had no idea how high was the penalty being paid by the men of the sea so that others could continue to eat.

The sun was well up and quite warm which made the shadow-encased small booking hall feel quite cold, or was it fear returning as he made his first lonely move to communicate with the enemy, albeit only a station clerk.

"Single to Cardiff please," and he placed the previously rejected ten-shilling note on the counter.

"First or third class, Hans?"

"Oh!" He'd not thought about that. "Third please; and why do you call me Hans, please?"

"There's quite a few of you chaps around here and I get to know the accent. Dutchies we call you, like I'm a Taffy. A couple of your officers just gone first class. You off the same ship?" The man was old and had been sitting behind the counter for many years, his only solace being able to talk to his customers as he dealt with their requirements and scrutinised them over the glasses perched precariously on the end of his nose.

The last thing Schultz needed at the moment was to have a conversation with the man but he was grateful for the unwitting information that there were genuine Dutch servicemen around. They were the very people who were the greatest danger! He took the proffered green ticket and, walking a few paces as he had seen another traveller do before him, offered it to another old man standing by the platform gate.

"This train here lad," the collector said, punching the ticket. "Have a good leave then," and returned it with a tired but genuine smile.

Schultz was grateful that his training, short though it had been, had included a session on how the British railways worked and how he should act when travelling on them. He said, 'Thank you', and walked onto the platform, relaxing a bit at the friendliness of the two men.

Turning left he saw two navy sailors wearing white gaiters and belts with 'Naval Police' on their arm-bands, come out of a door over which hung a sign saying 'Gents Toilet'. His heart missed a beat and he tried to look as nonchalant as possible as he passed them, but they took no notice of him, one saying to the other, "Christ Bill, I needed that. Nothing like a good crap!"

He walked almost the length of a carriage before finding an empty compartment. Entering it he carefully put the case in the luggage rack above him and then sat down facing the engine in the corner seat by the window. Drawing a deep breath he slowly let it out through clenched teeth and hoped that his pulse would stop racing.

The sun was now quite high, its rays penetrating the platform between the carriage and wrought ironwork of the roof. A roof whose glass panels had long since been shattered by air raids. He glanced at his wristwatch - seven o'clock; ten minutes to go. Surely they were the longest ten minutes of his life so far but pass they did. On the platform he heard a shout and a whistle blow, followed by a clanging as the train's couplings took up the slack. With a jolt the carriage moved and with loud hissing the engine strained to get on its way.

Very slowly the platform started to move past his window. There was the 'Gents' and the ticket collector at the gate, an empty porter's trolley, a door marked 'Ladies' and then the two naval policemen looking totally bored with their lot. He felt a stupid urge to shout at them, 'I am a German naval officer, you will salute me or I'll have you put on a charge!' Then, as things out there began to go by faster, he was almost seized with panic.

The bravado engendered when in the Hitler Youth and fostered to the point of arrogance in the SS left him; all thoughts of loyalty and duty to the Fatherland and *Führer* gone by the board. He wanted to jump out and race back to Gwen and hide with the quilt over his head until she could tell him that the 'Paddies' were ready to take him back to Ireland. There he could spend the rest of the war in a comfortable internee's camp eating good food while others, but not him, died.

Had there been other people in the compartment with him such thoughts would probably not have taken control, but for a moment or two he found his hands shaking so much he had to grasp his knees to control them. After half a minute his mind slowly returned to more rational thinking; this was not the way for a specially chosen German officer on a mission behind enemy lines to behave. Fear was something for others, not him! Fear must be toned down to apprehension. Apprehension would keep him on his toes. He wondered if all agents felt as he was or whether it was just because his training had been so quick that there had been no psychological aspect to it. Perhaps Weiner had fallen down on that aspect of things?

The station gave way to houses and then rolling hills bounded by hedges. Some of the fields had sheep in them, or a few black and white cattle. Others were growing crops, corn of some sort he thought and grown to about a third of a foot high and looking lush. It was all orderly and not at all the devastated and wasted land the *Luftwaffe* was supposed to have created.

He caught sight of a flying boat as it appeared from behind the hills, which ran down to the port he had just left. Its engines could clearly be heard as they strained to lift the ungainly Sunderland into the sky. Perhaps that aircraft now climbing upwards was the one that had made them dive so hurriedly back in the Bay. The irony of his situation was not lost; back there they had tried to kill him and now here he was on their doorstep! If only they knew?

The train started to slow down as more houses came into view and eventually drew to a stop in a small station. There were no signboards with the place name on them but a man walked along the platform shouting, 'Johnstone'.

In peacetime the train with its goods-vans full of fish at the back end would have gone through to Cardiff almost non-stop and then on to Paddington, its precious load bound for Billingsgate market. But now it stopped so that the airman stationed at the flying boat base and airfield were given a chance to go on leave.

The platform seemed quite busy with a predominance of men in the uniform of the RAF, but the three flight sergeants who got in with Schultz wore uniforms of a darker blue, which Schultz knew was that of Australia. One of their group was arguing at the platform gate with two RAF Police Corporals who, apart from the white belts and gaiters, wore holsters on their belts. Unlike the sailors before, they looked very professional.

A whistle blew and there was a hiss of steam preparatory to the train getting underway again. One of the sergeants held the door open and yelled, 'Come on, Jacko. Run for it or you'll miss the bloody train!' So admonished, the man grabbed his pay-book from the corporal and ran the few paces to the carriage, flinging his case in before jumping after it. One of the policemen started to follow but was called back by the other with a, 'Leave it Corp; those Aussies haven't a bit of discipline in them!'

"What the stuff was all that about, Jacko?" asked one of the others who wore the brevet of a wireless operator.

"Bloody drongo! Said the Boss had forgotten to sign my leave pass and said I couldn't come. It's time Poms like that understood we're volunteers and couldn't give a stuff about their rules and regulations." He looked at Schultz seeing the silver badge. "You chaps don't like bull either do you? That's why you wear civvies." His eyes took on a faraway look as he continued. "Lost a brother last year in your mob. He was a radio op. Bloody U-boats! Sod all Germans!"

"Yes, sod all Germans," Schultz replied. "I lost my parents in Holland." He'd been told in his training that such a remark might engender sympathy; he turned to look out of the window as if not wanting to talk.

One of the diggers muttered, "Sorry, Mate," and then they started to discuss their forthcoming leave at a farm near Cardiff, explaining to Schultz as they talked, that the owner had a distant connection with

Australia. They argued, apparently not for the first time, as to who would tell Smudger's fiancée, one of the farmer's landgirls, that he had been killed. One of them muttered, "Bloody 'eighty eights."

Schultz couldn't resist it, although he had made only non-committal remarks before when they had good-naturedly tried to bring him into the conversation. "What happened?"

"Got jumped by three JU88 fighters out over the Bay when we were about to have a go at a sub. Luckily there was a bit of cloud about and the skipper got us lost pretty damn quick, but not before they'd killed our navigator and badly wounded old Smudger. He died a couple of days ago. Suppose there'll be a few more of us clocking out before it's all over." He paused pensively and then added: "When we came over to the old country, like our Dads before us, it was all one big game and when they taught us to fly we thought all our Christmases had come together. Now it's not so funny and we've learnt what it's all about, just like you have." They all lapsed into silence with their own thoughts.

The train stopped at Swansea, by which time Willie Schultz had had time to reflect on his own position. It seemed that as long as he kept away from any real Dutchmen and amongst people like these airmen, and kept his wits about him, he was perfectly safe from discovery.

When the train started on the next leg to Cardiff, Schultz had the fliers tell him what their hometowns were like 'down under'. He found their descriptions quite graphic and interesting. When asked about Holland he stuck to his briefing.

As the train drew into the city the Aussies said that when on short leaves they always went straight to the nearest pub for a beer and insisted that, if he had time, he went with them.

Leaving the station no-one took any notice of either him or his companions so that, first having asked what time trains left for Bristol, he felt at ease enough to enjoy the two halves of mild ale and a couple of sausage rolls for lunch with his new-found companions.

CHAPTER 11

ENGLAND

Captain Weiner had told Schultz to go down to Bristol for three reasons. Firstly, he knew a bit more about Bristol than Cardiff, secondly, if British Intelligence had become aware of Schultz he hoped that by going south, instead of straight to Glasgow, it might help to throw them off the scent. Thirdly, most of the five-pound notes carried by Schultz were forgeries; real ones seemed to be in short supply when Weiner had tried to procure them. It was an accepted fact that British seamen were paid in these large notes after long trips away so their use by Schultz should not draw undue attention. The average shopkeeper would, anyway, be hard pushed to detect the forgery; nevertheless the more the changing of them was spread around the better.

After hearing that there were Dutchmen on the train Schultz thought that there might be more in Cardiff so it definitely seemed a good idea to go elsewhere.

He arrived at Temple Meads station without incident just before half past four. His orders were now to find secure accommodation for the night and let Weiner know that he had arrived in England. Following other people across the footbridge he surrendered his ticket at the gate and left the station completely unheeded by one railway policeman and two very large military police, complete with side-arms and conspicuous red cap covers. As he left the gate behind him a gas driven taxi, looking as if it should topple over backwards with the weight of the coke generator at its back, stopped to let its occupants, an American colonel and major, get out. Schultz seized his chance and asked if he could be taken to a hotel somewhere near the city centre.

"Sure, hop in. Could be difficult but we'll find somewhere for you. Most of the better places are full of Yanks on leave, or whatever, since they seem to have plenty of cash to throw around. Not that I can grumble for they tip well! Where're you from then with that accent?" The driver seemed friendly enough and wishing to chat.

"Holland, but I'm serving in the merchant navy now. I need a new uniform and some other gear. Do you happen to know where there is a tailor's or clothes shop? I was told that there was a uniform place in Avonmouth but I believe that is quite a way to go?"

"Certainly is. Half an hour by bus or you could go by train but I know a good shop near the Tramway Centre. I'll show you the street as we pass." The accent was broad Bristolian and again Schultz was almost defeated in the translation of some of the words. There seemed to be as many dialects here as there were in Germany – Platt Deutsche in the north and the almost indecipherable Bavarian in the southern Alps.

Passing over Bristol Bridge Schultz saw ample evidence of the bombing by the *Luftwaffe* but it did not seem as bad as that being suffered by his own cities back home. True to his word the taxi driver pointed out a tailor's shop before finding a small private hotel off Cathedral Square that had a vacancy sign up.

Schultz was lucky enough to secure a third-story room and although the furniture was old it was clean and the double bed did not look too uncomfortable. He took it for four days, explaining to the proprietress that it all depended on how long it would take to get his new uniforms. He signed the register and showed both his identity card and seaman's discharge book, not that the good lady took much notice, and went back to his room, carefully locking the door behind him. As in Ireland he took the only dining chair in the room and propped it under the doorknob. On the bedside table there was a bible, ashtray and a reading lamp, all of which he put on the floor and replaced them with his case.

Next he opened the case and removed his bits and pieces, exposing the wireless. The set, being pre-tuned, had a minimum of controls and to someone of Schultz's radio competency was simplistic in the extreme. He opened a small panel and taking out a power lead plugged it in where the lamp had been, then he turned a knob labelled 'Charging' to 240V.

The aerial of fine copper wire was wound on a drum. The end of the wire was threaded through a sleeve of toughened insulating mica and terminated in a small eye made of the same material. Taking the eye he carefully pulled out the wire, walking to the window as he did so; there he undid the lock and slid the lower section up enough for him to momentarily stick his head out. There was, of course, no reason why anyone should be out in the road looking up at this particular window but he checked nevertheless before lowering the wire until it was level with the top of the ground floor window. Next he adjusted the sleeve so that it was on the corner of the windowsill and carried the wire just clear of the brickwork before clamping it in position by lowering the window on it. It would not be the best of aerials but better than a short one across the room.

Going back to the set, he sat on the edge of the bed and switched on the power. While he waited the few moments for the valves to warm up he first clipped a shorting strap across what aerial wire remained on the drum and then placed one of two crystals in a socket and turned to the 6m\cs range. Gradually the miniature earphones he had donned began to come alive with the sound of static. Good, the receiver was working; now for the transmitter. He moved a switch situated at the bottom of the set from 'RX' to 'TX' and pressing the Morse key watched as the needle of the only meter started to rise. Quickly he made the necessary adjustment to the 'Inductance' and 'Capacity' controls for the length of aerial in use. Satisfied that he had maximum power going out into the ether he switched back to receive and sat upright, realising that his heart rate had risen and his breath seemed in short supply. The crucial moment had arrived!

After *U-614* was clear of the Irish coast Petty Officer Telegraphist Openheim had been ordered to send a brief message to base, for onward transmission

to Intelligence H.Q., which read simply 'All is well'.
It meant that Schultz had been handed over to the Irish
pipeline.   Captain Weiner, in consultation with the
Signals Officer of KG 200, had decided that messages
were to be as simple as possible and in plain English.
His reasoning being that should the vast listening
network of the British monitoring service centred on
Bletchley be lucky enough to pick-up the few short
transmissions from Schultz they would assume that
such messages must be in cipher. They would spend
weeks trying to find out what it meant, by which time
the operation would be over.

Realising that his nerves were on edge, Willie
Schultz took a cigarette from the packet of Players
given to him by one of the Aussie sergeants, took a
few puffs before bracing himself and once more
changed to transmit and sent his first message. 'M M
M   DE Z'. Switching back to receive he waited with
the volume control right up; nothing, just static.
Watching the second hand of his watch he started to
get agitated but exactly half a minute later Cuxhaven
started to come through. 'Z Z Z DE C C C K'.
The signals orders read that if the station called, in
this instance Merimac, which was designated the
control, failed to respond in half a minute first
Cuxhaven then Trondheim and lastly Greenland
would answer. Those orders also stated that once the
message from *U-614* had been received all stations
would keep a twenty-four hour watch with
transmitters on standby. 'Had the operator in France
chosen this very moment to go for a piss without
calling for a relief?'

'C C C DE Z Going shopping QTC ?' The pre-arranged message saying he was in Bristol went out along with the question, 'have you anything for me'. The operator at Cuxhaven repeated it to ensure he had heard correctly, adding 'QTC NIL'. There were to be no preambles, no niceties of formal message sending, just short and sweet and if the Tommies did hear him let them scratch their heads wondering what it was all about! He wound the aerial in and packed everything back into the set. Even if the Tommies knew the operating frequency and all about the operation it was doubtful, with all transmissions sent at a speed of twenty-five words a minute, they would have been able to take a directional fix on him. He felt elated and decided that it was time he went out for a beer and a meal!

In the room was a wooden wardrobe with a key in its lock. He decided that wandering around with the case in the evening might look odd so decided to leave it in the wardrobe and, since the weather was still fine, left his raincoat and cap as well. Dropping his trousers he took out four more five pound notes from his belt; *that* he would most certainly not leave behind! Locking the door, after first placing a single hair on it so that he would know if anyone had been in the room, he went into the bathroom to empty his bladder and then slicked back his hair with water. What was it he had been told the RAF men were called? Ah yes, 'Brylcream Boys' because of the lavish use of the hairdressing they used; he must buy some of that tomorrow.

Going downstairs he asked the hall porter where he could get a meal and was told that 'if he didn't mind paying through the nose and no need for coupons' there was a restaurant up the hill where rationing appeared not to be an obstacle. The alternative was a café down by the docks where he could fill up with baked beans on toast. Thanking the man he passed over a shilling. Schultz thought that things here were not much different from Germany. If you had rank or cash anything appeared to be obtainable!

He left the hotel, walked down the three steps and out of the small forecourt. Hesitating on the pavement he looked around him making a mental note of its name and where it was located; heaven forbid he might come back later and not know where he was staying!

He eventually found the restaurant and noted the name of the licensee, 'Rosenbaum', over the door as he went inside. 'Shit', he thought, 'I'd be right in it if they knew back home. Must remember this one for closing when we take over. Bloody Jews.' Inside the place was hung with heavy dark maroon drapes and almost smelt of 'affluence'. A grey-haired Maitre'de clad in tails looked at him with obvious disdain since he was not in either uniform or dress-suit, before ushering him to a table for two. At the next table sat an American two star general, a colonel and two elegant looking women. Elsewhere were other senior ranking officers in both American and British uniforms with a few civilians in dinner jackets. 'Shit', he thought again, 'I'm really up with the brass!' But when one or two eyes were turned on him he began to feel a bit awkward and that his sports jacket and slacks really were out of place; more so when an equally grey haired and obsequious waiter took the napkin from his side plate and spread it on his lap.

Jewish establishment or not the meal was quite good; a thick vegetable soup followed by pigeon pie and a half bottle of white wine from some obscure French vineyard. He supposed that wine must be in quite short supply now. He refused a port with his coffee, knowing he dare not get the slightest bit tight. The coffee was definitely superior to that now available back home.

'If only they knew who I was,' passed through his mind as the general got up to go, his woman catching Schultz's eye and smiling at him. She was a good looker and half the soldier's age. 'Lucky bastard, wouldn't mind getting her between the sheets myself'. He wondered where he could find a woman like that for he was sure neither woman was her escort's wife.

Schultz had been given a miniature alarm clock, Swiss made of course, and now its subdued tones woke him. Rubbing his left eye he belched; pigeon pie! Time to visit the toilet before he had to use the wireless. Orders were to listen as near as possible to 0600 and 1800 hours on a daily basis. Obviously from now on any information on the 'Queen Mary's' movements would be vital to Schultz and accordingly, without knowing the reason, New York had been told to let H.Q. know when she arrived or left and anything else the agent could glean.

Repeating yesterday's procedure he listened to the crackling of the ether for five minutes before, exactly at 0600 hours, Merimac came on the air: 'Z Z Z de M M M QTC 1 QRK?' Jesus, they had a message for him! Rapidly he acknowledged the call and let out a sigh of relief when told that they were able to hear his signals without difficulty. The message said simply, 'Auntie is getting ready to leave'. The pre-arranged code which told him the 'Queen Mary' was loading troops; something that normally took two days. If that was the case he had probably six or seven days before she arrived at the Tail o' The Bank.

Putting away the aerial he found his hands were shaking and his heart thumping more than they should be from the realisation that the whole reason for his being in Britain was now starting to come together. With it came the possibility, if he were unlucky, that his own end might be in sight. With the wireless returned to the wardrobe he once more sat on the bed and took out a cigarette, a du Maurier bought with no difficulty at the restaurant last night. He would have to get his uniform quicker than he thought.

Weiner had debated whether to give him a uniform to take with him but had decided against it on the grounds that it would be more for him to carry around during the journey across Ireland. He could have worn it for the landing but then he would have possibly been too conspicuous - civilian clothes with the small silver badge would be best.

Cigarette finished and with his adrenalin now running he felt his bladder needed emptying yet again.

Back in his room he doused his face with cold water at the hand basin. Drying it he looked in the mirror where those cold blue eyes stared back at him from beneath the fair eyebrows. For some time he stood there unmoving while *Leutnant* Whilhem Schultz in the mirror seemed to be telling him to get a hold of himself.

The hour until breakfast took ages to pass but pass it did and by the time he left the hotel bound for the tailor's shop he was quite composed, although disconcerted by what he had read in a paper while waiting for the meal. If it was not all propaganda the *Reich* was suffering setbacks in Russia and the air raids were increasing. Italian lines of communications too were now being heavily bombed.

He was in luck at the tailors where they had an officer's uniform in stock which required only minor alterations and those would be completed by tomorrow midday. "What gold-braid would Sir want?"

"Chief Radio Officer, please. I want three shirts, half a dozen collars, a couple of sets of underwear as well. Oh, and a raincoat." He looked around the shop, trying to remember what else it was that had slipped his memory. "Yes, two each of collar studs and I'll take a set of those MN cufflinks."

"Certainly Sir," and the man measured his neck. "What size cap?" He tried two on before he got it right. "Any particular company cap badge or the ordinary merchant navy one?" The man was almost grovelling and when Schultz paid a deposit and saw the name on the invoice - A Jacobs - he almost recoiled in disgust. 'Another fawning shyster of a Jew. The bloody town seemed to be full of them!' He needed to get out in the fresh air!

He walked back to the Tramway Centre, bought a paper and a second-hand copy of one of C.S. Forester's Hornblower books. The weather was still fine and mild and as he studied the narrow strip of water, which formed the town's docks, he saw in the distance, amongst other bombed buildings, the blackened shell of a large warehouse. A street sweeper, wearing a bar of three soiled medal ribbons from the last war, seeing what he was looking at, leaned on his broom.

"Bleeding Jerries! Christ knows how many fags went up in that lot. Burned for days it did and after you boys…" He pointed to Schultz's badge, "risked yer lives to bring us the baccy. Sodding war!" and he went on sweeping the gutter.

Schultz thought that he could remember the way to the station, but to make sure walked up to a policemen and asked for directions. It all seemed so simple. Could all the Tommies really be as stupid as these people seemed to be?

Before walking back to the hotel he asked a porter at the station the time of trains and where he would have to change to get to Glasgow. He stopped at a café for a lunch of baked beans on toast and something he hadn't had for years, a milkshake. It was not exactly the Ritz but was obviously popular and from a heated argument between three workmen at the next table, frequented by dockers. Seeing a poster on the wall which read, 'Walls have ears' under a cartoon-like picture of Hitler, and another reading, 'Careless talk costs lives', he almost felt like telling the men that he was a spy and they should definitely not be discussing the cargo of the ship they were unloading. Of course they would not believe him and he smiled to himself. Was it like this down on the waterfront of Hamburg or Bremen where, being an officer, he would not normally go?

Later, back at the hotel, he locked his room door and laying back on the bed studied the route from Bristol to Glasgow in the school atlas; read a couple of chapters of the book, set the alarm and dozed until it went off. He was worried about letting the aerial out of the window for fear that someone might just happen to spot it so used the suction cups provided for indoor use and strung it across the room. Control could still read him but not as strongly but since there were no messages it did not matter.

Sprucing himself up he left the hotel. Wandering past the cathedral he thought he saw a pub sign down a side road and crossed the square towards it. It was just past opening time and only half a dozen customers propped up the bar. He ordered a half of bitter and a packet of crisps, taking them to a table in the corner. Idly he watched as an effeminate looking man of about thirty, in a crumpled and ill-fitting grey lounge suit detached himself from the two sailors he was talking to and sat at a table. Schultz had taken a few sips of his beer when he felt the man's gaze on him and began to feel uncomfortable; there was no doubt that he was being scrutinised but why? He took his time finishing the beer all the while feeling the man's gaze on him. When the two sailors left he decided to go as well.

Outside he turned left towards the city centre not sure of what he would do. He did not fancy going back to the atmosphere of yesterday evening's restaurant but was there anywhere else to go other than the café? Once again he went down to the docks, which he now realised were no more than a wharf on either side of the water and the three ships there were quite small; thousand tonners or so, and all painted almost the same dull grey as their own merchantmen back home.

The thought of 'home' brought him back to the reality of his present position. Turning, he looked away from the ships and noticed a cinema. A film, that should pass a couple of hours, but he found that the programme was already well into its second half and went to the dockside café instead.

When he had nearly finished a pie and potatoes, washed down with lukewarm tea he realised that the effeminate man from the pub was also eating there and was sitting so that he could watch Schultz as he did so. After a while, inadvertently as far as Schultz was concerned, their eyes met and he gave the German a watery smile, causing him again to feel ill at ease. Who was this fellow? Could he be a counter intelligence agent who became interested when he had heard Schultz's accent while ordering his drink back in the pub? The man did not look particularly fit and perhaps that was why he was not in uniform, but what did an MI5 agent look like anyway? For that matter did Schultz look like an enemy agent? 'Christ, it was unnerving!'

He cursed inwardly and to cover his agitation went up to the counter and ordered another cup of tea, although he still did not like the way the English made it. Despite the place being now fairly full with the atmosphere smoky and noisy Willie Schultz began to feel he was becoming very conspicuous and suddenly longed for the friendly Gwen and the feeling of safety she had given him. 'God Almighty,' he had never felt so alone as now; it was not quite the panic he had felt as the train had pulled out of Milford Haven yesterday but damn near. He sipped from the cup only to recoil and spill some of its contents as this time it was hot and hurt his lips. He lit a cigarette and waited for the tea to cool, making himself look at as many of the other occupants of the room as he could, trying to guess what they did for a living which was not difficult for the name 'Dockers' Café' said it all.

By the time he had finished the tea he could see, before a waitress started to draw the black-out curtains, that the evening was closing in so he got up to go while he was still able to see where he was going. Tomorrow he must buy a torch for, as at home, the city was totally blacked-out, but unlike home the people seemed little worried about further air-raids on their battered city.

Outside he took a deep breath, glad to be in the fresh air and started back towards the Tramway Centre and his hotel. Coming to a sign that read, 'Public Convenience', he went down the steps in the Gentlemen's section and after fishing in his pocket for a penny, went into a stall. With the physical changes to routine since leaving the U-boat and the present psychological turmoil his bodily functions had become erratic.

When he came out there was that damned effeminate fellow by a urinal. Hearing Schultz behind him he turned, still doing up his fly buttons.

"Wait, please," he said in a pleading tone and stretched out an arm, clutching the German's sleeve.

Willie Schultz panicked. No one should be addressing him like this. The whole reason Weiner had him operating on his own and not asking for help from the established spy network was for total security. Had he been a fully trained agent with months and months of going over every situation that he might encounter, he would probably have realised what this man, holding his sleeve, was; but he did not. The man must definitely be a counter intelligence agent in disguise and would turn on him at any moment. In one movement he shook the arm free and, grabbing the man's ears, with the full weight of his body propelled the fellow backwards, smashing his head hard against the wall with such force that the eyes momentarily almost came out of their sockets.

The force Schultz had used was that required for the survival of life. The fellow went limp and his body slid to the ground as his knees buckled under him, the head eventually coming to rest in the trough of the urinal, where the urine, still not drained away, started to turn pink. The eyes were open and staring in a face that held an expression of complete surprise!

'Scheisse!' Schultz in the heat of the moment relapsed into his native tongue and, worst still, uttered the word out loud. There was the sound of movement behind the closed door of the farthest lavatory. He had to get out of there and quickly.

Because of the difficulty of enforcing an effective blackout the light bulbs had been removed so that even in daylight the place would be a twilight zone; now it was almost in darkness but despite this he bounded up the few steps two at a time. Despite the turmoil in his mind he had the sense to drop to a walk once he was on the pavement. Running would only draw attention to himself and there were quite a few people nearby waiting at a bus stop. He felt no remorse at what he had just done. The man could be dead or just badly injured but either way he was an enemy agent and in a war people got hurt. It was a simple case of 'him or me' and Lieutenant Schultz of the *Kriegsmarine* meant to stay alive as long as possible.

CHAPTER 12

SCOTLAND

On the walk back to his hotel Willie Schultz stopped several times to make sure he was not being followed. He desperately wanted a cigarette but dared not light one lest he draw the wrath of some air-raid warden and thereby focus attention on himself. Finally, back in his room he was able to do so and sitting back on the bed pondered the events of the evening. Even with the smoke from the cigarette close to his nostrils he could still smell the stench of that lavatory; urine intermingled with disinfectant and that fellow's body odour. However long he might live he would remember the foetid smell of that place.

In his mind he was now certain that the fellow who's head he had just smashed, was an enemy counter agent. It must have been pure luck that he had been in the pub and heard Schultz's accent, or perhaps they had MI5 men stationed at all the west country ports just waiting for German saboteurs to land…. No, that was a stupid thought. It would require an army to cover all the pubs and cafes frequented by seamen. There was really only one answer and that was that MI5 had been tipped off about his arrival and he had been shadowed ever since he had landed. 'Jesus! He hoped that Gwen had not been picked up', and for once in his life realised that he 'felt' for someone else's well-being instead of his own. But he must think of his own well-being. He was here to do a job and in the last hour that job had taken on a very sinister outlook.

Schultz had deliberately kept his eyes on his food whilst he ate so for all he knew the dammed fellow could have used the café's telephone to call in a report. But if he had not then the best thing was to sit tight in the hotel until his uniform was ready and hope that they did not know where he was staying.

Sleep was not easy. Once he woke in a sweat, only to find that the police breaking down the bedroom door was only a dream. He had been awake for over an hour when the alarm went off. He duly 'listened out' on the wireless but there was no message for him and he decided, just in case, that he would not send anything to say he would be leaving today. The wait for breakfast seemed interminable but eventually it came; afterwards he went straight back to his room with a copy of the Daily Mail. Being a national newspaper there was, of course, nothing in it about a minor incident in a public toilet in the centre of Bristol.

By eleven o'clock Willie Schultz was beginning to regain confidence. He was sure that if MI5 had known where he was staying they would have picked him up if for no reason other than he had attacked one of their own. Having made sure there was no one in the reception area he dialled the number of the tailor and enquired whether his uniform was ready; only to be told, after a brief delay, 'We are terribly sorry but one of the tailors has not turned up for work, but the uniform and everything else will be ready at four o'clock without fail'. For the benefit of anyone behind the closed office door he said gruffly. 'It had better be or I'll miss my ship,' but inwardly he fumed.

He decided to pay his bill and knocked on the office door. Confronted by the proprietress he was told that he would have to pay for tonight as well as he had not vacated the room before ten in the morning. He supposed that he could well have walked out without paying but if the local police were told and happened to be very efficient, they might just pick him up at the railway station.

Back in his room he swore and cursed all Jewish tailors. He would have to stay where he was and go without something to eat at midday, for there was no way he would go near the pub or café or ask anyone where else he might go for a meal. He consulted the school atlas and decided that rather than go straight up to Glasgow via Crewe he would take a train to London and thence to Edinburgh, hoping thereby to confuse the issue for anybody trying to follow him.

By the time he arrived at the tailors he was not in the best of moods but knew he had to keep his wits about him and that it would be unwise to vent his spleen on the Jew; that would have to wait until victory for the *Reich*. Since he needed to check the fit of his new clothes he decided, if all was well, to change completely and stay in uniform. Making sure that the shop assistant and an army officer, who had come into the shop, would not see him and the slight bulge of his money belt, he drew the fitting cubical curtain tight and stripped off his civilian clothes.

Once back into the dark navy blue serge, almost identical in shade to the one he was used to wearing back home, he felt, for no real reason, considerably better. Drawing back the curtain he passed out the discarded items and told the tailor to pack everything in a case before stepping back in front of the long mirror to admire himself.

Yes, he had to admit, it was well cut and he looked very handsome in it. Even if it was not as an officer in the *Kriegsmarine*, he felt better for seeing the gold braid on his sleeve. The two wavy stripes with a diamond between them looked like nothing to be found in the German service but nevertheless were of the best quality. Yes, the taxi driver had definitely done him a favour in recommending this place, Jewish or not. Back in the shop the young second lieutenant in a khaki battle dress nodded to him and noticing the gold braid said, "Good afternoon, Sir". To be deferred to by rank dispelled the last of his black mood and Schultz felt almost elated that yet again he was being accepted as an allied officer. He paid the bill and surrendered the required number of clothing coupons.

Outside the shop the sunshine had disappeared and a fine drizzle set in. Schultz asked if the assistant could 'phone for a taxi, which eventually turned up quarter of an hour later, during which time he engaged the army man in conversation and smoked a cigarette. The boy, for he seemed no more than that, had just been commissioned and was ordering his dress uniform while on leave before joining a new regiment. There was no hint of doubt in the young officer's mind that Schultz was what he said he was, a Dutchman fighting for the liberation of his country; just as all the allies were, the youngster vehemently assured Schultz.

"With all these American troops arriving in the country surely the invasion of the Continent could not be far away, could it Sir? Especially now that Rommel has been kicked out of North Africa?"

"I expect you are right Lieutenant. I've noticed there certainly seem to be a lot of Yanks around, particularly black ones here in Bristol." Inwardly Willie Schultz wondered what the *Führer* would think when his *Werhmacht* had to fight Negroes, who were considered even lower than the Popovs.

"Those here at the moment are mostly Pioneer Corps but rumour has it that there are some fighting units and even an air force squadron. It seems damned unfair but the Snow-drops, that's what their MPs are called because of their white helmets – but perhaps you know that already Sir? – try to segregate them from the white troops. I live on the outskirts of the city and it has caused quite a bit of ill feeling between us and them. Another thing that bugs us is that they all have such high pay; even a private is paid more than I am!" And he lapsed into a pensive silence.

In the taxi Schultz thought back over his recent conversation. It was to Germany's advantage if there was dissension between the Americans and British, even if it was only at a lower level. 'So what if we have been kicked out of Africa'; that would

214

shorten the supply lines and he was sure that the reverses in Russia were only temporary despite what the paper had said this morning. When the *Führer's* promised new secret weapons became available next year things would change.

At the station he bought a first class ticket to London and purchased a copy of the Evening Post from the newsstand.

"This platform here Sir. You've missed the express so there'll be a half hour's wait for the next one and she'll stop almost everywhere," the ticket collector told him, and once again the military police were not the slightest bit interested in him. On the platform he looked up and down and seeing a sign saying Buffet went inside. It was fairly crowded and stuffy in the warm evening air. Almost everyone in there was in a uniform of some sort and there was the constant hum of conversation; that no doubt centred on either the leave just over or the prospect of one to come - as it would be in such a place back home in Germany.

'Really, it did not matter which side you were on when it came down to the poor buggers who did the fighting. They were all the same', Willie thought

He noticed a table with two officers seated at it. Although there were other-ranks standing at the long serving counter and he could see no spare seats at any of the tables, there were two where a naval sub-lieutenant and a marine captain sat; apparently the divide between officers and men functioned even here. Brazenly, and buoyed with having been accepted by the young fellow at the tailors, Schultz took the

215

few paces across the noisy and smoke-filled room and asked if either of the seats were vacant.

"Sure, one is, the other's for our chum. He's in the gents." Schultz then noticed the teacup and empty plate in front of it.

"Do you mind if I take this one then?" he asked, taking off his Burberry and hanging it over the back of the vacant chair, having first placed the small case with the wireless in it on the seat. "I'd be grateful if you would keep an eye on this," he said tapping the case, "while I get something to eat?" Somehow he knew that the all important item would be safe.

"Not a problem, old man." And once again it was the captain who spoke.

At the counter Willie asked for a cup of tea, "with no milk please and a slice of lemon." Why had he not thought of that before? The somewhat frazzled lady looked at him as if he was mad. "Lemon!" she exclaimed, "you foreigners have funny ideas. May be you get it on yer ship but certainly not 'ere, Ducks!" and she went to the huge urn and filled a cup. "Want anything with it. Slice of cake?"

"Thank you. I'll have two please."

"Not likely you won't. Only one per person. There's a war on, or don't yer know?" Somewhat taken aback by the annoyance in the woman's tone he offered five pounds in payment thinking of his orders to change as many of the forged notes as possible before he got to his final destination.

"Gor luv us! 'Aint yer got no change?" She snatched the note, muttering something about 'bloody foreigners' as she went to the till, and deliberately short-changed him by five shillings.

Back at the table another naval type with the braid on his sleeve of a lieutenant in the volunteer reserve was now occupying the other chair. Sitting down the German agent nodded to the man who remarked, "Merchant navy eh? Christ you fellows didn't half take a pasting in my last convoy. Managed to save a few but the other poor sods? Water is bloody cold off Iceland," and he shrugged his shoulders.

"Well you chaps I must be off. Got a wife and kid waiting for me. Nice talking to you. Have a good war," and so saying the marine rose and, picking up his case, left them.

The young subbie spoke next. "Guess we should get to our platform Peter. No sense in wasting any of our leave by missing that train to Taunton." And to Schultz. "Not meaning to be rude old man but where do you hail from; can't place your accent?"

"Holland".

"Oh, then you'll hardly be going home on leave". A slight pause as he rose. "Anyway chum, jolly good show on your getting out and joining us. Must have been frightful leaving everything behind. Good luck," and then both men were gone.

Willie sipped his tea, took a bite of cake and opened the paper. On page three he found what he was looking for, a small headline catching his eye. 'Body found in public convenience'. He read on. 'A cleaner found the body of a well-known homosexual in the Tramway Centre convenience yesterday morning. It is thought that he may have fallen backwards and fractured his skull. He was last seen alive leaving the Dockers' Café. It is known that the man had a penchant for blonde men and Police would like to interview a fair-haired merchant seaman seen leaving the café shortly before him.'

'Christ Almighty!' the Police were looking for him. The sooner he got on a train the better'. He wondered about the man occupying the last lavatory; in the gloom he probably thought the fellow was drunk and had just left him lying there. Subconsciously Schultz put his cap back on, he had taken it off when he sat down. Had he panicked by thinking the fellow was an MI5 counter-agent? The fact that he had killed yet another man did not worry him, but what did was that he had almost jeopardised the whole operation. 'Shit, it had been a near thing!' What was it the IRA girl had said to him? 'God help you when you are on your own,' or something like that, and she was about right!

He was still hungry. Carrying the wireless case he went to the counter and, avoiding the woman who had served him before, obtained a Spam sandwich. Back at the table he mulled over happenings of the last few hours as he ate. Thinking rationally, it was unlikely that the Police would pick him up; they wanted to interview a seaman who had been in civilian clothes and not an officer who normally would have been in uniform. Even if he were questioned his papers were all in order and anyway, no one actually saw him with the fellow. No, he could forget the incident. There was another point that had cropped up several times and that was people asking him where he came from.

Weiner had given him shoulder flashes to put on his uniform with the word Netherlands to fit that part of his cover story. Indeed, not far away was a petty officer in a dark blue navy uniform with the word Australia just below his shoulder. When he had ordered his uniform Schultz had thought about the flashes but decided that they would most likely attract any real Dutchmen to come up and say 'hello', and that was the last thing he wanted; so he had decided not to wear them. Particularly if, as Big Red had said, there were Dutch crewed scows being used up on the Clyde. On this point he felt he was doing the right thing.

Outside he sat down on a bench and opening his new case took out the C.S. Forester book, he might as well read on the train. He had sat there for not more than five minutes watching as people began to arrive on the platform when a loudspeaker came to life. 'The train now arriving at platform one is for Swindon, stopping at all stations. Passengers for Paddington please use the front four carriages. Those for Oxford the rear two,' a tired female voice announced.

As the engine came past emitting a loud hiss of steam Schultz stood up. Counting off four carriages he noted where there was a first class compartment and followed it along until the train came to a shuddering halt. Entering the compartment he put his cases in the luggage rack above him, closed the door and settled into a corner seat facing the engine. No sooner had he done so when a large lady, perhaps in her sixties, carrying a very small Schnauzer dog, opened the door and demanded, "Young man help me up with my case!" in a peremptory manner.

For a moment he sat there not moving. *Frau* Klein! No it could not be but the likeness was incredible. Wearing a military type fawn raincoat with its belt drawn tight around an ample midriff, she was stoutly built with a large bosom and heavily made up. An exact *doppelgänger* for the woman who had lived at the far end of his street and been a constant source of provocation to the local children with her 'do's and don'ts' as they tried to play. She complained incessantly to their parents mostly about imaginary misdemeanours. When he and another boy had joined the Hitler Youth they got their own back by threatening to report her with a concocted story about her having no love for the *Führer* and actually taking her dog between the sheets of her bed after her husband finally died from the results of being gassed in the Great War. He remembered how they had sniggered at the very thought of it!

Automatically Schultz fetched the case from the platform and put it up in the rack above the far corner of his seat, then held the dog as she hauled herself up into the compartment. The woman plumped down on the seat without a word of thanks, which was typical of *Frau* Klein. God they must be long lost twin sisters or something! The door opened again and an elderly major wearing the last war ribbons on his chest, got in, acknowledged them with a nod and sat down, and was immediately engaged by

220

the woman in mundane conversation. Majors were obviously far more important than two stripers from the merchant navy and Schultz was grateful for it. He took out his book and partly read and partly eavesdropped on the conversation, which was kept up until two stations past Swindon when she got out, the major helping. When he pulled the door shut he grinned at Schultz.

"Thank God for that. What a bore. Imagine being married to her!" and he settled down to read his paper.

By the time the train arrived at Paddington station it was nearly eleven o'clock and Schultz was both hungry and tired. On enquiring where he would catch the train for Edinburgh he found he would have to go to another station called Kings Cross and if he did not want to walk would have to wait in the queue for a taxi as buses and the Underground had stopped at ten o'clock until early morning. Following directions he found the taxi queue and joined it. It consisted almost entirely of officers from the services – he supposed that other ranks could not afford the fares and would have to wait until the morning, much the same as they would back in Berlin.

It took half an hour before the civilian policeman controlling the taxi queue called out, 'Anyone for Kings Cross. Room for one.' Climbing in, Schultz took his place with four RAF officers one of whom said, "God, a sailor. Have to behave ourselves chaps. Senior service and all that. Tell you what, old man, one of your Wrens," and he leered at Schultz, belching as he did so, "sure gave senior service last night. Bloody wizard she was!" From their subsequent talk he deduced that they were a bomber crew returning to their station after a few days out on the town and were considerably inebriated.

Unlike the Australians back in Wales they did not include him in their frivolous and mostly ribald remarks. Sitting on a drop down seat with his back to the driver Willie Schultz realised that the airmen were too far into their cups to realise he was not a navy type. He wondered if a British agent in Berlin could get away with what he was now doing; he did not think so. Someone would surely have asked to see his papers long before this!

Arriving at Kings Cross the fly-boys argued with the driver over what the journey had cost and to save any altercation which might involve authority, Schultz paid for them all before asking the driver if there was any chance of finding a hotel room for the night.

"Shouldn't think so, Guv, not at this time of night. That's unless you want to mix with the high and mighty at the Savoy or somewhere like that and pay through the nose as well. Best kip in a waiting room." He was momentarily non-plussed by the cab driver's use of the word 'kip', until its meaning dawned on him. He thought that mixing it with the 'high and mighty' might be a little risky and opted instead for the waiting room. Thanking the man he entered the main concourse. Although the first class counter was closed he was able to purchase his ticket to Edinburgh at one of the only two third class positions open.

Once again the few people around were almost all service men or women without the need to buy tickets as they travelled on railway warrants and went straight to the platform gates. However, as he paid for his ticket, a Redcap walked toward him and his heart skipped a few beats. Was his luck at last going to run out with a request to see his papers? The man strode past him and asked a woman sergeant at the second counter for her leave pass, presumably alerted by the fact she apparently had no warrant. He heard her say, "Been in town for the afternoon Corporal and am going back to my battery," mentioning a name he could not catch but it satisfied the MP who strode off without even a glance at Schutlz. Somewhat relieved he studied the board for the next train to Edinburgh and which platform it would be going from. He had missed the night one and would have several hours to wait. He looked for the Buffet but found it closed.

The next few hours were spent trying to sleep on an uncomfortable waiting-room bench until, feeling dishevelled and with an aching neck, he went to the gents and shaved in cold water. He tried to console himself with the thought that he could be far worse off than he was; if it had not been for that damned tailor he might have slept in a bed....bloody Jews!

There was just time to get an indifferent sandwich and cup of tea before the train pulled out; coincidentally at almost the same time of day he had left Milford Haven and he momentarily again thought of Gwen.

He shared the compartment with two sub-lieutenants and a midshipman of the Royal Navy Volunteer Reserve whose uniforms were as new as his own. He gathered from scraps of their conversation that they were on their way to join their first ship as officers. A flying officer was with them until York. In the corridor there were plenty of other ranks standing or sitting on kit-bags or cases and although there was a spare seat in the compartment the divide between officers and men ensured it remained empty – just the same as in Germany he thought. The other occupants seemed to be as tired as he was and in consequence their conversation was minimal, for which he was grateful. They all dozed most of the way to the cathedral city.

There was some time before leaving York and he was able to partake of more black tea – he had learnt his lesson and did not ask for a slice of lemon. Upon his return to the compartment he found the airman's seat now occupied by a naval Commander of some maturity. The very presence of a senior officer made Schultz more alert. The younger officers he felt he could easily cope with but this man would be a different kettle of fish if he engaged in conversation; would he have been safer if he had travelled in civilian clothes in a third class compartment? Perhaps he had let his vanity and liking of comfort get the better of him.

Arriving at Edinburgh two hours after the scheduled time of three thirty he was glad he did not have to stay on the train all the way to Aberdeen. Other than having to tell his cover story to the

Commander, who obviously believed him, the journey was uneventful even if it was somewhat tedious. Here there was not such a mass of people milling around as in London or Bristol. A taxi was readily available, whose driver found him a decent hotel where he had a tolerable meal and a good night's sleep before keeping the morning w/t schedule.

Merimac could hardly read him but Cuxhaven once again came to his rescue and passed on the message that, 'Auntie had left yesterday afternoon.' So he now had, say, four days before he would see his quarry! As he packed away the wireless he was not quite sure what his feelings were. Was the adrenalin starting to flow or was he beginning to feel afraid again? He shaved and finished dressing, replacing his now somewhat creased collar with a clean one. Feeling more like himself he went down for breakfast, after which he surrendered a coupon from the ration book and paid the bill, waited half an hour for a taxi and returned to the railway station. There, thinking to himself that having survived the long, and at times tedious, journey so far, he might as well travel in comfort, he purchased a first class ticket to Glasgow.

CHAPTER 13

SCOTLAND

Glasgow was more like Bristol with servicemen and women everywhere. Before starting for the exit Willie Schultz waited a while to watch as a troop-train full of American soldiers went slowly along the next platform heading south. He assumed that they had just come from Greenock and for a moment he worried that 'Auntie' might have arrived already, but that was impossible. Other troopships must have come in and he remembered hearing someone in the carriage saying that the delay in reaching York was probably due to 'another load of Yanks arriving', and that 'their trains often stuffed–up normal schedules'. Back home it was not the troop-trains, unless perhaps in Poland, which played havoc with train timetables but the RAF bombers! Why was the *Luftwaffe* not doing the same here?

Following his idea of shaking off any agent who might be following him, although he was now pretty certain that this was not the case, he left the station and went into the first pub he could see. After a half pint of beer and a so-called sausage roll, he returned to the station and bought a ticket for Greenock. After a short wait, only slightly longer than the journey itself, he boarded a train, most of whose occupants wore naval uniform.

He shared a carriage with four officers, two of whom wore the uniform of the Free French. As if it were the precursor of foreboding at thoughts of returning to their ships, the war at sea and possible death, the blue skies became dull with heavy clouds. Rain began to fall and with it conversation ceased as each man pondered what the future might bring.

For the German agent, now so close to his final destination, he knew his prime object was to find accommodation near enough to the docks at Gourock, where he would be able to watch closely the disembarkation and then the embarkation of 'Auntie's' passengers. His knowledge of what he would find in Greenock, other than that it was a massive terminal for troop convoys, was minimal. *Kapitän* Weiner could have found out more by ordering an agent, already operating in Scotland, to go and see how things were but that might have led to someone putting two and two together as to where Schultz was going and that was the last thing he wanted. He knew that even in the *Abwher* one hundred per cent security could not be guaranteed.

So far the journey had been easy by comparison to what lay ahead and Willie knew that from now on everything would be up to himself; only the W/T schedules would have to be conducted on orders already dictated. He glanced surreptitiously at the two Frenchmen. Like himself they were in a foreign land far from home but at least they had each other and probably a whole ship's company to talk to. He had no-one, and once again he thought of Gwen and vaguely wondered how long he could survive on the almost one thousand pounds in his money belt if he were to forget the whole operation and just lose himself amongst the enemy? As he was realising that whilst the money might last quite a while, the ration-books would not, there was the squeal of steel on steel as the engine driver applied the breaks.

One of the Frenchmen said, *"Nous somme arrive, Jean"*. As one they stood up and started to don their Burberrys, balancing themselves against the jerking movements of the train.

Schultz waited until they sat down again and then did likewise as the train crawled into the station and came to a juddering halt. 'And I too, have arrived,' he said under his breath as all thoughts of abandoning his mission left him. The compartment now empty he took down his two cases from the luggage rack and following the others to the platform exit surrendered his ticket without anyone giving him a second glance.

At the station, taxis were in short supply and after a lengthy wait he had found himself sharing one with the two naval types who had been in the same compartment on the train. The driver dropped them off at the Princes Pier railway station, which was occupied by troop-trains loading more Americans, then took Schultz to the Bay Hotel. With difficulty Willie understood that to try and find any accommodation in Gourock or Greenock was almost impossible. When the southern port of Southampton and the London docks were closed to all troopships, because they were within easy range of enemy bombers, some six hundred workers, in many cases with their families, were brought north to handle the work created by the convoy terminal. They were now billeted all over the place, almost anywhere that a bed could be put and even the base naval officers had great difficulty in finding somewhere for their wives.

Herr Leutnant Schultz of the German navy and, as he now thought of himself, Special Agent, surveyed the lounge of the Bay Hotel in Greenock. Its occupants were almost all in naval uniform, wearing the gold braid of commanders and above. At a nearby table a captain with the purple stripe of an engineer between his braid was earnestly talking to a grey haired civilian who appeared to be making notes as they talked.

Schultz, with his two wavy stripes, felt almost out of place and the receptionist, when he booked in, appeared to be about to say, 'This is for senior officers only, Sir'. But she did not and allocated him a small room at the back of the hotel. "That room is the best I can do for you, Sir, particularly if you wish it for several nights."

At least Schultz could understand her without difficulty but it had been a different case with the taxi driver. His use of colloquial words such as 'wist, awa' and others had led to several requests for a repeat and had almost defeated the German.

Schultz went to the bar and ordered a half of bitter. He chose a table by a wall to while away the time until the evening meal. Again, in the presence of so much 'Brass', he felt uneasy. There was a W.R.N.S. officer with her two and a half blue strips contrasting the gold of the two commanders seated with her. Both she and one of the men wore the shoulder flash of Canada.

He studied as many of the other occupants as he could and with a feeling of relief saw no indication of the Dutch navy, or for that matter, any Merchant Navy officers. If he could not find lesser accommodation he would keep clear of the hotel save for sleeping and dinner. From what the receptionist told him it would be easier regarding ration coupons to dine in the one place. Anyway Schultz reasoned that if the place was for senior officers there was a good chance that the menu could be better than was normal.

Willie Schultz's seventh night behind enemy lines was again uneventful and on the morning's w/t schedule he advised control that he was 'waiting with Bert', the pre-arranged code that he was now in position. The memorising of such small phrases had not been difficult and he definitely felt that Weiner had been right in keeping messages to a minimum, thus eliminating the need to carry an incriminating code-book should the unthinkable happen. From now on, unless something drastic happened, he would only keep a listening watch in the mornings.

After breakfast – his surmise about the food had been correct even if some of it was not prepared the way he was used to – he asked directions to Gourock. Since the distance was not great he decided to walk along Union Street and look at the window advertisements in any newspaper shops he came across. Perhaps he might be lucky and see a 'digs vacant' notice; on the other hand if 'Auntie' arrived in the next two days and he was extremely lucky and was able to work out how to get aboard her this time around, a move would not be necessary. Then again would it be possible to 'create' a vacancy but he dismissed that idea as being too risky.

The drizzle of yesterday had disappeared and by the time he reached the tramway terminal at Guorock and found his way down to the pier it was a pleasant summer's day. He walked to the west of the pier and onto the esplanade and leant on a rail put there to stop people falling the three or four feet down onto the narrow beach. As in Ireland there was the scent of seaweed and saltwater. The beach shelved rapidly to deep water and the sea became a dark blue. He gazed across to Kilcreggan and then down the Firth of Clyde towards the far shore and the houses of Dunoon.

All along the far shore the hills rose steeply towards a now clear sky, their earth covered in the browns, greens and purple of the Scottish Highlands. He knew nothing about the history of Scotland, or anything of the British Isles for that matter, but even with his insular outlook on life he felt moved by the grandeur of those hills. He had been to the Bavarian Alps and seen their jagged peaks reflecting the red and gold light of a setting sun, even appreciated the magnificence of such a scene, but those hills across the Firth, although not as high, were nevertheless just as awe inspiring. In the Alps there could be landslides and shapes altered but those hills looked so solid and immobile and, he thought, almost threatening in their majesty.

Out in the anchorage were several medium sized troopships. He supposed it was they who would have brought the American troops he had seen in Glasgow station. One of them had a paddle steamer alongside and another a coastal tanker. Yet another had a tug towing two barges towards an open loading port to do what, at this distance, he could not tell. A ferry was halfway between the troopers heading, he assumed, for Greenock. A destroyer, with colourful signal flags flying from her yardarm in contrast to her drab grey paint, was steaming slowly up from the west; apparently on her way to join three smaller navy vessels already at anchor. Further up-stream were various cargo ships, some riding high out of the water and others in deep draft. Amongst them all a plethora of smaller craft dodged their way across the small white-capped waves. With the sun shining he thought how different this was to that dismal day when he left Lorient in the U-boat.

The 'Tail o' the Bank' presented a picture of being totally 'busy'. Despite being a naval officer he felt strangely remote from it all; as if something there resented his presence and it had, he knew, nothing to do with his being one of the enemy. He thought of Hashagan and was sure that he would have been welcomed and not rejected as he himself felt. There was about the scene an aura which could only be recognised by those who, unlike himself, were genuine men of the sea and it made him envious! Once more he felt that pang of loneliness. Irritated, he ground his half smoked cigarette under heel. This was no time for introspection or even to think of anything that had no connection with the job on hand.

He walked west along the promenade for five minutes before stopping and once more surveying the scene. Two women in their early twenties, wearing naval uniform with the word 'Canada' at the top of their sleeves came towards him. When they were near one of them said, "What's up sailor? You shouldn't be looking glum on such a nice day." Realising as he turned that he was an officer added, "Sir".

Good lord, were these two trying to pick him up or were they, with that intuition that some women have, genuinely concerned? "Sorry, just a bit down in the mouth" – he had not used that expression before, nevertheless it rolled easily off his tongue. "The war you know, gets to one sometimes." They were not bad looking, he thought, and his male hormones began to make themselves felt. Maybe this was the moment to mix business with pleasure. If they were stationed hereabouts they might have some information that could be useful.

"If you are going back towards the docks may I walk with you?"

"Of course. You off one of the ships out there, Sir?" He had yet another dialect to deal with although this one, as she spoke it, was pleasantly soft and easy to understand.

"No. I'm waiting to take passage in one of the big ones over to your side of the ocean, but I don't quite know when she is due."

"Oh! Well, we're signallers in the port control station and as soon as we see Scrutton's tugs come down from their berths further up river we know one of them is due. Otherwise they come and go and only the Big Brass know when! By the way, I'm Ellen and this is Bronwyn."

"My name is Wihelm Schultz, called Willie for short. I'm from Holland. So you are over here doing your bit then?"

"Absolutely. My brother was killed by the Japs in Hong Kong; at least that's what we believe as we've not heard anything since those bloody little bastards took over. Sorry Sir, shouldn't swear; it's not lady like is it? Anyway, being over here we're nearer to the battle and we're doing something positive towards helping beat the Jerries. As bunting tossers we release a chap to go to sea." She turned her head and half smiled at him. "What about yourself? You say you're from Holland. You grow tulips and other flowers and have lots of canals or something. Sorry again, don't know much about Europe really."

"That's OK. Yes tulips, lovely sight." He had never seen the tulip fields and changed the subject. "Tell me girls what does one do of an evening up here. I only arrived yesterday?"

"Well, if you dance there are one or two almost every night. The Town Hall one only costs a buck, sorry, a shilling, if you are in uniform. It gets a bit crowded there but if you want to go up-market there is one at The Imperial Ballroom. That costs three shillings but the band, Kenney Green, is really good. Bronwyn here is a really good dancer so we go most evenings when we're not on watch. Of course then there's always the flicks. The best film on at the moment is 'Casablanca' with Ingrid Bergman and

Humphrey Bogart. I should buy the local paper. It's all in there!" She had hardly stopped to take a breath. "We're off this evening and could show you around if you wished. Couldn't we Bronwyn?" She turned to her companion who had said nothing so far and now just nodded.

Films! He knew little about Hollywood other than that the traitor Marlene Dietrich had made several films there and not returned to Germany when war broke out. The name Bogart was vaguely familiar.

"You do dance of course?"

"Well, yes but I don't know if its exactly the way you do?" He needed to fish for information. "No regular partner then?"

"Only when he's not at sea, which isn't often. Time we started off to our billets for lunch. We're in a big mansion, Lyle House, and right alongside is the 'Old Sailors Home', only now that's full of young navy types. You'd be surprised at how convenient that is!" She looked at him with eyes wide in mock horror.

They had now returned to the Gourock quay, really he did not quite know what to call it. Originally a terminal for ferries and the pleasure cruising steamers of the Clyde, it had been enlarged and a railway line built right on to it to cope with the troop shuttle service to and from the United States. A few hours ago it must have been a hive of activity but now it was comparatively quiet, yet far from the sleepy backwater of pre-war.

Before the two wrens left they made arrangements to meet outside the Imperial Ballroom at half past seven to go dancing. Willie Schultz was feeling less despondent with the thought of what the evening might bring. The sun was still shining and on the quay a long canteen had one of its windows open and was serving customers from those working around the place. The atmosphere was one of laissez faire with four ferryboats tied up alongside and no train cluttering up the railway lines. He nodded to a policeman and walked boldly up to the canteen.

"Of course you can have a cup of black tea and would you like a sandwich?" the woman replied to his question. He paid her sixpence and joined a number of workmen who were leaning against the unopened portion of the building.

Alternately sipping his tea and taking bites of the sandwich he looked across at the ferries, surprised to see that one was called *Queen Mary II*. His mind returned to the job on hand. When he had finished his meal and returned the tin mug he sauntered over to the vessel and mounted the gangway, asking of a man leaning on the rail above him if he could come aboard and possibly speak with the captain?

A few minutes later he was seated in a small stuffy cabin under the wheelhouse and taking another cup of tea with a man who well qualified for the title of 'an old salt'. In his sixties, slightly rotund with a florid face, thinning grey hair and prominent sideburns, the atmosphere he generated was one of competence and a man who would brook no nonsense. He apologised for not being able to offer his visitor a 'wee sup', for the captain was temporarily without a bottle. He had, as yet, been unable to visit his friend who was master of one of the cargo ships at anchor.

"Ye see, laddie, not leaving these shores the supplies are not quite as plentiful as a chiel would like, ye ken!"

Schultz was lost as to what a 'wee sup' was; indeed he was hard pushed, as any Englishman would have been, by the old sea-dog's use of a number of pure Scottish words.

His host readily accepted Schultz's cover story and that he was now waiting for his transit papers to come through before he would be able to board the troopship. In the meanwhile he had noticed this vessels name and wondered how it had come about? With some difficulty Schultz finally understood that the ferry's name had been just *Queen Mary* when she had been launched in nineteen thirty-three but after secret discussions between Cunard, the Government and the ferry's owners she became *QM ll*. The master added that she was triple screw and turbine driven, making her a joy to handle and he was very proud of her.

He was very forthcoming on how the ship went about off-loading the mainly American troops and then back-loading various groups of civilians and service personnel. Also there now seemed to be a considerable increase in Jerry prisoners going to the States; 'got to make room for all those Yanks'. With mostly Polish soldiers guarding them he thought that the POWs would not have a very smooth crossing.

237

'Serves them bloody well right after what they did to Poland'!

"It must take quite a bit of organizing to move all those troops, Captain?" Schultz remarked.

"Aye, that it must.   My owners give me twenty-four hours notice to be ready to disembark the troops and from which ship it'll be.   In fact, we're under orders for our namesake right now.   I expect she'll arrive tonight, then as soon as she's anchored we start; generally takes about thirty-six hours to disembark them all.   Then we take out the Mrs. Mops who help the crew to clean her out.   The whole operation takes about four days before she's off again. Perhaps she might be back in three or four weeks, who knows?"

The German agent smiled inwardly at that statement.   At the moment he must be the only man in Scotland to know well before those twenty-four hours. The captain's next remark sounded a warning bell.

"'Tis most unusual to find a single chiel like yourself coming here.   Most times fowk are mustered elsewhere and then arrive here in a party or crew, get off their train, have a cuppa and straight on to us. Would hold up her turn-around if they did head-counting here."   He paused a moment in contemplation.   "Och, aye.   You could say it was organized!"

They talked about this and that for a few more minutes before Schultz said that if the trooper was due soon he should be getting back to the Pool office to see if his papers had finally come.   He thanked the ferry skipper for his time and went back ashore and thence to the hotel.

Little did Captain MacBride, for that was the old man's name, know just how much Schultz had to thank him for! In one ten minute discussion he had learned about the system by which his target would be loaded and the all important time parameters that would take. All he, Schultz, would now have to do would be to watch the operation and decide which would be the best way to board. It was obvious that a person on his own would be unusual so he would have to be careful.

As he walked down the street no one was in the least bit interested in him. What was it with these Tommies that they appeared not to care about possible espionage? What made them so gullible or was he an extremely good actor? Certainly Captain Weiner had planned the whole operation with consummate skill and Schultz radically revised his initial appraisal of the man. Maybe he was not a party member but in this case so what? He had to admit that there were a few million who were not but they still fought for the *Führer* and the glory of the Fatherland; or was it just because they had no option? If their heart was not in the fight was that part of the reason why Rommel had been kicked out of North Africa? There seemed little doubt now, according to the papers, that that had really happened. God, what he would not do to be able to listen to Radio Hamburg now.

Back in his hotel room, having failed to find alternative 'digs', he read another chapter of his Hornblower book and dozed until it was time for the evening meal and then to meet the two girls outside the Imperial Ballroom, where he paid for them both.

When the band started up with a quickstep Ellen stood up and held out a hand. "Come on Willie, no sense wasting time!" He dutifully obeyed, being reminded as he did so of the imperious character of the Irish girl back in Tralee.

That first dance was not a success, indeed, he felt that if ever he was to be exposed it would be now. He was used to the 'two step' rhythm of continental dancing rather than the very strict Victor Sylvester tempo played by the present band. It seemed that he was stumbling around and was sure he had stood on her toes more than once and must be very conspicuous. In fact there were, of course, a number of other men and women who did not dance correctly and he was no more obvious than any of them.

Returning to their seats at the side of the floor he apologised to Ellen who grudgingly, or so it seemed, said it did not matter. When the next dance, a foxtrot, was announced she was in no hurry to get him on the floor. Instead Bronwyn who, as with their meeting earlier in the day, had up to now hardly uttered a word said, "William, I think I see the problem, let me help. Let's try shall we?"

Once on the floor she explained where he was going wrong and led him into the less complicated steps until, by the third tune, he was far more relaxed and no longer stumbling. On the dance floor Bronwyn lost her previous demureness. As her companion had said, she was indeed a very good dancer. Walking beside her after the music had

240

stopped he was amazed at her apparent change in character. True Ellen had the more dominant personality and was slightly taller than her but here, on the dance floor, there would be few who could surpass her. Schultz also decided that with her rounded face and soft brown eyes she was the better looker of the two.

When they got back to Ellen she was talking to a Free French petty officer who had little difficulty in understanding his own language as spoken by a Canadian from the predominantly French province of Quebec. She introduced them before continuing an animated conversation with the man, who now gave the impression that he would be in their party for the rest of the evening and, for this, Schultz was thankful. He definitely did not feel 'at home' with Ellen although he had felt that she would have found somewhere to make love after dancing. With Bronwyn it would be different and, amazingly, he found it did not bother him!

By ten-thirty, when the dance finished, Bronwyn had made considerable progress in Schultz's dancing education. Fortunately he had an ear for music and enjoyed dancing so the transformation was not difficult. They walked together in the late evening dusk towards her billet, until she pointed out the shortest way back to his hotel with not much further to go for herself. Ellen and the Frenchman had left them some while back – the shadows were deepening and much could be achieved before her late pass expired.

CHAPTER 14

RESPITE

When he had said goodnight to Bronwyn, Schultz had not tried to kiss her. This was definitely not the way he normally acted where an attractive woman was concerned and he wondered why. There must be something about this woman that had dampened his ardour but what, at this time, he did not know. Gwen back in Milford Haven had been different, almost maternal and anyway she had taken him to bed; he had then been far too much on edge to think about sex, but this girl?

She would be on duty until midnight for the next four days, which suited him since he needed to watch how things went down on the Gourock quay. On the other hand he most certainly felt an urge to see her again, so they had arranged to meet once more at the Imperial Ballroom on the first night she was off.

The next morning Willie Schultz took an early breakfast and catching a tram to Gourock quickly made his way to the quay. The sight that greeted him on his arrival was totally different from the previous day. Two long trains sat with steam hissing from their valves as if impatient to be on their way. One of the ferries was alongside with a stream of American GIs in full webbing, carrying rifles and kit bags, coming down her gangway and then being ushered onto the train nearest them. As each compartment was filled an MP checked the number of soldiers crammed in it then slammed the door shut.

While this was going on another ferry started to berth with a minimum of fuss. The scene was one of movement with very little noise or the shouting of orders. It was, as Captain McBride had said, 'organised' and the German agent was quick to realise it.

There were some movable barriers, presumably to keep unwanted persons such as himself and people without any specific job to do, clear of the troops. The civilian policeman to whom he had nodded yesterday was standing near an opening in the barrier. Schultz ambled over to him and bade him good morning, adding, "Things are certainly not as quiet as yesterday. When did she get in?"

"Just after one. Once either of the two big ones arrives nothing stops until they are gone again. Somehow there always seems far more of a rush than when a convoy of smaller ones arrives. There probably isn't really, just seems like it. I saw you hanging around yesterday. Can I help you with anything, Chief?"

The question put Schultz on his guard. "Thanks but no. I'm supposed to be going out on her with a crew for one of the new ships. I've got a special lifeboat wireless to take to the States for testing. I suppose that not being a member of a specific crew and Dutch to boot, is the reason for my papers having gone adrift. It's a right mess! The Pool office told me to come up here and wait, so I thought I'd come and watch how things went. I see one end of the canteen is open so I think I'll get a cuppa."

"You do that, Chief."

While drinking the tea he pondered on what his next move should be. If he could attach himself to one of the merchant crews when they got off the train he could go aboard with them. Could he manage it this time round? No, better watch and make sure he got things right and go next time she came in. Maybe Berlin, assuming he lived to tell the tale, would eventually want to know why he did not go this time round but better safe than sorry.

His tea finished he felt it prudent not to hang around too long so walked back in the direction of Greenock until he came to a shop where he brought a daily paper. With that under his arm he changed direction and went down to the foreshore, found a bench seat and sat there, ostentatiously reading the paper but mostly watching what was happening out there on the water.

He decided that he would have to watch each phase of the disembarkation and then the embarkation making careful note of when the merchant crews turned up. That really would be the crucial point. He could hardly hang around the quay with his case for hours just on the off chance. What if there were no crews for next trip? He felt goose pimples rising on his neck. Suddenly he could envisage all sorts of 'ifs'. Once again complacency left him.

On the quay he had noticed an office hut, which appeared to house the naval transport staff. Off course they would know when the trains with the crews were due. For a moment he toyed with the idea of brazenly going in there and asking them direct; could he get away with that or would that be pushing his luck too far? Then he remembered something Captain McBride had said. Because many of the merchant crews were mustered down in ports such as Swansea, Cardiff and Bristol they spent many hours on a train without the chance of a meal so they were given sandwiches upon arrival on the quay. The canteen! They would know because they would have to get the meals in beforehand and extra staff to serve them!

After the time when dockers would have had their lunch break he made his way back to the quay and when the one open window was deserted he ordered more tea. The woman serving remembered him. "That's without milk, ain't it luv," in an accent that was definitely not local, which gave him the opening he needed for a conversation.

By the time he had finished his tea he had been told all he wanted to know, as well as the information that the woman was the wife of one of the dockers brought up from the south, in this case Tilbury on the Thames. Also that their home had been bombed early in the Blitz by those 'bloody Jerries'. Fortunately they had been ''aving a drop down at the pub when it 'appened or they'd 'ave bin 'istory right now!'

He was saved from hearing the rest of her family's history by the arrival of another customer. It was all so easy, would the canteen helpers in Hamburg or Bremen have been so accommodating? The information he had gleaned was that the manager here was told the day before and to the nearest hour, when the meal boxes would be required to be served.

They were made up elsewhere in Greenock and then delivered either the evening before or early on the day. All he would have to do was to order a cup of tea from 'Rosie' when the cleaning ladies were aboard sweeping 'her' out and he would have a reasonable time frame within which to make his move! It was interesting that nobody seemed to use the vessel's name. 'Her' or 'she' were all pervading when at the Tail o' the Bank; just as her size dwarfed other shipping, 'she' dominated all happenings.

According to what he now knew the disembarking of the Americans was likely to carry on for the rest of the day and into tomorrow so there was little to be gained by waiting around the quay. He decided to take a long walk to the west and finally stopped for a rest by the lighthouse at Cloch Point, overlooking the southern end of the anti-submarine boom that stretched across to Dunoon. Fascinated, he watched as two small naval vessels, he thought they might be minesweepers, came up and waited for it to open. Unlike the tender at Milford Haven the ship operating the boom here was no 'rust-bucket' but a small smartly painted naval ship with a gallows over her bows.

Willie Schultz arrived back at the Bay Hotel almost too late to take the evening meal. Indeed he tied with two commanders for being the last to finish. They looked tired and strained and from their conversation the two men had recently come in from sea, although in different ships, and had imbibed rather well before the meal. The volume of their voices was now well above that of the decorum

246

required in such a hotel – as the Maitré de said to the head waiter, 'such things had to be tolerated in a war'.

Willie would have liked a few drinks himself. Because he dared not become too talkative he had decided to limit his intake to no more than one beer before the meal and one after; although if the bar was too crowded, as it had been, he would have to go without or visit a pub. He still felt worried in the presence of too many senior officers.

The walk had made him quite tired and although the evening was fine and mild he went to his room and slept until his alarm woke him in time for the morning w/t schedule. The day went according to his plan. In the afternoon, when the last troop train had pulled out and been replaced by a ferry full of cleaning ladies going the other way, he brought a cup of tea and a piece of cake and engaged Rosie in conversation. It took some while before finding out that the staff had not yet been told when they would be required to serve the meal boxes. "Probably tomorrow luv. Anyway what's it to you?" And he had to give her a brief outline as to why, adding, "They could tell me over at the office but I'm sure your information would be more accurate. You know what officialdom is like." And, as expected, she almost visibly preened herself at the thought that she was more reliable than the old chief coxswain across the way.

The activity on the quay had now changed as lorries arrived and unloaded various boxes and crates labelled 'TT.QM', which in turn were loaded into barges. Again Schultz was impressed by the organisation that coped with such huge logistical problems while also trying to keep a certain degree of secrecy. He supposed that his own people must be able to deal with such things although, until now, he had never thought about this side of the war.

Safely cocooned in the *Oberkamando Kriegsmarine* the war, other than the now more frequent air-raids – which always seemed to happen just at the crucial moment when a girl opened her legs – and the lack of decent rations, had little real hardship for him. But there was one thing that had disturbed him and that was the sight of the hospital trains from the Russian front; mostly they arrived during the night but not always.

After dinner that evening he again went down to the quay and found that Rosie had left a message with her relief that 'the lunches would be dished out from ten o'clock to morrow'.

It was such a small, innocuous sentence that nobody would have thought it of any interest to an enemy agent, if such a person were to hear it! For her to have done that made him feel she must have 'taken a shine to him', as she would have said. His conceit told him it was his good looks!

Amazing! He now had all the information he required. Tomorrow he would be watching discreetly from nine-thirty onwards. It would be as if he were an understudy of the lead role in a play with tomorrow being the dress rehearsal. He felt elated and in need of a drink!

He was so elated that, in the first pub he came to, he almost slipped up by asking for a *steiner* of beer instead of a pint. Drinking it he thought how nice it would be to hold a good heavy mug again instead of these glass ones, or to watch the famous barmaids in Munich as they carried several in each hand. They had hands like gorillas; he had only ever managed to carry two.

He became morbid with thoughts of home. As the imminent finale of the operation loomed he was realising that his chances of seeing the Fatherland again looked rather slim. He could be killed in the bombing and subsequent fire or drown when they abandoned the sinking liner, either way he would be dead.

Schultz did not sleep particularly well that night. Once he woke in a sweat as *Fraulein* Becker, his last conquest, came to kiss him and as she touched his face all the skin peeled off revealing his charred skull. Shaken, he lay watching as the grey of the dawn changed to daylight.

It was a quarter past nine when he sat, paper in hand, where he could hear the arrival of any train on the quay before moving to where he could watch its passengers alighting. Just after one o'clock the sun disappeared and a drizzle set in. Having heard one of the waiters tell another guest at breakfast that it might rain he had bought his Burberry with him but even so by mid-afternoon he felt damp and uncomfortable and was glad when he was able to get to the canteen and have a cup of tea.

Apart from the effects of the fine rain he felt dishevelled. He had forgotten all about arranging with the hotel to have his laundry done and had consequently found he had run out of clean shirts and was down to his last collar, to say nothing about underpants. Assuming that 'Auntie' would sail tonight he would go shopping in Glasgow tomorrow, which would also enable him to change more of the counterfeit five pound notes in a place other than locally. If he now faced three or four weeks of waiting for the liner to return he felt it would be prudent to consider moving to another town where there was not such a big naval presence.

During the next evening with Bronwyn he mentioned that he wanted to go elsewhere but was not sure where. She said she had a maternal grandmother who lived in a quiet town called Colwyn Bay in North Wales, which was not too difficult to get to by train. By the end of the dance it was arranged that she would 'phone her grandmother tomorrow and ask her to find bed and breakfast accommodation for Schultz.

It had been Bronwyn's intention to spend a ten-day leave with Grandma next month but she would see if she could bring it forward and join Willie. She had visited Grandma for four days last year but otherwise did not really know the lady since her parents had emigrated to Canada twenty years ago, when she was two.

When Willie Schultz met the Canadian wren at ten o'clock the next morning, after he had checked that 'Auntie' had indeed sailed during the hours of darkness, all was arranged. One of the girls in the signal station was happy to swap dates with Bronwyn as her boyfriend's ship would not now be returning for goodness knows how long. Today and tomorrow

Bronwyn had to go on watch at midday but the day after tomorrow she would be free and then they could catch the first train out. As she said the last sentence she hugged his arm and gazed up into his face – she was just that little shorter than he – and what he saw in her shining eyes should have warned him, but he missed it.

Colwyn Bay! *Leutnant* Schultz had given little thought as to what he would find on the north coast of Wales. He had spent holidays on the Baltic coast near Keil and on the East Frisian Islands with their low-lying and long sandy beaches. Here it was different with just a narrow strip between hills and sea accommodating the various towns along the rail route. There was sand when the tide was out but when it was in the water lapped the edge of the promenade!

Bronwyn stayed with her grandmother, a kindly lady in her early sixties whose hair was just beginning to show grey streaks. It was easy to see from which side of the family the girl inherited her good looks. The lady had arranged for her grand-daughter's friend to sleep at a house a few doors down the road towards the beach; he would, however, take breakfast with them. Excellent arrangements, thought Willie.

The following twelve days – she had added a weekend pass to her ten days – became, for her, sheer bliss and for him, towards the end, a time of introspection and rumination. They attended afternoon tea dances at the Grand Hotel in Llandudno and often dined there of an evening – it was amazing how the sight of a ten shilling note would conjure up something which had been 'off the menu' to other diners. On Wednesday and Saturday evenings they danced in the Colwyn Bay Pavilion at the end of the pier, where his gold braid seemed to be held in awe by the young cadets at the local wireless college.

They went past Llandudno to the old slate mine at Penmaen-mawr, where her father had looked after all the machinery. In the mornings, when the tide was high, they sometimes swam. Neither had swimming costumes so he bought her the most expensive one in the shop. Indeed he spent lavishly and when she had become a little worried after an over generous tip to a waiter and asked about it he told her that while in the Resistance he had never received any pay. Now the Dutch Government in exile had rectified that so for the moment he was well off.

'What', he said, 'was the point of not spending it since I might well become a statistic of the dead'. When he had said that she had been unable to hold back the tears as her hand sought his under the table and gripped it tight.

"Oh NO! Dear God, please no!" she sobbed.

Perhaps he should have seen then what was happening to the girl but it was not until the next day, a Sunday, when everything except the chapels were closed, that he became aware of it.

The weather had so far been kind to them with sunshine and balmy gentle breezes throughout. Grandma had made a small picnic for them so they walked up the steep leafy lanes until they reached the top of the hill behind the town. Climbing over a style they sat on a rug he had been carrying and admired the magnificent view out over the Irish Sea. After their meagre meal they stretched out, letting the warmth of the sun filter into their bodies.

Without thinking he placed a hand on her knee and started to move it up to the thigh. He felt her stiffen as she whispered. 'Please no Willie. I want to, but not until we're married."

Marriage! Now, breaking through the arrogance indoctrinated in him from the days of the Hitler Youth, he got the message! For the first time ever, as far as he could remember, he had no wish to force himself on a woman and, withdrawing his hand, respected her wishes. Marriage. He'd given no intimation that was on his mind.

Respect for a woman? Love? Marriage? These things were for the older men in the Party, not for young bloods like himself. In his view it seemed stupid to tie one's self down financially when there were plenty of women around who enjoyed a good fling. True you could still have a bit on the side even if you were married and he knew there were wives who did just that.

There was the recent case of the *Gauleiter* down in Bremen who had thrashed his wife near to death when he had caught her in bed with the local Party secretary, but why shouldn't she? Did getting married change your outlook on life? Was there really such a thing as this so called 'love'? Previously he would have said emphatically, 'No'. Now he was suddenly not so sure.

Perhaps it was being brought up as an only child by an overbearingly doting mother who had, in his early years, dressed him as a girl because she had wanted a daughter rather than a son. Was it that, combined with the dictates of the Hitler Youth, which had made him even scorn family love to the extent that he had reported his father to the Gestapo for criticising the Führer?

No, family life was for the peasants not the officer corps. Free love was about the only thing he could agree with in the Communist doctrine and now there was this girl saying that she loved him and wanted to get married. 'Shit, what a mess', and for the first time he realised that he had some sort of feelings for her.

As the last few days went past these new feelings did not dampen his enjoyment of her company. Could he throw overboard his love for the Fatherland for a woman? Again there was the thought of what it might be like to live here. These people seemed to live a much freer life without the ever-present subliminal thought that the Gestapo was not far away.

According to the Party the British lived a decadent life but from what he had seen so far it certainly did not appear to be the case. Perhaps from a purely military or disciplined point of view they certainly did not live in the same regimented way those at home did. Did he miss that way of life or was he beginning to like the way things were here in Wales? If that was the case was he, therefore, on the way to becoming decadent also?

As each day had passed he marvelled more and more how easy it was for him to remain undetected. It seemed that his 'cover' was impeccable and daily his confidence grew. He reasoned that with such incompetent allied security the Reich was bound to win the war in the end.

On the last day of her leave they travelled back to Gourock and the following morning he kept the w/t schedule. There was no way that 'Auntie' could be back in two weeks so he had disobeyed orders and, on Bronwyn's assurance that it would be safe, actually put the wireless in a 'left-luggage' locker in Glasgow station before they had changed trains for Chester. Back in his room at the Bay – he had pre-paid to retain it – he listened at the appropriate time for the message he knew would not be there. In fact, that message did not come for another nine days. Nine days of killing time before the adrenalin started to build up as the *Queen Mary* raced across the ocean towards Scotland and, luck being with him, their mutual demise.

When Bronwyn reported back to the harbour signal station she found she would be on duty for the next five nights. This meant that, apart from a few hours sleep both before and after duty, they had most of the day together. As the weather was still fine they took a bus into the countryside calling into a pub for a drink and whatever snack there might be on offer.

As he became more convinced of his seeming invincibility he bemoaned the fact that he was not a demolition expert. A few sticks of gelignite here and there and he could cause havoc with the railways.

The French Resistance did it so why on earth was it not being done here? He racked his brains as to how he could cause the enemy a bit of mayhem without endangering his immediate operation but could think of nothing so that frustration started to build up making him moody.

There was another reason for his moodiness. Other than that night with Gwen in Milford Haven he had now been several months without his regular indulgence in the pleasures of the body and *that* he was definitely not used to. Being celibate while training on that damned airfield had been one thing but now why on earth hadn't he had 'it off' with Bronwyn, or any other woman for that matter? The time he spent with Bronwyn now definitely exacerbated the physical annoyance.

On the second evening back from Colwyn Bay, with Bronwyn on the late watch, he decided to try to find a women for a one night stand. He felt that perhaps he would have more chance of a quick pick up if he went to one of the cheaper dance halls which would probably have more patrons and be mainly frequented by 'other ranks' rather than officers. Not that the sexual desires of officers and other ranks differed but he had found back in Berlin that the women of the so-called 'officer class' took more time to make their minds up and that a couple of nights could well be wasted before bed was forthcoming.

Donning his sports coat and slacks he made his way to the Town Hall where an 'H.M.Forces Dance' was billed. The girl on the ticket counter, because of his civilian attire, glanced up at him but seeing the silver MN badge accepted his shilling to go in. As expected he found the hall crowded with service men and women but also a number of girls in civilian clothes. Buying a cup of tea from a nearby counter he found a vacant chair at a table on the edge of the dance floor and began to survey the 'field'. The band, the 'St. Louis' according to the writing on the base drum, was playing a quick- step and several couples were jiving in the American fashion. As a sailor swung his partner up and out and then down and between his legs Schultz was given a good look at her thighs and noted that she should have been wearing tighter knickers; his hopes rose.

When the music finished and the dancers returned to their seats he carefully noted which women were accompanied or in groups and which appeared to be alone. Of the latter there were not many but after a session of waltzes he picked on one and made his play. She was not particularly good looking and wore glasses but her body was not out of proportion and looked inviting in a loose-fitting summer dress of a cheap floral design. The MC called the next dance as the Palais Glide so he went across and asked if she would care to dance, adding that he was not quite sure what the Palais Glide was.

She was not the dancer Bronwyn was so there was more than one occasion when he stumbled and trod on her toes but she did not seem to mind. By nine o'clock she was telling him that she was grateful to him for asking her to dance as not many did. When asked what he did he just said that he was in the Merchant Navy on a Dutch ship. In return she gave a potted version of being a very humdrum housewife who had been sent into war work at a factory in Glasgow. Her husband was a leading seaman in the regular navy and had been overseas since almost the beginning of the war and only two months after they had been married.

When he had been left a small terraced house in east Greenock by a distant aunt a year ago, he had told her to move into it to avoid any resumption of the bombing around the naval housing in Chatham. Normally she came to the dance with a friend but she was sick at the moment. Feeling lonely, for she had not made any other real friends only acquaintances, Mavis had come by herself. They were dancing a slow foxtrot, the final one before the last waltz, when he stumbled again and pulled her tight against him and for a moment as they regained their balance, they were stationary. He felt her move her pelvis against his as she looked up into his cold blue eyes. He knew then that he had reasonable expectations.

The house was one of a line built of cold grey stone and in the gathering dark looked drab and uninviting. The street was deserted as she unlocked the door. During the fifteen-minute walk they had not spoken, the understanding between them needing no words. Once in the narrow hallway she flicked on a light.

"If you need the 'little house' it's down there through the kitchen and the first door on the left, but I'll go first and show you. No light out there 'cause of the black-out." She took his hand and he noticed she had started to breath heavily so that her breasts moved up and down despite her brassiere. He began to get an erection which, when his turn came, was fortunately not too stiff. She waited and then, once again took his hand, leading him upstairs and into a poky, musty smelling bedroom.

"Don't use this room except…'wouldn't be right to use Charlie's' bed would it?" He failed to see any logic in her statement

She made no move to switch on the light as she closed the ill-fitting door, which allowed just enough light to filter through so that he could just make out the bed. "Wouldn't be right to Charlie for you to see too much 'o me."

'Shit,' he thought, 'what sort of woman was this?' They both undressed and she flopped back on the bed, drawing her knees up and apart. Obviously there was to be no foreplay. Perhaps that 'wouldn't be right for Charlie' either?

He climbed on top of her and she caught hold of him to guide it in. "Christ, 'ain't you got no rubber on?" She pulled him hard to one side causing him some pain and tried to close her legs. "You can't 'ave it like that! Charlie 'ud kill me if he came back and found me with a kid!"

"Fuck Charlie," he snarled and realised he had said it in German, not that she would know the difference between that and Dutch. He grabbed her arm and pulled it away from him. "Stupid cow, I'm not stopping now!" She cried out in pain as he jabbed at her trying to get in. "Stay still." Whether it was right for Charlie or not, when he got there she was ready but after the first few thrusts she started to scream so that he had to pull the pillow from under her head and hold it over her face to shut her up. Frantically she clawed at the thing stopping her breathing, managing to move her head sideways and gulp some air.

"You bastard get off me!" And she started to scream again as she felt him finish. Schultz now knew only the lust of a rapist and with the power he felt pressed the pillow hard down, ignoring the scratches she inflicted to his back with her free hand. Her cries became muffled and after a minute or so her struggles became weaker. He let the pillow up for a moment. She was still breathing but feebly and remained quiet. Thus he lay for, perhaps, five minutes before the urge took him again, the movement seeming to give her new strength, for she resumed her cries. This time he kept pressing on the pillow until all signs of struggling ceased and he himself felt exhausted and rolled on his side.

After half an hour he got up and dressed. He felt elated before his situation began to become apparent. 'Shit, he was stupid and should have stopped'. The fact that he had just taken the woman's life gave him not a moment's remorse. 'Wasn't there some saying that all was fair in love and war?' One less enemy woman for Charlie, if he ever came home, to breed from. What mattered now was to get away from here without being seen.

He put the pillow back under her head and went down to the kitchen for a drink of water, turned off the hall light and, sitting on the stairs, decided to wait a couple of hours. She had said her friend was

260

sick and she had no relatives in the area. The factory where she worked would probably just think she was ill and wait a few days, expecting someone would telephone saying what was wrong. The friend? He could do nothing about her.

Slowly he opened the door and, with eyes now well accustomed to the dark, peered up and down the street. Empty! Quietly he closed the door behind him and briskly, keeping in the deepest shadows, walked in the opposite direction from the dance hall. He had only the vaguest idea of where he was but knew that if he turned left he would eventually come to the railway. When he found it he turned again but continued in the direction of Glasgow until he found a station. He waited in the shadows opposite until the first train went westwards just after dawn and, half an hour later, could be heard returning. With his cap pulled well down over his eyes and having removed his MN badge, he brought a single third class ticket to Glasgow.

The train was quite full with workers going to their jobs and no-one paid any attention to him. In Glasgow, once clear of the station area, he asked someone the way to the nearest dock, eventually finding a café, not unlike the one in Bristol, where he had tea and baked beans. Despite the noise and smoke-filled atmosphere, exhaustion overcame him and he slept, head on arm, until a waitress shook him, demanding to know if he had no work to go to?

From a near-by telephone kiosk he put through a call to Lyle House and left a message for Bronwyn to the effect that he would be out of town

261

for a couple of days and would call her when he got back. He then caught a train back to Greenock and went as unobtrusively as possible to his room where he put the 'Do not disturb' sign on the door handle. He slept through until dinner-time and afterwards, until the following morning's w/t schedule.

Undoubtedly it was unfair to Bronwyn that he should keep up such a false friendship but, as with the Irish girl, it helped to keep his cover intact. He told himself that it was for the sake of the operation but, other than the fact that he got an erection at some time whenever he was with her, he did enjoy her company. He was sure that, once his hand reached the top of her thigh, there would not be a lot of resistance if he persisted but after the incident with Mavis he held himself in check.

The next two days were spent in his room. He went downstairs only for breakfast and dinner and to get the morning and evening papers. After the scare he had taken in Bristol he did not want to take any chances, also he did not feel like coping with a cloying Bronwyn. On the third day, with no mention of the woman being found he contacted Bronwyn and, since it was her day off, they took the ferry across to Kilcreggan and climbed the hills behind the village, admiring the excellent view of the Tail 'o the Bank. Before the afternoon was out the sky clouded over and turned the blue water to grey, while the wind increased and waves appeared.

The rain stayed with them for the next three days, curtailing their activities to sitting in shelters down on the promenade, followed by an early drink before she went on duty at midday. The afternoon and evenings he spent mostly in his room, the inactivity and strain of waiting starting to make him more irritable. He could have gone dancing but thought he might be too conspicuous on his own. When Bronwyn, sensing that he was moody, asked what was wrong he told her that he'd had to go to Crewe to meet someone from the Dutch Government, who had come up from London, and what he had told him was not good. She assumed that it had something to do with the resistance and did not pursue the matter.

After her next day off he told her he had to go away again and actually spent two nights in Edinburgh. He picked up a prostitute and spent the two nights with her in a very third rate hotel room, making sure that she left well before the morning w/t schedule time. That second morning he received the message that 'Auntie' had left so he went back to the Bay. Going down to the landing stage he had a casual chat with Captain MacBride and a cup of tea at the canteen with Rosie, before resuming, with very mixed feelings, his cover with the Canadian Wren.

During the four days of waiting for his quarry to arrive he spent all the time he could with Bronwyn and made sure he was seen down near the landing stage with his 'girl'. Twice they made up a foursome with Ellen and her Frenchman and went dancing. He took her down to the dock canteen and introduced her to Rosie. It all looked so natural: a girl and her man making the best of things before he went back to war, knowing that each meeting might be the last. In the meanwhile he still used the excuse for not discussing marriage that he could well become a causality of the war at sea and steadfastly avoided the word love.

More than once he wondered how their last meeting would be. She would know when the big trooper anchored and therefore be fore-warned. She had said that when the Chief Yeoman was in charge of the watch he did not mind an occasional private incoming call but, for security reasons, never an outgoing one. The Yeoman, newly made up to petty officer, liked to throw his rank around and was not so accommodating; it was unfortunate then that having answered the 'phone he refused point-blank to pass a message to Bronwyn. Schultz wanted to let her know that he would be down at the quay when she came off watch at midday and that his papers had finally come through, which meant that tonight and tomorrow would be his last.

Ellen, the other Canadian wren happened to be near the 'phone when Willie called and recognised his voice but only caught the word quay before the P.O. hung up. Knowing what Willie had come to mean to her friend she called across to Bronwyn that she thought he would be on the quay at midday. Then, in her very forthright way, turned on the Yeoman and said -"You're a bastard you know!"

The P.O. went a puce colour and threatened to put her on a charge for insubordination. At the time, another girl was using the big ten-inch signalling lamp with a shutter that made quite a racket. When the irate man almost screeched to the room in general, "Right, you lot heard that! You'll be witnesses!" he was met with a universal, "Heard what P.O.? Signal lamp; too much noise!" And, as if to put the final touch on his outburst, the telex machine started to click and, turning their backs on him, they returned to what they had been doing.

It was half past midday before a very tired and red-eyed Bronwyn found him watching the Americans come ashore. She had obviously been crying so he took her gently by an arm and went a hundred yards away from all the activity before he turned to face her. Before he could say anything she looked straight into his eyes.

"Please take me back to your hotel room. Now, dearest Willie." And she started to sob so that he pulled her to his chest.

If the policeman back there had come up to him and said - 'You're a German spy and I'm arresting you!' he could not have been more surprised than he was now. Another new feeling overwhelmed him; compassion, and he felt truly sorry for what he had unintentionally done to this girl. He then did something that a couple of months ago he would have thought totally impossible. He refused a woman.

"No, dear Bronwyn. No, you wanted to wait and surely one day you will regret it if we do." Now her sobbing turned to acute crying as the pain in her chest became all-pervading until she thought it would make her sick, all because she loved this man so. Some female intuition told her that he would never come back to her.

When the girl's crying became less he walked her to the other side of the Esplanade and turned in the direction of her billet. When they drew level with the quay again a taxi stopped and a small man with a thick gold band on his arm and a captain alighted. Seizing the opportunity he left her and sprinted across the road to secure the empty vehicle.

On the way back to Lyle House she stopped her sobbing and asked for an address to which she might be able to write to him. He said, and quite honestly, that for now he did not know but would let her know when it became possible. Outside the big gates of the mansion he alighted first and then helped her out, saying in a voice that was soft and gentle so that he hardly recognised himself.

"I'm so sorry. I never meant it to be like this. Tomorrow I might well be aboard. It would be better that this is our parting. Now go to the sick-bay and ask for a sleeping pill." And before she could reply or he do something that would prolong her pain he got back in the taxi and told the driver to drive off.

CHAPTER 15

THE QUEEN

Leutnant Wilhelm Schultz had paid off the taxi over an hour ago and now leant against the railings listening for sounds of the train bringing the next lot of passengers for America. In the distance he heard a whistle and if Rosie was right this should be the one he was waiting for.

Gone were the knots in his stomach and the rising bile at the thought of possible death. Gone were any thoughts about 'why should he die for the Fatherland'. His mind was clear and, if at all possible, his blue eyes were colder than ever. His job was to be the catalyst for the demise of that giant ship out there at anchor and that job, he now knew, he would carry out to the best of his ability. As the smell of the seaweed at the water's edge caught his nostrils he thought about that night, only a few weeks ago, although it now seemed longer, when the U-boat had taken him into the Bay of Tralee.

Again he wondered who had dreamed up this operation, which had so captured the imagination of the *Führer* that he had personally signed the special and so very secret order and which now placed his life on a knife-edge.

He picked up his two cases and moved to a position just out of sight of those at the gate but from where he would see the train arrive with the crews for yet more Liberty ships. The time spent talking to

Rosie in the canteen would now be put to the test. Had he been given the right information? Would any of the dock staff suddenly become suspicious when he finally turned up with the set he had spoken about but no one had yet seen? He lit a cigarette and was halfway through it when a train came slowly along the line letting off steam as it did so. This disturbed a flock of seagulls from the platform, which rose screeching into the air as they flew over the waiting German, one narrowly missed him but hit the wireless case with its droppings. Did he remember something about that, like a black cat crossing one's path? It was supposed to be a sign of good luck. If so then the fate of that giant of the seas was sealed.

Schultz finished his cigarette and ground it underfoot on the damp pavement. Above the noise of the steam came shouts of 'all out' followed by that distinct sound of compartment doors being opened and flung back against the side of the carriage. The overnight drizzle had disappeared and a watery sun crept out from behind the few remaining clouds. He took off his Burberry, so that it could clearly be seen he was an officer, and slung it over a shoulder. The time had come!

Purposefully he strode towards the entrance in the barrier, trying to give the impression that he had every right to be there. He need not have worried; there was no one to challenge him. The expected policeman was some way away talking to a naval chief petty officer who, by his well weathered look, had been called back to service after several years of retirement.

Despite the apparent disorganisation of the crowd milling around between the train and the quayside with its attendant ferries, it was not too difficult for Schultz to pick out four groups of ships' crews. With officers in uniform and most of their men in civilian clothes there was a quieter, rather non-official atmosphere about them. By way of contrast a large group of airmen was being berated by a flight sergeant barking a seemingly never-ending stream of orders.

The first batch of merchant seamen was now being ushered towards the long open serving hatches of a canteen. Leaving their kit-bags and cases where they had been mustered, the men each gratefully received a food box and mug of tea from the ladies of the Women's Voluntary Service. Schultz quickly took in the situation and joined the third group of officers. Putting his own cases on the ground he said, "Morning, don't mind if I join you fellows? The Pool told me to tag on to one of the crews going aboard. Thank goodness the rain has stopped, it would have been a bit miserable otherwise."

"Be our guest." An older officer with a gravely voice, who had gold oak leaves on the brim of his cap, answered. "Which ship you going to then, Sparks?"

"Don't know till I get there, Sir. Got a new lifeboat set here for the Yanks to copy. A Phillips engineer developed it for the Resistance and when I had to get out in a hurry I brought the original set with me. Can't really say more, Sir, it's a bit of a long story as to how I came to be here now." At that moment someone called for them all to fetch their meals, for which Schultz was thankful as, for a while at least, conversation would lapse.

The captain, if that was what he was, accepted without question Schultz's cover story and merely replied. "Right. Best come along with us then. 'Could do with that cup of tea. It's been a long time in the train since Newport!" Putting on his coat – it had kept trying to slip off his shoulder – he went with the others to the canteen and drew his food box and mug of tea; the fact that it already had milk in it he had to accept. He had been successfully integrated with this crew and did not want in any way to be seen to be different from them. God, it had been so easy. That seagull certainly seemed to be bringing him luck!

Someone passed the word that if they needed a pee they could go behind the canteen, but 'to make sure they didn't fall in!' They were given ten minutes to take their meal before two women with large trays came to collect their tin mugs. The airmen were ordered to 'fall-in' and then with a 'left, right, left, right…right wheel' marched towards the gangway on to the ferry, where an irate Mate yelled – 'For Christ's sake this isn't a bloody parade ground. Sergeant. Break step before they break my bloody gangway!' And then to the seaman beside him, 'Jesus, stupid fly-boys!'

A mixed group of air-force officers and civilians followed the airmen before the groups of seamen were told by a naval petty officer to follow on, and not to forget to disembark in the same order as they were boarding, officers leading. Once on the

270

ferry another petty officer ushered them into a pre-selected position and told them to stay put. They were, in fact, lined up facing a long armour-plate glass window looking into the engine room. A similar window behind them gave a view of the impressive looking paddle wheel. It was not long before there was the clanging of the engine-room telegraph bell and one after another, the pistons started to rise and fall, turning the paddle wheel so that it churned the water into foam as the vessel got underway.

'Now that's what I call a real engine room!' one of the engineer officers exclaimed.

A crewmember in spotless white overalls came into view with a large oilcan in his hand and proceeded to apply it to various cup-like receptacles over the main bearings of the shining engines. Everywhere copper or brass pipes were polished so that they looked like mirrors. Another and older engineer remarked, 'There's nothing like the good old triple expansion for reliability. It's polished as if she was still engaged in the holiday trade, Marvellous!'

From the bunch of seamen near enough to hear the remark came an, 'It's all right as long as you don't 'ave to do the bloody polishin', Chief! Some sodding 'oliday we're going on!'

It was about fifteen minutes before the engine-room bells clanged again for 'stand-by' and then rang again and again as the master up on the bridge, with consummate skill, manoeuvred the old paddle-steamer alongside the waiting liner. There was a slight bump and without the necessity for orders, because it had all been done so many times before and

271

mother nature was being kind to them with a calm sea, the vessel came to rest.

Schultz had appreciated the smartness of that engine room as he did for a wireless that had been wired with, as far as possible, its wires in straight lines, or a power distribution board with polished busbars and knife switches.

He was not left to his thoughts for long; orders were shouted and passed from group to group and soon the crew destined for the *Empire Regina*, the men he had tagged on to, were told to follow on those in front. Now another testing time was about to happen. Would he be accepted aboard the *Queen Mary* without question? So far it had all been too easy. Would his luck still hold?

From the ferry they went onto a pontoon moored alongside the liner. He had no time to look around and was only aware of a vast grey steel side full of rivets and a large entry port from which another gangway came down and up which they were directed. Either side of the entry-port was a table behind which was some sort of official who gave each man a ship's boarding card as he stepped into the trooper, officers to the right, other ranks to the left.

Had he mustered down in Newport with the rest of the crew of the *Empire Regina*, he would have been briefed that this card was to be its holder's bible while aboard the troopship. It would show them which part of the *Mary* they were berthed in and where and at what times they would take their meals. Schultz, as with the other officers of his group, was given a card without question. As far as the trooping staff were concerned, all the paperwork had been done ashore and they were not in the least bit concerned as to 'who and why' but only in a given number of passengers to board. Perhaps, but highly unlikely, they would find they had one extra in the two thousand odd they expected. Perhaps Schultz might cause an overflow from one cabin to another, but it would be of little consequence and most certainly no one would want to waste time finding out why? On these westward trips there was plenty of spare room and the ship had a schedule to keep.

Schultz found they were in a large flat, which went across the whole width of the ship. There was a notice saying 'C Deck'. To the right was a double staircase and lifts, on either side of these were doors into, according to signs, the Tourist dinning room. To his left was an office – now converted to a canteen – and several doors to various cabins; one even bore the title 'Bank' and fleetingly he wondered, if it were still in use, whether he would he be able to change a few of his forged 'fivers'! The dark timber panelling would, in normal times, have given this entrance hall an air of semi-opulence; now it had a more sombre effect on the men passing through it, almost as if they were in limbo between two time warps.

His berthing card had a room number on 'A' deck. It told him when to take his meals, which was at the first sitting in the Officer's dinning room where, in more peaceful times, Tourist's class passengers would have dined. Someone told them to go up the stairs until they came to 'A' deck and when he found his room, port side fairly well aft, he felt things could hardly be better. Those days spent studying the *Queen Mary's* plans now became worthwhile as he remembered with clarity that it would mean he only had to go up three decks to get to the mainmast and the gaff halyard where it had been decided he should hang the aerial.

He found he was sharing the cabin, originally designed for two people to occupy in considerable comfort, with three radio officers, the second, third and fourth officers and two apprentices. The numbers, since there were only eight bunks, of course did not add up and the second, as the senior man, told the two youngsters – they could not be more than fifteen, thought Schultz – that they would have to share a bunk. So, there had been an allocation of cards per the number of officers for the *Empire Regina* and the fellow who handed them out had spotted the discrepancy and just issued the lads with one between them; or was it that they, being so lowly in the chain of command, had to double-up anyway? He laid claim to a lower bunk by placing his two small cases on it and sat down.

On the door into the bathroom there was a whole list of 'do's and don'ts'; where they had to muster for emergency and fire drills etc. One of the radio men started reading it out as a voice over the loudspeaker system in the corridor told all passengers to do just that and for now to stay in their accommodation where, the voice reiterated what was on a separate notice in large red letters, there must be no smoking!

Schultz felt the adrenaline rising. He had arrived. Now all he had to do, until the trooper was at sea and it was dark, was just do whatever the loudspeakers told them to.

He placed the case containing his spare clothes in a drawer under the bunk and, with the other at his feet and hands under his head, lay down. Above him the two apprentices were arguing as to who would lie on the inside of their bunk. Two of the wireless operators started a conversation and he was sure that sooner or later he would be drawn into it with the question, 'this set you've got, can we see it?' The thought did not particularly worry him and he knew that he would be far more advanced technically than either of the two junior men. The fellow who wore the same braid as he should be able to understand the intricacies of the circuits. Anyway if they did ask it would help pass the time.

The argument between the two youngsters stopped, to be replaced by the sound of apples being crunched – there had been one in each food box. When the smell of someone having broken wind reached him he was glad that he would not have to put up with such cramped and crowded accommodation for long.

It was, perhaps, about an hour later when they were summoned to their emergency station where they were further harangued, albeit in a reasonable tone, about how they were to act in the case of fire or an attack on the vessel. Fire was undoubtedly the most likely of any emergency situation with the possibility, they were told, of a lone reconnaissance aircraft sighting and trying to bomb them. A torpedo striking them was considered highly unlikely, thanks to their speed, to which more than one merchant seaman who had sailed in the painfully, and almost suicidal slow convoys and survived, gave a sigh of relief.

Should an aircraft attack occur the ship was well armed against such a happening and in order that the gunners had clear access to their stations the upper deck was out of bounds at all times. This last order, Schultz foresaw, might cause him a problem.

On the trip from the pier to the *Queen Mary*, because of where they had to stay, he had not had the opportunity to even see the ship yet alone study where the anti-aircraft guns were. As he remembered things he would be able to go up the main after-stairway as far as the sun deck. He would then have to go outside and up an exposed stairway to gain access to the sports deck and thence the mainmast and the all important gaff halyard.

He had discussed at length with *Hauptman* Swartz, and the radio engineer from the *Abwher*, where the most practical place would be to put up the aerial. Without doubt up at the gaff would be the optimum – where at sea but in sight of land or other ships the ensign flag would be flown – and they had carefully measured the height available to them from the plans. Accordingly the aerial wire had been cut to a full wavelength for the frequency the set would be operating on, thus give maximum radiation.

If for any reason he could not use that position he would have to bring the suction cups into action and stick it on a rail on the eastern facing side so that at least it would not be totally screened from the advancing aircraft. Once again he used his favourite expletive, 'Shit, it was all so easy on paper but was far from being child's play when it came to putting things into action!'

"Also," the voice on the loudspeaker continued. "All the main-deck accommodation is totally out of bounds. Under no circumstances are you to enter it. As you may have seen or heard by now, we have a host of very important passengers aboard."

Schultz heard someone near-by say, "Yes, I heard one of the trooping staff tell another that it's old Winnie himself and about all the gold braid in the Kingdom."

The German agent's mind raced. 'Winnie', wasn't that what Churchill was affectionately called? If that was true then he was about to bring off the greatest victory of the war; not only would this ship go down but with it the *Führer's* greatest adversary, the British Prime Minister! Something inside him made him feel as if he had just run a mile and at a speed greater than any Olympic record. For a brief moment his mind went numb with the thought of it. Now, more than ever, failure of his mission could not be contemplated!

If there had been any thought of staying aboard with these Tommies and then losing himself in America – after all he still had a considerable amount of cash on him – they vanished at that moment. His success would place his name amongst the greatest of the fatherland's generals and a hero above all heroes. For the revere and love he had for his Leader he would succeed!

For another half hour they were kept at their emergency mustering station and all the orders repeated before being told to go back to their cabins. It seemed they had only just had time to each use the cabin toilet when they were told to muster once again and this time to ensure that everyone carried their lifebelts. This last reminder caused a bit of concern to the two boys since there had been only one such item per bunk.

"Sod it Jack," said the darker of the two. "I had to swim without one last time. I'm having it!"

"Shut up you two," the second officer admonished. "I'll sort it out when we're topsides."

Once back at their mustering point they listened yet again to all the orders. Schultz had to admit that those who ran the ship were making sure everyone knew just what they had to do and where. With so many people on board such knowledge was essential and he realised the utter chaos there would be if they did not. Briefly he wondered how his fellow countrymen, presumably down on the very lower decks, would fair if the ship were attacked - as surely it would be. Was there any way he could warn them? Perhaps tell them to over-power their guards as soon as they heard, if that were possible in the bowels of such a huge vessel, the Liberator coming in for its bombing run but not to come onto the upper decks? No, it would be too risky and might jeopardise the whole operation. The *Führer* had accepted that most would have to die, just as he most likely would do.

When they were dismissed this time they were allowed to kill the time before their evening meal in whichever way they wished. Schultz wanted desperately to get out on to the Sports deck and ensure that the practical layout around the mainmast was as shown on the plans. It could well be dark when he had to go out there with the set so it was essential that he had the picture well and truly impinged on his mind.

The *Empire Regina's* chief radio officer had been standing next to him during the muster and now asked the supposed Dutch Chief Sparks what he was going to do.

"Take some fresh air Chief." He found it vaguely amusing that they should both be addressing each other as 'Chief' but that seemed to be the way of things.

"Mmmind if I come along then?"

"Please do. Do you know anything about the ship?"

"Nnnot really. Just that she is damned big and must hhave some ppretty good radio gear aboard."

What could be more natural than two Radio Officers talking together and possibly looking up at the big, by comparison with a cargo ship, array of aerials that he knew he would find. He turned and with his companion made his way over to the main stairway and went up it until they could go no further, arriving on the Sun deck landing. Here on either side,

279

in large letters, were signs saying 'OUT OF BOUNDS TO ALL RANKS'.

Before turning to retrace their steps Schultz pointed out the location of the Transmitter room on the port side. They had to go back to A deck before they could get outside into the fresh air on what, in peace-time, was the tourist promenade deck. Right aft and looking up they could see only part of the transmitting aerials, but Willie explained what he knew about the rest as best he could. How did he know all this? Well he'd had to study the whole installation for one of his exams back in Holland. The other man was quite happy with that explanation. The fellow had a bit of a stammer but otherwise he was easy to understand with a slight northern accent to his soft voice. In a way he reminded him a bit of Hashagen, only older.

It was not long before the speakers called them for their evening meal. Because it was their first gathering for a meal it took some while before they got the hang of how and where they were to eat. After the meal was over Willie Schultz thought it was the best he'd had since leaving the Irish trawler. He was also impressed that he could take a couple of sandwiches for later on in the evening. After the meal they were called to yet another emergency station muster, where the same 'do's and don'ts' were told them all over again.

By following what the other officers in his group did Schultz was able to keep a low profile and felt totally inconspicuous. During the muster he promised to show the chief sparks the 'lifeboat' set in the morning. Later he found the canteen for his section of the ship and was delighted to see it well stocked with chocolate, albeit made somewhere in America. He bought two bars of plain to see if it was as good as that in Germany before the war. He thought that staying aboard for the whole trip might be, at least for an officer, not too hard a passage.

When Schultz awoke after a surprisingly good night's sleep he found that they were at sea. Like most on board he had heard or felt nothing when the giant vessel got under way. Only those right up forward might have been woken by the clanking of the anchor cable as it was hove aboard, or perhaps those on the last passenger deck near the engine room might have heard the hum of the giant turbines as they came to life. Built for passengers paying high fares the designers' only thought had been for their comfort. Her underwater lines were exquisite so that she glided through the sea. It was only in poor weather that she tended to roll more than those designers had wished.

He took his turn in the bathroom to shave and generally spruce himself up. When they were called to breakfast he almost felt like one of those peacetime passengers and when reality once more set in he was almost sorry that tonight he would have to end it all. When the emergency muster, now apparently obligatory every few hours, had been held after breakfast Schultz kept his word and, sitting on his bunk opened the case and showed its contents to the Chief R/O, who ordered his two juniors to listen as well.

It did not take long to go through the simple transmit/receive circuits and explain the controls. While he explained the latter the sight of a panel bearing the words 'HIGH VOLTAGE', with the usual lightening flash danger sign reminded him that he should have set the automatic frequency changing circuit back in the hotel room. He could hardly do that in the cabin with the others looking on for that would have negated his claim about the simplicity and yet high efficiency of this particular set. After all lifeboat sets were not exactly a new idea, in fact two of the *Queen Mary's* own boats were fitted with them. Instead he told them that under that panel was the vibrator to change the low battery voltage to the higher one required by the output valves.

Before lunch he retraced his steps of yesterday to the Sundeck and back. When he went outside he saw that sailing in company with the *Queen* was an aircraft carrier and three, what he thought, were cruisers and, farther out, a screen of four destroyers. The latter, he had been led to believe, was normal for the first day but the larger ships were not. If they did not leave with the destroyers this evening then the men from KG 200 would have more on their hands than they bargained for. This was very perturbing but something he could do nothing about, or could he? Perhaps send a warning message? He had no sooner thought about it than he dismissed the thought. The target was now far too important to warrant aborting the operation. Surely at least one of the 'planes would get through?

Despite the next two meals and another drill, time seemed to drag on interminably and, because they had apparently steamed north west all day, it seemed ages before the sun set.

He lay fully clothed, having pretended to fall asleep before even taking off his shoes. Finally, at half past ten, with all the other occupants fortunately asleep he made his move. To avoid cracking his head on the bunk so close above him he bent outwards and picking up the case swung his feet onto the deck. Putting the side of his foot down first before going onto its sole, exactly as he had been shown back in France, he stole silently out of the cabin.

CHAPTER 16

ZERO HOUR

Willie Schultz paused on the main deck landing; there was enough light here to make the final adjustments he had forgotten to do while still ashore. He opened the case and then took one of those pocket knives that so many men carried which had a tin opener and a screwdriver attachment. On the front of the set there was a small panel with the inscription H.T. and the usual lightening sign for danger. Carefully he undid the four screws and removed the panel; a switch labelled 'single/double' he changed from single to the double. To the right of this was another switched labelled, 'Time', and this he changed to 'on'.

He had now switched in a circuit that automatically changed the frequency output from the 6 megacycle band to 12. Each would transmit for two minutes followed by an eight- minute break of silence thus prolonging the battery life. With the advent of the new miniature valves it had been possible to add the second output frequency with almost no increase in the overall size and weight of the set. The *Abwehr* engineer and Klaus Schwartz, together with the best clock maker they could find, had done a brilliant job with the final construction. Klaus particularly had been overjoyed at being able to put all his knowledge into play and with total access to all the latest materials – even if there had at first been cries of alarm by inventors and valve manufacturers alike. He had been like a child with a precious new toy.

Willie Schultz had just finished replacing the panel and closed the case when the door to the main deck accommodation opened and a voice demanded to know 'what was going on here?' The German agent almost jumped out of his skin and quickly stood up, turning to see who it was. Although the windows of the inside communication door were not blacked out he had not noticed the marine sentry who patrolled the after end of the corridor between the main deck cabins. Now the man, seeing the gold braid on Schultz sleeves said, "Got a problem, Sir? You're not supposed to hang around this deck you know."

Willie's mind now moved into very fast gear. Assuming that the man would not know much about the layout of the *Mary* he replied, "Forgot to make an adjustment to the set down in the workshop before making a night test on it."

"Well, I don't know? My orders are that no one should be around at this time of night. Let me have a look." He moved forward, pushing Schultz back a step who, now quite alarmed, surreptitiously withdrew the garrotte with his right hand and then passed it behind his back where the left took hold of one end. If the man became too inquisitive.....

Looking into the case the marine saw a radio, which appeared not unlike one of the smaller field sets he had seen. Standing back up he repeated, "Well, I don't know, Sir. Perhaps..." but he got no farther as the garrotte wire went around his neck and started to cut into the flesh, changing his words to a gurgling sound. When Schultz had murdered Hashagan he had done it almost apologetically. He had used the minimum of force, throttling him slowly. But this marine was different. He was one of the enemy and could stop *Operation Königin* in its tracks.

Savagely Schultz brought his left knee up into the small of the man's back and exerted all his strength on the instrument of death. Frantically the marine clutched at his neck, forgetting all he had learnt in unarmed combat – if you are being throttled from behind catch hold of the little fingers and snap them back until they break or, like now, if it is a rope or something reach back until you have hold of your antagonist's head and smash it into the back of yours, hopefully breaking a nose in the process. Either way the grip should be broken and give you a chance to buckle your knees so that your assailant became off-balance and you then simply rolled him over your head. He forgot all the pain the instructor had caused him counteracting the move until he did it correctly. He went on clutching at the wire until a moment later the jugular vein was severed and, because he forgot, he died.

Quickly Schultz recoiled the wire and shoved it back in his pocket, blood smearing his hands as he did so. Catching the body under the arms he dragged it up the stairs to the half landing where it was out of sight from the door window. He unclipped the marine's revolver lanyard and taking the gun out of its holster pushed it into his belt, something he wore as well as braces when in uniform, before retrieving the radio and running up the remaining stairs to the Sun deck. He was by now panting hard and he stopped for a moment to regain his breath, wondering how long it

286

would be before the sentry was missed? 'Shit. This wasn't in the plan at all!'

Following his planned route of yesterday he went out on to the Sundeck and was surprised to find that it was in twilight and not darkness as he had thought it might be. Again this was not according to plan; it meant he could be seen and yet on the other hand he could more easily see where he wanted to go and what he wanted to do. This time he went up the stairs, dodging under the chain that held a 'STRICTLY OUT OF BOUNDS' sign and arrived on the Sports deck. He hesitated for a moment as he took in the fact that the Oerlikon gun emplacements were manned; there was one immediately to his left just forward of the engine room skylight armour plating. A gunner there was looking at him, grateful to have the monotony of his watch broken by the unexpected appearance of an officer. Schultz took the bull by the horns and waved, receiving a tired smile in reply. Another emplacement was far more alarming; situated as it was half way between the mast and the rail to which the gaff flag halyard was secured. There the gunners would be overlooking him from only a few yards away.

Trying to muster as much confidence in his stride as he could to show that he had every right to be there, he walked the few yards to the rail, looking up at the gunners as he went past, greeting them. "Morning fellows. Got to test this lifeboat set. Would normally fly a kite to hold the aerial up but we're going too fast for that, a twenty-seven knot breeze would just about break everything! So, going to use

287

the flag halyard instead. Careful you don't shoot it down if you have to open up. That would cause an awful lot of bumf work!"

Someone replied, "Not much bloody chance of that, Sir. Two years of doing this and never fired a shot in anger yet!"

Carefully keeping himself between the gunners and the halyard cleat he attached the aerial to one end of the rope and then slowly hoisted it up to its extremity. With a bight of the now spare halyard he secured the handle of the case to the lower rail. With the adrenaline once more pounding in his system he switched on and tuned the aerial circuit. Using the transmit/send receive switch to over-ride the automatic settings he had put in just now he started to send. As he crouched there with one knee on the deck planks he felt terribly exposed, expecting a bullet to enter his back at any moment.

'BT', the two middle letters from the *Queen Mary's* official call sign. He sent this three times and then listened, holding one of the earphones to his left ear. He waited for the half minute, which now seemed more like half an hour. Nothing. He repeated the call but all he heard was one of the gunners saying, "Thank Christ it'll soon be light enough for a smoke." And then someone else, "Hookey, I need a piss again. OK if I nip down to the rail?" and the reply by the leading gunner, "Bloody hell, Chalky, reckon you must have caught the clap last time you was ashore. Best see the Quack when you gets off watch."

'BT'. Schultz followed the set procedure and tried for a third time, but again all he heard was the crackle of static. He was not surprised by this failure to get through and he switched to the 12 megacycle band. Now he heard it! First Merimac then Cuxhaven followed by Trondheim and finally the weather station in northern Greenland.

'Dear God, it was really working. Sure, all stations only reported a weak signal but that was enough to set everything in motion.' As the aircraft became airborne and got closer they would eventually hear the 6 m/cs signal and be able to home directly on to it. He pulled over the waterproof cover for the set and got up, still feeling that he might be shot at any moment.

"That should do it lads. Got to leave it where it is for a few hours," he called up to the gunners as he retraced his steps to the ladder down to the Sundeck. Once there he leant against the rail, hoping that his heart rate might return to something like normal at the same time as he tried to visualise what would be happening back at the KG 200 base.

It took the aircrews exactly seven minutes to be in their cockpits ready to taxi to the runway. Since Schultz's message saying he was going to board their target an engine mechanic had been in each plane so that when the control tower fired off a green Very light they started up the motors. One by one the ground crews removed the chocks from under the wheels and the planes began to roll forward, the Liberator leading. The weather was not particularly good for flying, there being some rain and a cloud base of only two hundred metres but the cloud over France would be of no import once the planes were far out over the Atlantic; out there the Greenland station thought skies would be more or less clear. At three thousand metres the small flight levelled out and steadied on a westerly course until they would be clear of approaching too near to the English fighter bases in the West Country. The Kondor from KG 40 with the life rafts had followed them into the air, knowing only that he had to take orders from the flight leader once airborne.

Hauptman Swartz received the first set of bearings, all stations adding that they were 'woolly' and passed them to the navigator. He, in turn, applied the 'half convergence' factor necessitated by the long distances involved before plotting the result on his ocean chart. After half an hour he gave a new course to be flown direct to the last position given by further bearings. Swartz passed this to the Ju 88s and, by now somewhat behind the others, the Condor. In the Liberator, as with the four ground stations, the *Gruppefermeldeoffizer* had installed three new receivers so that he could listen direct to the signal from the *Queen Mary* on both frequencies, with the third set as standby. He received the bearings from the ground in the non-transmission periods from the target and kept the other planes informed by using the aircraft's normal R/T installation. To check the accuracy of the bearings the navigator took half hourly star sights and while he was doing that Schwartz had bearings taken on their own aircraft. Both men were glad of the checks for there was a very large area on the chart where the bearing lines crossed.

After over three hours in the air the position of their target on the chart could be seen to have altered and showed the general course the liner was steering. Then, just when that course had been noted and as a result a few degrees taken off their own, the still very weak signal on the 6 m/cs band doubled in intensity! It had no call sign on it and was transmitting continuously. The signals officer switched through to his direction finding loop aerial but the new signal – Shwartz knew from its tone that it was a different transmitter – was not yet strong enough to actuate the needles for the beacon response. The flight signals officer had not the faintest idea what Schultz must be doing on the ship. It certainly was not their 'Lifeboat set', in fact, at the appropriate time interval the latter heterodyned with it. The man must be creating some sort of a miracle down there.

Leutnant Schultz did not know what to do next. The beacon was actuated and it would be several hours before his countrymen would start their bombing run. When that happened he intended to be several decks down until they had finished, after that all would be in the lap of the Gods. Having recovered his breath he walked to the after end of the deck. How long before the dead marine would be found? He knew he had blood on his uniform and would be hard pushed to explain it away if he went back to his cabin and someone saw it. He thought again about the

291

aircraft carrier he had seen yesterday; were she and the three cruisers still shadowing them?

The barrel of the revolver was causing pressure on his stomach and he shifted it more to the left side feeling, as he did so, the shape of the two crystals in his jacket pocket.

When on automatic sending the transmitter used two much smaller crystals so that they had been built into it leaving the plug-in ones surplus to requirements. The object of this had been to reinforce the cover story of the set being able to be used on various marine frequencies. The crystals! Now he knew what he would do!

The decision he took was ultimately to lead to the manner of his death. If he had just left his own set working and, throwing his uniform coat overboard, gone below and lost himself amongst other passengers he might well have survived. But he thought only of increasing the chances of his mission succeeding.

His interest in reading the article about the Marconi equipment in the Wireless World Journal during training had been one of technical curiosity; he had never thought that knowledge would be of any use in this operation. 'Yes by God, he'd use one of the ship's powerful short-wave transmitters as the beacon!'

He was already on the same deck as the ship's transmitting room so he made his way back to the entrance door and going into the flat turned right. He remembered the plans of the radio installation showed the entrance to the transmitting room was from a small hallway off the main corridor in which he now stood. Also from that hallway was the cabin for the radio electrician.

He turned the handle to the entrance door very slowly and gently opened it. To his right was the radio spares store, the electrician's cabin in front of him and to the left of that the transmitter room. Would the latter be locked? Perhaps in peacetime it would be and the key kept in the receiving room but now nothing, other than perhaps the bullion room, was locked. (Locked doors on ships that might come under attack could cost lives.) Gingerly he turned the handle and gave a push. 'Shit, he was in luck!' That seagull certainly was working for him.

He closed the door quietly behind him, letting out his breath, which he had unwittingly been holding. The room was ten metres long and arrayed down it, just as the pictures had shown in the article, were the four transmitters and their associate equipment. As a wireless engineer he appreciated the complexity of this most modern of all seagoing radio installations and momentarily he thought what a pity it was that in a few hours it would all be destroyed.

He was in no hurry since the 'planes would still be quite a way off. To his immediate left was the Local/Remote control panel now showing that all the equipment was switched through to the receiving operators' positions and on Stand-by. Next came one of the two short-wave transmitters with the second opposite it.

Of course he had no idea just where this ship was in the Atlantic, other than somewhere between the British Isles and Iceland, probably nearer the latter than the former. He only remembered that the aircraft would cruise at two hundred and fifty knots in order to conserve petrol. He had started the beacon at midnight by his watch so he decided to switch on one of these transmitters at three o'clock. Now it would be a case of staying awake, or could he still trust his alarm? He re-set it and then, to make sure, summoned as much saliva as he could and swallowed one of the four Benzedrine tablets he had been given for such an occasion.

Kneeling down in front of the transmitter he removed the bottom panel and there saw the row of ten crystals; he had remembered correctly. Selecting the crystal which was the nearest in frequency to that used by the beacon he replaced it with his own. Good, only minimal re-tuning would be required when he switched on and he carefully took in the various controls he would have to use. Satisfied, he moved to the workbench space in the corner behind him. There was a stool wedged there but it looked uncomfortable so, with his back to the vacant bulkhead, he gently slid to the floor and sat there with legs out-stretched, placing the revolver on the bench before he did so. The room was temperature controlled and began to feel stuffy so he undid his coat, smelling the now dried blood as he did so.

Two hours to kill, but in his self-imposed prison what could he do to pass it? There were a number of workshop manuals on a shelf above the bench but reading of any description would only increase his drowsiness. Since the transmitters were not in use and would not, therefore, require the occasional visit to check that all was well, he felt confident that he would not be disturbed. There seemed no alternative other than to sit and think and possibly doze for just a few minutes at a time despite the Benzedrine. Also he had one bar of chocolate, although now somewhat crumpled, in his left jacket pocket.

He was already on his feet when his watch told him it was time to start the transmitter. His full bladder had broken into his thoughts of the last few months but he did not want to risk going past the radio-electrician's cabin. So, very carefully, not wishing to give himself what at least could be a very unpleasant electrical shock, he urinated in a far corner where there was no wiring or machinery. Thus relieved he went to the Local/Remote control panel and switched the controls for the number one transmitter to local and then the transmitter itself to tune. Meters started to come to life and quickly he made the few minor adjustments until his knowledge told him that everything was working as it should be before he put the local standby/send switch on Send. The die was cast.

When Willie Schultz switched control from remote to local he knew that at least one of the duty operators in the receiving room four hundred feet further forward would soon realise that something was not as it should be. The question was 'how long'? In fact it was ten minutes before the operator on that circuit noticed the indicator said the transmitter was on local control.

Because of the presence aboard of the Prime Minister and his staff, and despite the fact a special naval communications centre had been set up, the traffic for the *Queen Mary* had considerably increased. With the transmission blackout no acknowledgements were being given for messages received so that, coupled with the duplex system in use, he was not over-worried and thought that it might just be a fault on the indicating circuit. It was half an hour before he had the chance to mention it to his colleagues on watch with him and who were likewise extremely busy.

The delay enabled Swartz up in the Liberator to use his own D/F loop to get an accurate course to fly directly to the *Queen Mary* and eventually a strong enough signal to be able to 'fly down the beam'.

After a while the senior radio officer of the watch sent someone aft to the transmitting room to check things out, an eventuality which Schultz had foreseen. He now sat on the stool, revolver in hand on his lap, with a clear view of the door. He was just beginning to think that he had got away with things when the door started to open and a figure appeared. He fired without taking proper aim. There was a cry of pain and a curse, then the sound of running feet disappearing down the corridor.

Although it was only a point thirty-eight revolver, in the confined space the noise almost deafened the German as it echoed around the room, which now smelt of cordite. A moment later the man sleeping next door came out of his cabin. Fortunately for him he knew what the smell was and realised the noise that had woken him had been a shot!

'Jesus! What the hell was happening?' With alacrity he ducked back and turned the key in the lock. His cabin was on a direct telephone line to the receiving station and he was asking one of the other radio officers there what on earth was happening well before the wounded man got back, panting and with blood dripping down his sleeve, to his colleagues. Astounded at the story he heard the senior man on watch 'phoned the chief radio officer who arrived almost at the same time as a hastily summoned master-at-arms.

"Are we transmitting, John?" asked the Chief. He reached out and swung the receiver dial over to where their transmitter should be. "You other two keep to your posts or we'll have chaos!" Being slightly off balance he moved the dial further up the band and came across the signal from their own transmitter, which was so strong it blanketed out the beacon. He put the dial back to the shore station frequency.

"John, get one of the off-watch fellows to take over this station. Mister Brown..." with such a huge crew he was lucky enough to know the master-at-arm's name... "Get a doctor here, also the staff captain. Tell him this is very much an emergency! Do it from the passenger's office next door, don't want to disturb these fellows more than we need. Brian," he turned to the wounded officer. "Let's get out of here. How's the arm?"

"I think it's only a flesh wound, Sir, but it stings like hell!"

"Making a bloody mess on the deck whatever it is. Come on!" and he went in to the clerical office. The chief radio officer had spent years tackling emergency situations, although nothing quite like this. Mostly it was dealing with irate passengers whose telegrams, or whatever, had gone astray, or they expected an answer before the one with a question in it had even been transmitted! Now, with a dressing gown over his pyjamas, – unlike those on smaller and slower vessels where the risk of having to abandon ship was very real, some of the senior officers who did not keep watches, actually still wore their pyjamas in bed – and with what little grey hair he had left ruffled, his glasses almost on the end of his nose, he looked comical but acted with decision. Checking the 'phone index he called the electrician's cabin.

"Mac, any movement down there?"

"No Chief, not that I can tell. How's Brian?"

"He'll live! Get on to the duty electrician down below and tell them to cut off the power to the transmitting room. Make sure they understand that. God help them if they cut off this place as well. Got it?"

"Yes Chief, right away".

The radio rooms each had their own separate power supplies from generators seven decks below near the engine room. If they could not get into the transmitting room because of some madman with a gun they could at least stop the transmitter.

The staff captain and the doctor arrived more or less together. While the latter attended to the wounded man the captain was briefed on the situation and took control.

"Mister Brown, get on to the C.O.S.'s duty officer and tell him that by the look of things we could do with some armed help!"

"Right Sir. I was talking to him a short while ago. Seems they lost one of their marines. Couldn't find him when they went to change sentries."

"Those accommodation sentries are armed aren't they?"

"Yes Sir. 'Can't take a risk with Winnie aboard just in case one of those POWs down below gets out'; that's what he said."

"Good God! Then it looks like we could have one of our own marines gone troppo?"

"If it is, Sir," the chief R/O interjected, "then he must know something about radio, and why put our 'mitter on air and on a different frequency, broadcasting to the world where we are? I think we should take this to the top, both our own and the PM's. Unfortunately the signal was broadcast for at least half an hour. Plenty of time for any subs around to get a D.F. fix on us!" He placed great emphasis on this last sentence, which was greeted by silence for a moment as its import began to sink home on his listeners.

" 'Struth! Yes, you're right, Michael. This is getting complicated. I'll tell the Commodore and then get down to the Powers That Be. Mister Brown, please warn them I will be down shortly."

It was shortly after this meeting that the captain in-charge of the marine guard, with two of his sergeants, made a very cautious approach to the transmitting room and its occupant. Assuming it was the missing man – his body was only found shortly afterwards – he called out, "OK Troubridge, throw out your gun and come out before anyone else gets hurt!"

Schultz's reply was to fire a shot in the direction of the door. He had by now realised, when the room and all its equipment became dark, that the power had been cut off, a possibility he had overlooked. About all he could do now was to keep the people out there concentrating on him, hoping that they would not find the beacon. Again the captain called for 'Troubridge' to come out and Schultz grinned to himself at the confusion he was causing. Naturally he had no idea as to who the owner of that name was.

Five minutes passed during which he heard the murmur of voices. Then a gruffer voice called out irately, "Right you bastard, whoever you are, come out or I'll personally come and blow you to hell." The missing Marine had been found.

Again the German fired, the bullet hitting something metal so that it went whining down the corridor and made those outside crouch even lower. The sergeant who had called out, suggested that they back off a little and let the sod stew for a while. He had been a commando and wounded in the Dieppe raid, to the extent that he was now, much to his disgust, assigned to supposedly less stringent duties.

His captain was not a bad chap but had so far only served on sea-borne duties. He was more than a bit out of his depth in this situation and tacitly acquiesced to the suggestion.

"I reckon this is how we oughter play it, Sir," the Sergeant went on to say. "No bullets were missing from Troubridge's pouch, so I reckon that fellow has three left. With these lights on 'ere we're sitting ducks as soon as we get near that doorway; silhouetted nicely for 'im." He turned to the master-at-arms who was with them but well out of the line of fire. "So, Chief, can you get these corridor lights doused?" Brown nodded. "OK. When you've done that 'phone the bloke in the cabin next door to open his door a couple of times, but from behind. Chuck out a shoe or something; I want to draw that bugger's fire. Tell 'im I only want two shots fired. Got the idea?" Again a nod from the master-at-arms. "Right, go do it." He turned to the other sergeant and explained his plan.

"When the lights go out we waits a couple of minutes to get our eyes used to things, then I'm going to crawl in and when I says 'now' you fire a couple of shots into the ceiling of the hallway. I need him to fire once so I know where he is. OK George? Memorise the angle you've got to use. Don't want you putting one up my arse!"

In the transmitting room Schultz was filled with apprehension as to what would happen next. Something inside told him that the end was near.

Outside, the sergeant muttered to no one in particular as he waited for the lights to go out. "They

301

say I'm not fit for this sort of skylark. Stupid cunts, I'll show 'em." And he inched his way forward so that he was in the best position for what he had to do. As the lights went out he started to count down two minutes. He heard the cabin door being opened and something land near his head. Schultz fired. The next time the shoe landed behind him and again there was a shot from within, but he had seen where it came from. He rolled partly on his side and held his gun in both hands in that direction. "Now!"

Schultz fired again not realising it was his last bullet. *Reich* officers were used to automatics with eight or nine shots. For the commando on the ground it was all he needed. Three rapid shots rang out, rewarded by a cry of agonised pain and then a thump as two of the bullets swung his target around. Schultz's head caught the edge of the power distribution board and the darkness became even blacker.

The sergeant's breath came in short gasps. Perhaps he was, after all, past this sort of skylark.

EPILOGUE

What happened after Schultz collapsed is left somewhat to conjecture.

Since there were not many aircraft-carriers in the fleet it was easy by a process of elimination to ascertain that it was the *Illustrious* which had been escorting the *Queen Mary*. However, five months more passed before I was able, through the Royal Naval Association, to track down someone who had been in the carrier at that time.

He had been a petty officer radar mechanic and although all on board had been admonished never to refer to the incident he was quite happy to tell me, as he understood things, what had happened. 'After all, the war had been over for years so what harm would be done if he talked to me' – particularly as he was getting a good dinner out of our meeting!

When the *Queen Mary* had flashed a message about the incident aboard, the escorting naval ships had been piped to battle stations. At about breakfast time, radar reported an aircraft echo approaching from the south east at a hundred miles. Since there was no intelligence of Allied airborne patrols in the area and some radar sets still had a 'hiccup' every now and then my acquaintance was sent-for to check things out. Backed-up by his Radar Officer the set was declared to be working correctly.

The *Illustrious* had been ordered to escort the *Queen Mary* with her all-important passengers to ensure that there was continual close anti-submarine patrol and for her fighters to take care of any enemy long-range aircraft which might come across the ships. As soon as there had been enough light to make it possible, a flight of its Barracudas from number 810 squadron had been air-borne to keep an eye out for any U-boats. Next, the captain ordered 894 squadron to place a flight of Seafires on 'stand-by' and, in accordance with his instructions, called the Admiral.

By the time the Admiral reached the bridge three smaller echoes coming in on the same bearing were reported and one of the cruisers had also signalled she had an unidentified echo. This was most disquieting particularly after the earlier aldis-lamp signal they had received from the *Mary*.

With the all-important 'Identification Friend or Foe' sets failing to get any response from the approaching aircraft, two flights of the Seafires were ordered to be flown off to investigate. The liner was signalled to ensure that her own gunners were closed-up.

When the fighters subsequently closed the approaching aircraft the flight commander was momentarily baffled by the Liberator, which did not seem to have the usual configuration of those used by Coastal Command. He throttled back and flew alongside, giving its pilot a 'thumbs-up' sign. It was at that moment that the leader of the second flight identified the three Ju 188s as enemy 'planes. After all, with its large bulbous cockpit, there was not another aircraft flying that had such a peculiar shape. He did not even need to see the German markings to convince him of the need to attack, especially when they were so far out of their normal operating range.

Although brilliantly handled by their pilots who, apart from their single front gun, had nothing other than their slightly superior speed and flying skill to avoid their attackers, their fate was sealed. They were almost in sight of their quarry but with no worthwhile cloud cover they had nowhere to hide, so they weaved, side slipping, climbing and diving, around their original course but to no avail. They were no match for the cannon and multiple machine guns of the Seafires.

In a matter of minutes it was all over as one became engulfed in flames, another spiralling down to a watery grave, whilst the third literally flew into the waves as it tried to avoid its pursuer.

In the Liberator, the front and rear guns, the former manned by *Hauptman* Swartz, fought back and severely damaged one of their attackers before their load of depth charges blew them and their aircraft into little pieces, almost taking another Seafire with it.

Some hundred miles astern of the four attack aircraft the slower-flying Kondor, not yet picked up on the ships' radar, turned back on its course when Swartz warned it on the r/t that enemy fighters were coming towards them.

It was from the debriefing of this aircraft's crew at KG40 and the subsequent record of it, which had somehow failed to be expunged, that I was able to confirm, after more delving, this part of *Operation Königin*. All records of KG 200 activities seemed to have disappeared.

Willie Schultz was apparently vague and either did not wish or, due to his medical state, could not communicate to my father much of what took place after he was gunned down in the transmitting room of the *Queen Mary*. He said he thought he was in and out of a coma for several days. In Halifax he was landed and placed under twenty-four hour visual surveillance in hospital until transferred to the sickbay of a naval vessel, which he thought to be a battleship, and taken back to Britain.

When fit enough he was interrogated at length by several naval officers and two civilians, he assumed the latter to be from MI5. After much difficulty he finally convinced his interrogators that he was indeed, *Leutnant* Schultz of the *Kriegsmarine*. Perhaps that was why he was executed by firing squad and not hung, or perhaps the reason was as I had conjectured when asked by *Kapitän* Weiner. The manuscript did not tell me and any inquiries were rebuffed with, 'Such a situation never existed'.

I prefer to believe *Kapitän* Weiner.

EITHER WAY DEAD

GLOSSARY OF
GERMAN/ENGLISH

Abwehr	German Military Intelligence
Alles in ordnung, Herr Kapitän	All finished, Captain
B-Dienst	Special service
Deutchland Über Alles	Germany above all (National anthem)
Doppelgänger	Identical copy
Flughaven	Aerodrome
Fraulein	Girl
Frühstück	Breakfast
Führer	Leader
Funkeroffizier	Radio Officer
Gasthaus	Guesthouse
Glauwein	Mulled wine
Gestapo	Internal Secret Police
Gross Admiral	Admiral of the Fleet
Gruppefermeldungoffizier	Squadron Senior Signals officer
Gutten abend, mein Herr	Good evening, Sir
Hauptmann	Army, Air Force captain
Heil	Hail
Herr	Mister
Holle	Hell
Himmel	Heaven

Heute die Luftwaffe hat London wieder gebombardieren	Today the air force again bombed London
Ja	Yes
Kampfgeswader	Air Force squadron
Kapitän zur Zee	Naval captain
Keblewagon	German type jeep
Kondor	Long range aircraft
Kornetten Kapitän	Lieutenant Commander
Kriegsmarine	German navy
Kriegsmarine Kommando	Naval H.Q.
Langsam achteraus backbord	Slow astern port motor
Lebansraum	Living space
Leutnant	Lieutenant
Lieber Gott	Dear God
Lipziger Platz	Lipziger Square
Luftwaffe	Air Force
Mein Gott! Darf ich	My God! May I…
Mein Kampf	Hitler's writings
Milag Nord	North camp
Naturlich	Naturally; of course
Nachtrichtendeinst aus	News service from Bremen
Oberfunkermann	Chief petty officer telegraphist
Oberteilgeheim	Top secret
Oberschreibermann	Chief petty officer writer
Oberst	Colonel
Oberkommando der Abwehr	Intelligence H.Q.

Operation Königin	Operation Queen
Oberbootsmannmate	Chief Botswain's mate
Prost	Cheers
Paperien bitte	Identification papers please
Rathaus	Town hall offices
Reichsminister	Senior minister of Germany
Reichsmarshall	Marshall in the German forces
Reichsführer	Senior Nazi party post
Reichsleiter	Lesser senior Nazi party post
Reiperbahn	Famous street where nightlife abounded
Scheisse	Shit
Schinken	Ham
Schnellboot	Fast naval craft
S.D. Einsatzgruppen	Special squads charged with the murder of Jews etc
Siegalhafen	Harbour named after the old sailing ships
Selbstopfermanner	Suicide mission
Staffel	Flight of airforce planes
Standartenführer	Colonel in the S.S
Steiner	One litre tankard
Storch	Light communications aircraft
Tirpitzufer	An avenue by the river
Unterseebooten Kommando	U-boat Headquarters
Vielleight noch einmal Lieber…	Perhaps just one more time darling..
Wehrmacht	German army
Waffen SS	Fighting unit of the SS